"Don't say no, Moira."

Like that day outside the obstetrician's clinic, Will's face spasmed with some emotion Moira couldn't read any more than she could understand her own. His voice was hoarse. "Please. Don't say no."

When she still failed to say anything at all, he let her hands go and leaned forward until he could draw her into his arms. Gently but inexorably he tugged her forward until her brow rested against his broad chest and he could settle his chin on top of her head.

"Marry me, Moira," he said, so low she barely heard him. "Let me do this for both of us."

Dear Reader,

Those of you who read *Charlotte's Homecoming* might remember Moira Cullen, who was the hero's best friend and his partner in an architectural firm. For me, linked books are usually planned that way; secondary characters rarely linger in my mind the way Moira did. There was just something about her....

For one thing, it's unusual for a woman to be such good friends with a man, and an attractive one at that. I hint in that book that Moira, although successful professionally and an attractive woman, lives with quite a bit of self-doubt. And she had to be lonely, didn't she? So...what if she reaches desperately for intimacy and ends up in a one-night stand with a man who can't give her more—because he's leaving for a two-year job commitment in Africa? And what if Moira then discovers she's pregnant? What kind of man *was* he, and how will he react to the news that a woman he hardly knows but who haunts him is carrying his baby while he pursues his dreams half a world away? And this is a man who'd already given up his dreams once, to raise his two brothers and sister. Two lonely, conflicted people...

Of course I couldn't resist Moira, any more than I could resist Will Becker! I hope you feel the same.

Janice Kay Johnson

The Baby Agenda
Janice Kay Johnson

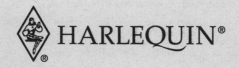

HARLEQUIN®

TORONTO • NEW YORK • LONDON
AMSTERDAM • PARIS • SYDNEY • HAMBURG
STOCKHOLM • ATHENS • TOKYO • MILAN • MADRID
PRAGUE • WARSAW • BUDAPEST • AUCKLAND

Recycling programs
for this product may
not exist in your area.

ISBN-13: 978-0-373-71674-6

THE BABY AGENDA

Copyright © 2010 by Janice Kay Johnson

ABOUT THE AUTHOR

The author of more than sixty books for children and adults, Janice Kay Johnson writes Harlequin Superromance novels about love and family—about the way generations connect and the power our earliest experiences have on us throughout life. Her 2007 novel *Snowbound* won a RITA® Award from Romance Writers of America for Best Contemporary Series Romance. A former librarian, Janice raised two daughters in a small rural town north of Seattle, Washington. She loves to read and is an active volunteer and board member for Purrfect Pals, a no-kill cat shelter.

Books by Janice Kay Johnson

CHAPTER ONE

EVEN THOUGH THE GALA was part of a professional conference, it looked as though almost everyone had arrived two-by-two. Moira Cullen had known they would, and decided to come anyway. So what if this, like most social occasions, had too much in common with Noah's ark? *She* was supposed to have been half of a couple tonight, too, until she'd gotten the email this afternoon from Bruce.

I'm sorry, Moira, but I won't be able to escort you tonight after all. Something has come up. I know you hadn't planned to attend until I asked you, so I hope it won't be too big a disappointment.

He'd signed off with "Bruce." Plain and simple. No "Love, Bruce," or "I'll think of you tonight and wish we were dancing together," or even "I'll call tomorrow and explain."

She still had no idea what could have happened since this morning, when they'd parted after a conference session. She and Bruce Girard both had been attending the conference held in Redmond, across Lake Washington from Seattle, for members of the building trade. He was a real estate attorney, she was an architect. They'd been dating for nearly six weeks, and she'd decided that tonight was a fitting time to invite him into her bedroom for the first time.

And she'd bought the most beautiful dress!

In a spirit of defiance, she'd decided to come to the gala anyway. Lots of attendees were from out of town and had come without significant others. A single woman would surely be asked to dance. It could be fun, she had decided, surprising herself with her determination. Bruce was probably disappointed, too, and would undoubtedly be in touch. They'd have other nights. She had no reason to feel hurt.

She hesitated only momentarily in the lobby, then walked toward the ballroom, telling herself she looked voluptuous in her new dress, not fat.

Repeat after me: I am not fat.

She *knew* she wasn't. Believing, though, that could be another story.

Right by the open doors, she saw a man she knew. She'd worked with Stan Wells on a job a couple of years ago. He appeared to be by himself.

He turned, looked her up and down, and said, "Well, *hello,*" then did a double take. "Moira?" He sounded stunned.

Stan had never once looked at her as if he'd noticed she was a woman when they had worked together.

She smiled pleasantly and said, "Hello, Stan," then strolled past him, enjoying the knowledge that he'd swiveled on his heel to watch her walk away. The dress must be as flattering as she'd imagined it to be.

It was also form-fitting, which meant that she scanned the buffet table with a wistful eye but didn't dare partake. So what. She wasn't here to eat.

Moira made her way around the outskirts of the ballroom, pausing to chat a couple of times and to promise a dance once the musicians started to play. She'd been right to think she'd have fun—it was nice to come to a party where she actually knew many of the people.

Then her roving gaze stopped on a tall, handsome man with sandy hair and a lopsided grin. Bruce Girard, wearing a well-cut suit, had his head bent as he talked to a beautiful, slender woman in a fire-engine red dress cut short to bare long legs. Moira stared in shock. She wouldn't have dared wear a dress that short, because she didn't have legs like that. On her, the razor-sharp, chin-length bob wouldn't have emphasized sculpted cheekbones, because she didn't have those, either. And—oh, God—if she'd worn a red dress, never mind the slash of scarlet lipstick, her hair and freckles would have looked orange.

They *were* orange.

She had to quit staring. Moira knew that, in some distant part of her mind. It would be humiliating if Bruce were to happen to glance her way and catch her gaping.

Maybe, at the last minute, his plans had changed and he'd come on the chance that she would be here. If he'd tried calling her at home, and thought that because she didn't answer…

He laid his hand on the brunette's lower back. Really, almost, on her butt. The way his hand was splayed there was unmistakably proprietary and…sexual. Recognizing it, the woman smiled and tilted her head so that it, very briefly, rested against his upper arm.

Pain squeezed Moira's chest. Surely he hadn't been seeing someone else all this time. Or was even married? They had several mutual acquaintances who knew they were dating each other. Wouldn't someone have said something?

And—face it—why would he have dated her at all if he had a wife or a lover who looked like that?

The backs of her eyes burned, and she suddenly felt homely and *fat*. Probably Stan Wells had turned in incredulity at the amount of flesh she'd squeezed into this damn dress.

Breathe, she told herself, and couldn't.

She couldn't seem to make herself move, either. She was frozen between one step and the next, excruciatingly self-conscious. What she'd convinced herself were curves were really bulges. And no one thought a woman whose skin was spotted was sexy. With self-loathing, she wondered who she had been kidding.

Then, to complete her misery, Bruce's head turned and their eyes met. His face went still. Knowing a riptide of red was sweeping up her neck to her cheeks, Moira forced herself into motion. With her redhead's skin, she didn't blush, she flamed. Even from a distance, he would see.

Her eye fastened desperately on a bar ahead. She could pretend she'd been looking for a drink. That gave her a goal. Made her feel as if she was less pathetically, obviously alone.

Except, of course, that she was.

There was a short line. The couple ahead of her were strangers and paid no attention to her. She wished someone else would join the queue, someone she could hide behind. Unfortunately, in her peripheral vision she could still see Bruce and the woman. He spoke to her, then left her watching him speculatively and approached Moira.

If only she could cool her cheeks, she might be able to handle him with savoir faire. A surprised glance, an, "Oh, you made it after all?" If only she had any actual confidence.

"Moira." He was here, at her side.

She tilted her chin up and, somehow, smiled. "Bruce. I didn't expect to see you."

"I didn't think I'd see you, either."

Anger was her salvation, or maybe it would embarrass her, she didn't know which. She went with it anyway.

With raised eyebrows, she glanced toward his date. "Yes, that's obvious."

"Ah…I'm sorry about this. I should have told you."

"That we weren't dating each other exclusively?" She was proud of her level tone.

"It's not like that." He frowned at her. "We were. I was. It's just that I ran into Graziella and…" Bruce spread his hands and shrugged. "We'd broken it off, but as soon as we saw each other again we both knew we'd made a mistake."

In other words, Moira realized, he'd been in love with another woman the entire time he'd dated her. No wonder he'd been so patient. He'd been filling time with her. Licking his wounds. She couldn't even flatter herself that he'd been on the rebound. He hadn't been interested enough in her for their relationship to qualify.

It hurt. Her heart or her pride, she wasn't sure which, but either way, it did hurt.

The couple in front of her stepped up to the bar. She moved forward.

"Honesty would have been nice."

"I didn't lie—"

"Yes, you did. If only by omission." Anger was still carrying her along, thank goodness. "I didn't understand that I wasn't supposed to come tonight. You've embarrassed me. That wasn't necessary, Bruce." Drinks in hand, the couple stepped away. To Bruce, Moira said, "Please excuse me," and turned to the bartender. "A martini, please."

By the time she'd paid, Bruce was gone, striding across the ballroom toward his Graziella, whose name was as exotic as her looks.

Moira took a huge gulp of the martini and wished she could go home. But if she did that, the jerk would know that she wasn't just embarrassed, she was humiliated and wounded. And she refused to give him that satisfaction.

She'd dance, and maybe even get a little bit drunk. She would clutch at her pride, because that's all she had. And she wouldn't let herself think until she got home about the fact that Bruce Girard hadn't wanted her, not really.

Men never did.

WILL BECKER LEANED AGAINST the railing, his back to the view of dark woods that somehow still existed within a stone's throw of the Redmond Town Center mall and the surrounding upscale hotels and restaurants. Instead, nursing a drink he didn't really want, he looked through the floor-to-ceiling glass at the ballroom where other people seemed to be having a fine time.

Him, he hated affairs like this. He was content lurking outside, glass separating him from the gaiety within.

Circumstances being different, he wouldn't be here at all. As it was, he and Clay had attended a few conference sessions together, but the real point of the weekend had been for Will to introduce his brother to everyone he knew. This had been a four day long changing of the guard, so to speak.

"Yes," he'd said dozens of times, "Clay will be taking over Becker Construction. He knows the business. Hell, better than I did when I stepped in for my father." *Got stuck,* was what he really meant. "I have confidence in Clay."

That was the important part: to convey to everyone

that he believed Clay could replace him without one of the county's biggest construction companies suffering even a minor hiccup.

"I have plans," he'd said vaguely when asked what he'd be doing. Only to a select few had he admitted that a week from tomorrow he was flying to Zimbabwe to begin a two-year commitment to build medical clinics. He only knew how to do one thing—build—but at least he'd be having an adventure. That, and doing good, instead of adding another minimall where it wasn't needed.

Now, he was lying low. He'd done his duty this evening and would have left if Clay didn't still seem to be having a good time.

Music spilled from the crowded ballroom, and he idly watched the dancers. Not for the first time, Will found his gaze following a redheaded woman whose lush body was poured into a high-necked forest-green dress that might have been demure on someone else—someone who didn't have a small waist, a glorious ass and breasts that would overflow a man's hands, even hands as large as his.

The guy she was dancing with kept trying to pull her closer, and she was refusing to relax into him. She sure as hell had no intention of melting against the guy, which seemed to be frustrating him no end.

When the music ended, he said something to her, his hand still resting against her waist. She shook her head and walked away, straight to the bar.

Will had noticed that, too. The beautiful redhead was putting away the drinks. Not enough yet to have her tanked, but more than was wise if she intended to drive home. And he guessed she'd need to, because he hadn't seen any sign she was here with anybody, friend or date. In fact, for all the dancing she was doing, she didn't look like she was having a very good time. Maybe a mistaken impression, but…he didn't think so.

She took her fresh drink and this time headed for the doors that stood open to the terrace where he currently lurked. Just like he had, the redhead went straight for the dark perimeter where light from the ballroom didn't reach. She didn't realize she wasn't alone until she was almost on top of him.

When she started, Will said, "Hey," making his voice soothing. Even if he hadn't been standing in the dark, his size tended to alarm lone women. "Want to hide out here with me?"

She blinked owlishly. "I didn't see you."

"I know. That's okay, I wouldn't mind some company." Hers, anyway. To himself, he could admit that he'd been humming with a low level of arousal since he'd first set eyes on her. He didn't like bony women, and this one had the most luscious body he'd seen in longer than he could remember.

He wished he could make out what color her eyes were. He knew she had a pretty face and a mouth made for smiling. But her eyes, he hadn't been sure of from a distance. Brown? Didn't most redheads have brown eyes?

"I don't want to intrude," she said after a minute.

Will shook his head. "You're not. I was watching you dance."

Her head tilted his way. "You were?"

Some undertone in her voice puzzled him. She sounded surprised. Or even disbelieving.

"You're beautiful," he said simply.

His mystery redhead snorted. "Yeah, right. That's me."

Oh, yeah. Definitely disbelieving.

He grinned at her. "You think I'm full of hot air."

The pretty mouth was mulish and *not* smiling. "I know what I look like."

He was tempted to end the argument by kissing her, but he didn't make a habit of grabbing women he hardly knew. And anyway…she wasn't being coy. The words had been pained, as if pushed through a throat that was raw.

"Did somebody insult you?" Will asked gently.

She took a long swallow of her drink, swayed and clunked it down on the railing beside his. Liquid splashed. "You could say that," she said in a small, tight voice.

He was hardly aware of his hands tightening into fists. Partly to keep them off her, and partly because he wanted to slug the bastard who'd hurt her feelings.

"Who?"

She blinked at him again.

"Who?" he repeated.

"Oh, it was my own stupid fault," she said finally. "I guess I was supposed to get the message when he let me know he wouldn't be bringing me tonight." She heaved a sigh. "The part I missed was that he was bringing someone else."

"He thought you wouldn't come."

"Bingo."

Will's eyes narrowed. "So he's here."

"Yes. With Graziella." She grimaced. "Of course she couldn't have a name like Ethel."

Not many women in their twenties or thirties were named Ethel, Will thought with a trace of amusement. But he liked the way she said it, and the way she spit out *Graziella*.

"I'll bet you're nothing as plain as Ethel, either."

"No," she mumbled, "I'm Moira."

"As Irish as your hair."

She reached up and touched the skillfully tumbled

mass of red curls atop her head as if to remind herself what was up there. "I suppose."

"I'm Will," he said, and held out his hand. "Will Becker."

She laid hers in it and they shook with an odd sort of solemnity. "Good to meet you, Will Becker."

She sounded as if the booze was starting to go to her head, as if she was having to form words carefully. He hoped she'd forget she still had most of a drink.

"Having a good time anyway?" he asked.

Moira sighed. "Not especially. You?"

"No. I'm not a real social guy."

She stirred. "You probably wish I'd leave you alone."

"No." He clasped her wrist loosely. "No. Don't go."

After a moment she said, "Okay." She didn't seem to notice he was holding on to her. "I kind of wish I could go home, 'cept…*except* I don't want *him* to catch me slinking out. You know?"

"Is he really worth the heartburn?"

"I thought so," she said sadly.

"Have you been seeing him long?" Will didn't actually want to know; he didn't want to talk about the scumbag at all. But he also didn't want her to go back in, and he couldn't think of anything else to talk about. Sure as hell not the local building trade, since as of Monday morning he was no longer president of Becker Construction.

"I don't know," she said in answer to his question. "A month or six weeks."

Will slid his hand down and laced his fingers with hers. It was almost more intimate than a kiss, he thought, looking at their clasped hands. There was something about being palm to palm.

She didn't seem to notice that they were holding hands now.

"I just want to forget about him," she declared. "And *Graziella*."

There it was again, the name as abomination.

Will laughed. "Definitely forget them. Talk to me. Did you grow up around here?"

She turned to look at him instead of the ballroom. "Uh-uh. Montana. Missoula. You?"

"I'm a local boy."

"So your family is here?" She seemed bemused by the idea.

"Yeah. Not my parents, they're gone. My mother when I was a kid, and then my dad and stepmom in a plane crash when I was twenty. One of those freak things, a sightseeing flight—" He stopped. Sharing long past tragedy wasn't the way to get the girl.

Not that he was trying to *get* her. Not when he'd be winging to Africa a week from now. He just wanted to enjoy her for a little longer.

"But I have two brothers and a sister," he continued. "From Dad's second marriage."

She nodded her understanding.

"The youngest just graduated from college. My sister, Sophie. She'll be going to grad school come fall." He smiled. "And that's more you wanted to know, I bet. Do you have sisters or brothers?"

Moira shook her head. "There was only me and my mom. I didn't really even know my dad. My parents split up when I was two."

And her father was a jackass who hadn't bothered to make time for his daughter, Will diagnosed. He really, really wished he could see her face better. Once again, she sounded a little sad, but he might be imagining things. He was surprised to realize that, for the second time tonight, he was feeling protective and angry on her behalf.

He thought he'd worn out all those instincts getting his siblings safely raised.

"Have you ever been river rafting?" he asked, at random, determined to lighten the conversation.

She made a little gurgle of amusement. "I can't swim. So no."

"You can't swim?" Will repeated. "How is that possible? Doesn't every kid take lessons?"

"Not this one." She opened her mouth as if to say something, then closed it. "And I'm not about to start now," she finished with a hint of defiance.

"So, is taking the ferry across the Sound your worst nightmare?"

"No, the ferry is okay. I keep a close eye on the lifeboats. Now, those I wouldn't like, but it's a comfort that they're there. My worst nightmare…hmm. Sailing cross the Atlantic."

"*The Perfect Storm* wasn't your favorite movie?"

"I never have liked horror movies."

He found himself smiling at the description. Standing here this way felt good. Somehow they'd come to be closer together than they had started. His much larger hand enveloped hers. Their voices were low, as if they were lovers murmuring secrets to each other.

"What's your worst nightmare?" she asked.

Will had to think about that. He didn't have any phobias, per se. He guessed he might be a little claustrophobic; he'd had a construction site injury once and when the doctor sent him for an MRI he'd found the experience hellish. Given the breadth of his shoulders, he'd been crammed in that damn tunnel as if it were the skin of a sausage and he was the innards. And he'd had to lie there for an aeon. Yeah, being buried alive wouldn't be high

on his list. But it wasn't the worst thing, although it was
oddly akin.

"Being trapped," he finally said quietly. "Any freedom
of choice taken away from me. Spending my entire life
doing what I have to do, no matter how desperately I chafe
at it."

Now where had *that* come from? It was true, every
word of it, but he didn't think he'd ever spoken the words
aloud. God help him, that's what his life had been like
since the day he'd taken the phone call in his college dorm
telling him his parents were dead. He hadn't known what
he wanted to do with his life yet, but it wasn't going to be
construction. He'd worked summers for his dad for the
past five years, and that was enough.

Until all choice had been yanked from him when he
realized his brothers and sister had no one else.

He couldn't regret the decisions he'd made then. He
loved Clay, Jack and Sophie. But these past couple weeks,
knowing the end was in sight, he'd felt like a kid who'd
suffered through his school years looking toward high
school graduation.

Free at last.

He felt Moira's scrutiny. Finally she nodded, but said
softly, "Life's made up of obligations, though, isn't it?"

"But we ought to be able to choose the ones we take
on, don't you think?"

Her head tilted, reminding him of a curious bird.
Perhaps the owl he'd likened her to earlier, with downy,
unruly feathers around the enormous, unblinking eyes.

With that tilt of the head, enough light touched her face
that he thought, *green.* Her eyes were green.

"Yes," she said. "I'm a big fan of free choice." Her
fingers wriggled in his, and she glanced down in apparent
puzzlement.

So she'd finally noticed that they had been holding hands for the past ten minutes. Although reluctant, he released hers.

"If you'll excuse me, my feet are killing me and I think I had too much to drink. I'm about to conk out."

"You're not planning to drive, are you?"

She shook her head. "I think I'll get a room."

Will smiled at her. "I'll walk you down."

"You don't have to—"

"It would be my pleasure," he said with a formality unusual to him.

After a moment, she murmured, "Then, thank you." She started toward the open doors, and he strolled at her side.

When they reached the ballroom, he could hardly tear his eyes from her face. She was indeed pretty, but in a way that contrasted with her curvaceous, seductive body. Her cheeks were round, her forehead high, giving her an unexpected look of vulnerability, and her milk-pale skin was dusted with pale gold freckles. Her eyes were green, but flecked with gold, too. And her eyebrows, like the hair on her head, were the pure color of copper.

She looked…innocent, which made him feel guilty for wondering if the rest of her body was freckled, too, if the nipples crowning her generous breasts were pink or dusky brown, whether her pubic hair was copper bright, too.

He almost groaned. Yes, of course it was. And, damn it, he had no business thinking this way when he couldn't start anything with her. He was tying up the last strands of this part of his life, not opening any new packages. However enticing this one was.

Moira greeted a couple of people, and he did the same. They even had a few mutual acquaintances, none of whom seemed to think anything of the fact that they knew each other. He wondered what she did for a living, but decided he didn't want to know. He'd prefer to remember her as his mysterious redhead.

Then she stiffened. Raising his eyebrows, Will saw the couple directly in front of them. Good-looking guy, beautiful woman if you liked hip bones sharp enough to draw blood and thought counting ribs was an excellent postcoital activity.

The scumbag, clearly, and *Graziella*. Feeling Moira's tension, Will wasn't nearly as amused as he'd been when she last said the name.

"Bruce," she said coolly.

Some instinct made Will lay his hand on Moira's back in a way any other man would recognize. *Mine.* He nodded, making plain his disinterest, and steered her around the other couple.

"Aren't you Will Becker?" the other guy said.

Will nodded. "Yes." And kept going.

Moira gave another of those little gurgles of laughter that sounded like a small brook tumbling over rocks. "Well, that was rude."

"Yeah, and I enjoyed it," he said truthfully.

She turned that laughing face up to him, her eyes sparkling, and said, "Thank you."

"You're very welcome." He kept his hand on her until they reached the front desk, at which point he stood back and let her take a credit card from the small, sparkly bag she'd carried over her shoulder. When eventually she turned around, he asked, "All set?"

"Yes. You don't have to walk me up, Will."

"Yes, I do."

She bit her lip and studied him for a moment, her eyes curiously vulnerable in a way that gave him a pang.

Twice now he'd thought of her as such, which had to mean something.

He knew what that something was. His gut was telling him to say good-night to her outside her hotel room door and leave. Don't kiss her. Don't step over the threshold. She wasn't a one-night stand kind of woman, and he wasn't interested in anything but.

Moira nodded and let him walk beside her to the elevators. One opened as soon as she pushed the button, and they rode upward in silence, side by side. He heard the soft sigh of a breath from her, caught an elusive scent that seemed old-fashioned. He had a flash of standing on the deep front porch of his family home, the sky purple with twilight, and that scent filling his nostrils.

Lilac.

The elevator opened and he said, "What's your room number?"

She stumbled, stepping out, and he wrapped a hand around her arm to catch her. "Um…" She looked at the small folder she held. "Two-eighteen."

Will nodded and directed her to the right. The hall was broad, the plush charcoal-gray carpet inset with maroon. He stopped in front of 218 and watched as she fumbled with the card, finally getting it into the slot correctly and turning the knob when the green light flashed.

"I should say good-night now," he said hoarsely.

Holding the door open, she met his eyes. "Did you mean it, when you said…" She seemed to lose courage.

"Said…?" His heart was hammering.

She whispered, "That you think I'm beautiful."

"I meant it." He lifted a hand, hesitated, then only

grazed her round, plush cheek with his knuckles. "You are."

Her tongue touched her lips; she took a deep breath. "Then will you stay?"

CHAPTER TWO

STUNNED PLEASURE BLOSSOMED inside him like the warmth from good whiskey.

"You're sure?" Will asked.

Had she really invited him in? Could he get this lucky?

But already Moira's eyes had widened, as if she'd shocked herself, and her face flushed. Even so, she mumbled, "I think so."

Despite the rising tide of hunger, he found himself smiling. "That wasn't the strongest yes I've ever heard."

Now her gaze was shy. "I haven't done this in an awfully long time."

His every instinct was to kiss her and keep kissing her until she was past any second thoughts. Damn, he hadn't had sex in…it had to be a year, since he'd parted ways with Julia. But as desperate as he felt, Will wasn't willing to risk making love with a woman who might hate herself or him immediately afterward.

"It's been a good long while for me, too," he admitted.

"Probably not as long as it's been for me." This mumble was so low he doubted it had been for his ears. It was a good reminder that his redhead had maybe had too much to drink. She was clutching onto the door frame pretty hard.

"Why me?" he asked.

She raised her chin. "You can just say no."

"I don't want to say no."

"Oh." Her lashes fluttered. "I'm attracted to you. I suppose…I needed someone to tell me I'm beautiful. You sounded like you really did mean it." Her shoulders moved in an oddly unhappy jerk. "This is only for tonight…"

"It can only be for tonight." His voice came out harsh.

Now alarm flashed in her green eyes. "You're not married?"

"No." He laid a palm against her cheek and felt the heat of her blush. "No," he said, softer. "Nothing like that."

"Okay." Her breath tickled his wrist. "Then…?"

"Are you on birth control? I don't have anything with me."

Now her cheeks blazed. "I do. I was planning…"

He got it. The jackass downstairs was supposed to be standing here, not him. He was a substitute.

This was one time, Will thought with amusement and a leap of desire, that he didn't mind filling in.

"In that case," he said huskily, "I'd love to stay."

He had a fleeting moment of being bothered that she looked surprised—had she really thought he'd say *no?*— but it was forgotten when he stepped forward until their bodies touched, chest to thighs. He took the hotel key from her hand and urged her backward, until the door swung shut behind them.

The room was dark; he fumbled for a switch and batted at it. The lamp beside the king-size bed came on, casting a golden circle of light. Perfect.

Damn, she was pretty. Will tossed the hotel key onto a dresser top and divested her of the small evening bag, sending it after the key. Then he cupped her face in his broad palms and bent his head.

He didn't feel gentle, but he made sure his mouth was. Simply a little friction on her lips, a nibble, a stroke of his tongue. He could taste the martini, and something more. Something, he thought, that was distinctly *her*. He lifted his head and looked down at her face where color still blossomed. This close he could see that her lashes were darkened with mascara. Their natural color was undoubtedly that same bright copper. He'd like to see her without the mascara, with no defenses.

Although she had precious few now. She might have started with lipstick, but it had worn off, and the roses in her cheeks were surely her own. It would take a lot of powder to cover her freckles, and why would she bother trying? He liked those freckles.

"Can I take your hair down?" he whispered.

Her eyes were dazed. "I… Yes. Of course."

When he delved his fingers in, he found an intriguing texture. As he removed pins, curls sprang free. One leaped around his index finger as if to entrap it. Her hair was thick and strong, strands sleek but not downy soft. Despite the sexual tension that gripped Will, he found himself foolishly smiling, imagining her trying to tame this mass every day.

"It's awful hair."

"It's glorious." Pins showered to the carpet; he was too busy playing to care. The curls tumbled below her shoulders. He guessed if her hair had been straight it might have fallen to the middle of her back. He could see that calling it *copper* wasn't right: a hundred colors seemed to be mixed, from hairs as pale as flax to ones a deep auburn, and every shade in between. It was beautiful in this light. With sun shining on her head, she must glow.

"Man," he whispered, and buried his face in her hair. The lilac fragrance was coming from it, and he let himself wallow happily for a minute. Then he pulled back enough to nip her earlobe and finally string kisses across her cheek to her nose and mouth.

This time he kissed her deeply, hungrily, sliding his tongue past her teeth to stroke hers. She made a muffled sound and wrapped her arms around his neck. Her body molded itself to his as if they were custom shaped. Sensation piled atop sensation: her tongue, slippery and sinuous against his, the plump, firm pillow of her breasts pressed against his chest, the vitality of the curls tangled around the hand he had cupping the back of her head.

He wanted her *now,* and fought to hold himself in check. That bastard downstairs had made her feel undesirable, and Will needed to fix that. Come morning, he was determined that she had no doubt in her mind how much he'd wanted her and how rich her own response was.

As he slid her zipper down and trailed his mouth over her throat, he murmured disconnected words meant to tell her what he felt. Her skin was unbelievably soft, and the leap of pulse under his lips aroused him like he couldn't remember being. He nipped at her neck, wanting to leave a mark but careful not to. He couldn't claim the right, not when he wouldn't be around tomorrow.

She let out little gasps as he eased her dress down and peeled it off her arms then over her hips. His blood surged at the sight of her deep purple satin bra and a skimpy pair of matching panties.

"Beautiful. So beautiful," he managed to say, although the words came out sounding raw. Her dress fell to her feet and he scooped her in his arms and moved her a few feet closer to the bed.

She wore no stockings, only strappy high heels and the bra and panties that were... His hands explored. Not a thong, but there wasn't much there except the generous curve of butt that had him so hard he hurt.

Damn. He kissed her again, both his hands gripping her ass to hold her tight to his hips. They rocked where they stood, as if they couldn't help themselves, and a groan tore its way from his throat.

He eased back and started yanking at his own clothes, flinging his suit coat to the floor, his tie after it the moment he got the damn knot undone. Moira was wrestling with the buttons of his shirt at the same time, and it fell to the floor, too.

Somehow he got the covers pulled down and laid her across the wide bed, her sprawl so wanton he couldn't do anything but follow her even though he wanted to finish stripping. He had to cradle his erection between her thighs or he thought he might die right now.

They kissed and rolled, his hands everywhere on her body, hers on his. Not until she rose above him, sitting atop him, did he manage to undo the catch on her bra and free the most beautiful breasts he'd ever seen. Her chest was freckled, and a scattering of paler freckles danced down over the creamy skin traced with faint blue lines, as though her skin was more transparent than normal. Her nipples were pink, the aureoles larger and just a little deeper in color.

Will heard himself making sounds that weren't even words as he tugged her near so that he could lave her nipples with his tongue, first one then the other. Kiss them softly, blow on the damp skin until she shivered, then suckle her, pulling the hard nubbin deep into his mouth as his cheeks flexed.

She clutched his shoulders and whimpered. Her hips rose and fell on his as if she couldn't help herself, but he was afraid he'd come right now, in his pants, if she kept riding him that way. He rolled her onto her back so that he was on top, able to savor her breasts for another few minutes before he rose to his knees and tugged her panties off. There were the curls as bright as the ones on her head, nestled between a smooth, freckled stomach and perfect legs that were freckled, too. He wanted to kiss every single freckle, but he knew he wouldn't last that long.

Her stomach. He'd start there. He loved the give of it; she had a tiny waist, but not the washboard abs of a woman who worked out every day. She felt intensely feminine, the ripples of reaction under his mouth amazingly erotic.

He finally had the strength of will to retreat enough to remove her shoes and, with clumsy hands, unbuckle his belt and shed his pants and socks. Then he kissed and licked his way up her legs, from the quivering arch of her feet to the sensitive back of her knees and the velvet softness of her inner thighs. He nuzzled her curls and inhaled her scent, his head swimming. A few strokes of his finger told him she was hot and wet and ready. Her cries had become something closer to mewls, and her head was flung back, her hair a halo against the white sheet.

He moved up between her thighs and got as far as pressing against her opening when his brain finally kicked in.

A condom! What in the hell had he been *thinking?*

He all but sprang from her. "Your purse?" he asked.

For a moment he could tell she didn't comprehend, but then her eyes widened in shock that matched his. They'd come so close. Too damn close.

"Yes." She swallowed. "Yes. I don't know where…"

"I put it…" He turned his head and spotted the glittery bag. He leaped out of bed. When he got his hands on the

bag, he dumped the contents on the dresser top, not caring
that some fell to the floor. Between folded bills was one
small packet, and that was it.

He wished she'd brought more than one.

Will ripped it open and put on the condom. Two
long steps and he was at the bed, where her legs were
still splayed wide. He ran his hands up them, caressing,
squeezing, until his fingers reached her damp center and
he stroked as he knelt there. Not until her hips rocked
again did he lower himself, taking her mouth in a deep,
hungry kiss even as he pushed inside her.

She was tight. So tight he had a brief, horrified moment
of wondering whether she might be a virgin. But he met
no barrier, although he had to quit kissing her to grit his
teeth at the exquisite pressure her body put on him. He
was a big man, but he'd never felt anything like this.

"Am I hurting you?" he asked roughly.

She was panting for breath and her eyes were dilated.
"No," she whispered. "Oh, no."

Will moved. Out, in, slowly this time. He was near to
exploding, but he had to give her pleasure first. Had to.

"Never felt…anything…this good," he groaned against
her throat.

"Please." She wrapped her legs around his hips and
rose to meet his next thrust. "Oh, please."

He knew what she needed. He just wasn't sure he could
hold out long enough. He tried to blank his mind as he
plunged, again and again, clasped so tight by her. He'd
been holding his weight from her on his elbows, but now
he reached down with one hand and gripped her hips, lifting her higher, changing the angle at which their bodies
met.

"Will?" She sounded…almost frightened. Stunned,
certainly. And then she cried out, and her body spasmed.

He drove himself in her as deep as he could go and let the climax roll through him, the pleasure so powerful he couldn't have formed a coherent thought if his life had depended on it.

He collapsed on top of her and couldn't move.

Through a haze, it occurred to him that he'd never felt this amazing in his life. That sex had never *approached* being this powerful. He didn't know how or why it had been this time. Maybe something about the night, about having watched her for so long through the glass. And they didn't know each other.

That was it: anticipation, and mystery.

Eventually he made himself roll to one side and tuck her against him, her head on his shoulder, her hair tickling his chin. Eyes closed, he smiled, imagining those tendrils reaching for some kind of toehold, like ivy scaling a brick wall.

"You're amazing," he murmured, his voice thick.

She snuggled closer and said nothing.

Will let himself drift, aware of the change in her breathing as she fell asleep. And, in drifting, he slept himself.

It was probably the unfamiliar weight of her head on his shoulder that awakened him. Will was disoriented only for a moment. He reached up with his free hand and brushed curls from his mouth, then tilted his head enough to be able to see her face. Her lips were parted, and a faint snore came to his ears.

His body stirred, and Will wished again that they had more than one condom. He supposed he could call down to the front desk… But she was sound asleep. She didn't surface when he gently disentangled himself. Wishing for another condom had reminded him that he hadn't removed the last one, or cleaned up.

What he should do was get dressed and go. Staying longer wouldn't bring anything but frustration and, come morning, an awkward conversation he'd as soon not have. She'd asked for one night; he'd told her it couldn't be any more than that. What else was there to say?

Will eased away, used the bathroom, then quietly got dressed. He found a pen on the desk and wrote quickly on the back of one of his business cards:

You *are* beautiful. I wish more than one night had been possible.
Will.

He underlined the *are* with a dark slash.

He picked up her clothes and laid them over a chair, then tucked the covers under her chin. She sighed and shifted before sinking back into deep slumber.

Will took one last look at her face and the vivid hair spread across the pillow, turned off the lamp and quietly let himself out of the room.

MOIRA WOKE WITH A START. Her mouth felt disgusting and she tried to work up some saliva. When she moved, a headache blossomed. Ugh. Was she coming down with something…?

She opened her eyes and remembered. *Oh, Lord,* she thought in shock. Had she really…? She squeezed her eyes shut. Yes. Yes, she had.

Behind closed eyelids, she pictured him, broad and tall in the darkness, the way she saw him first, then his rough-hewn face above her here in this bed, his short dark hair and the deep brown eyes looking so intensely into hers. She saw him so vividly, she expected to see him in reality when she opened her eyes, even though she knew better.

When she rolled enough to check out the other side of the bed and the room, it was to find herself alone. He was gone. They'd had sex, and he'd left her sleeping.

After, Moira noticed, picking up her clothes so they weren't left wadded on the floor.

With a groan, she got out of bed, snatched up her clothes and rushed into the bathroom. Her stomach felt queasy but not too bad. She couldn't exactly say she was hungover, although she wished she hadn't had the last drink or two. Maybe, with a clearer head, she'd have had more sense than to take a hotel room and invite a perfect stranger into bed with her.

Shame crawled over her skin like goose bumps. What on earth had made her do something like that? She'd had only one lover in her whole life, and that was a college boyfriend. All these years since, she'd never even been *tempted* to have a one-night stand.

Until last night. When she'd not only been tempted, she'd done it.

The shower was blessedly hot, and she stayed in it for a long time. Getting dressed afterward wasn't fun, given that she didn't have clean underwear and had to put on an evening gown and high heels. She'd have killed for coffee and breakfast to settle her stomach, but no way was she going in a restaurant dressed like this, advertising that she'd had a hard night. She could order from room service... But that seemed silly. She'd be home in forty-five minutes.

With no brush, either, all she could do was loosely braid her wet hair. Her evening bag...she spotted it lying atop the dresser, next to a TV schedule and some local promotional brochures. Her keys had fallen to the floor for some reason, and as she bent to pick them up she saw her lipstick, too. She grabbed the purse and straightened, stuffing the lipstick inside as she turned for the door. Moira had no idea where the room key was and didn't care. At last, gingerly, she picked up the business card with the short note written on the back. A painful lump seemed to form in her chest.

Why can't *we have more than one night?* But she wouldn't call him. He'd made clear his limitations. If he wanted to, he could find her.

Moira dropped the business card in her purse and let herself out of the room. All she wanted was to get to her car, preferably unseen, and go home.

Then she would try to understand why she'd so foolishly gotten naked with a stranger, however kind and sexy he was.

But she knew, of course: her feelings had been hurt and she'd needed consolation. *Foolish* was the word for it, Moira thought, blushing as she crossed the hotel foyer under the gaze of a woman behind the front desk.

And *risky.* That was another word for having sex with a stranger.

Except, he hadn't hurt her, and she knew he'd used the condom. Because *he'd* remembered, not because she had. She'd been lucky. Done something dumb, and escaped any of the myriad possible consequences. She should be old enough not to have to learn a lesson this way, but apparently she wasn't.

Moira got into her car and momentarily laid her forehead against the steering wheel.

I learned. I did.

Time to go home and... No, she wouldn't wish Will Becker would call. Instead, she'd do her best to forget last night ever happened.

THE SECURITY LINE at the airport lay just ahead. This early in the morning, it was short. He'd have plenty of time for breakfast and coffee once he got through it.

Will had intended to take an airporter to SeaTac, but Sophie insisted on driving him. During the past week, he'd signed over the title to his pickup to Jack and piled a few plastic tubs filled with his possessions in the basement of the family home. This morning, he had taken one last look at his bedroom, stripped of personality, and felt something unexpected: grief. He was saying goodbye to his entire life to this point. He had grown up in this house, played with plastic dinosaurs on the floor of this same bedroom, fought later with his stepmother over how clean he had to keep it. Sneaked a high school girlfriend in here and had sex with her after his parents were in bed and asleep. Returned the one summer after his freshman year in college, swearing that it would be the last time he'd work for his father, the last time he'd swing a hammer.

Then he'd come home to stay after his parents died. He'd never considered moving into the master bedroom, which was still empty. It was stupid, really, with Jack, Sophie, Clay and him all here, all in small bedrooms designed for children. He hoped, if and when Clay got married, that he'd have the sense to overcome the past and make the house his. Really his.

Something Will hadn't done, in part because he hadn't wanted the house, or the company, and he sure hadn't wanted to be a twenty-year-old stand-in father of three, responsible for the financial and emotional well-being of his young sister and brothers.

And now, he thought, standing in SeaTac airport at the crack of dawn, he was done with all of it.

He turned to face his sister. "Thanks for bringing me."

Sophie was the shrimp of the family, and still stood five foot ten. "*Somebody* had to see you off," she insisted.

"Yeah." He grinned at her. "Don't do anything I wouldn't approve of, okay?"

Her brown eyes filled with tears. "Oh, Will!" she wailed. "I'm going to miss you!"

His arms closed fiercely around her. "Damn it, Soph. I thought we had this goodbye crap out of the way."

She shook her head hard. "I know it doesn't make sense, when I've been away at college the last four years, but...you were always here. And now you won't be."

"I'm sorry," he heard himself say. "Do I still need to be?"

She shook her head again, then pulled back to give him a watery smile. "Of course you don't. I'm being silly. It's just...I'll miss you, Will. I'm *glad* you're going. I know how much you need this. How much you gave up for us."

He scowled. "Don't start with that. I did what I had to do. I have no regrets."

Her smile became more genuine. "Yeah, sure you don't. Just, um, have a fabulous time, okay? And email."

"Yeah, yeah." He kissed her wet cheek. "I love you, Soph. I won't disappear, I promise."

"Okay." She sniffed and swiped at damp eyes. "I'm going. You don't need this. Just...take care." She gave him one more fervent hug, then hurried away.

He watched her go, not looking back, and remembered taking each of his siblings to college to start their freshman years. Helping them haul their stuff into dorm rooms, wishing he was the one there to stay, then driving away with the feeling that a big hole had opened in his chest. Except for the envy he hadn't been able to help, he'd been all parent, a little shocked to find out how much he was going to miss first Clay, then Jack, then Sophie.

By the time Sophie started her freshman year, Clay was home again and working with Will. Unlike Will, he had loved the summers he'd worked construction. It seemed to be in his blood. He'd learned the business eagerly and had a natural air of authority.

Will shook himself now, surprised again at how alone he felt. Glad he was, but a little sorry all the same. Maybe he should have expected these mixed emotions, but hadn't. He'd expected to be celebrating this morning.

He went through security, taking out his laptop, putting his shoes on the conveyor belt, having to go back and empty the change out of the pockets of his pants. Then he put himself back together and headed for the closest place to have breakfast.

Although he'd brought the morning *Times* to read while he was eating, Will found himself thinking instead about his redhead. He kept thinking he should have tracked her down and called her. Maybe she felt fine about making love with him, but maybe she didn't. He hated to think she was embarrassed.

He wished…oh, damn, he wished he'd met her at another time and place. That he'd been able to call her the next day and ask her out to dinner. Let her know that she could be special to him, not merely a chance to get his rocks off.

Face it, he thought harshly; that's all she'd been. And she deserved more.

He'd feel worse if he was sure saying "Thanks, but no thanks," would have been the right thing to do. Will was still afraid that would have hurt her, that she'd been emotionally fragile enough to *need* a man to want her.

And maybe he was trying to excuse himself for taking

what she offered because he wanted to, whether it was a crappy thing for him to have done or not.

He hoped she didn't give the jackass another chance if he came begging.

Forget it, he told himself, frowning as he rose to walk to the gate. There was nothing he could do now. This was his new beginning. He should be rejoicing.

Too bad he wasn't already in Harare, instead of facing thirty-six hours on airplanes and airport layovers in Frankfurt and Addis Ababa, Ethiopia. He hoped like hell the promised aisle seats materialized; he was way too big a man to spend that many hours cramped between other passengers or at the window.

Half an hour later, his flight was called. Thinking, *Here goes nothing,* he took out his boarding pass and joined the line. But he was still picturing an apple-cheeked, freckled face with pretty lips and green eyes when he wedged himself into his airline seat and buckled the belt.

CHAPTER THREE

STANDING ATOP THE ROUGH concrete foundation, Moira studied the completed framing of the building that would house doctors' offices and an outpatient surgical center.

"Looking good," she told Jeb Morris, a contractor with whom she'd worked before. These visits were almost a formality with Jeb; he knew enough to spot problems before they tripped him up. And he maintained high standards.

A short, stocky man with a close-cropped beard, he pushed his hard hat back, his gaze resting on her. "Everything okay, Moira?"

She looked at him in surprise. "Sure. Why do you ask?"

He shook his head. "You seem distracted today."

Moira forced a smile. "I guess I am. Just things on my mind. Sorry, Jeb."

"Hey, no problem. I'll walk you to your car."

Because she was visiting several sites today, she'd worn her clunky work boots, jeans and a green flannel shirt over a T-shirt, in case the day got warmer. It was May, tulips were in bloom, but the morning had been chilly.

She was trying very, very hard to think about the job site and the wiring and electrical and plumbing that would soon go in, about spring flowers and how she was meeting Gray and Charlotte for lunch later. Gray Van Dusen was her partner in Van Dusen & Cullen, Architects, and her best friend in the world. Charlotte had quickly become almost as good a friend.

Moira was doing her best to think about anything and everything except the fact that she was almost positive her period was late. At least a week late. Maybe ten days. She didn't keep exact track, so she wasn't sure. But…it should have come and gone.

Sickening fear rose from her belly to swell in her chest, as it did every time she let this worry creep through her defenses. She felt Jeb's scrutiny and made a point of smiling again and asking about his oldest son, who was a senior in high school waiting to hear which colleges had accepted him.

Jeb's face brightened. "Didn't I tell you? He received early acceptance to Stanford. Can you believe it?" He wore a goofy grin. "My kid, going to Stanford."

She laughed. "Your kid, your tuition bills."

That didn't wipe the smile away. "Worth every penny." He slapped the top of her car. "Take care, Moira."

"Yeah, thanks, Jeb." She put the key in the ignition and closed the door as he walked away. Not wanting him to turn back and see her sitting here, she reversed then drove across bumpy ground toward the street. Meantime, her stomach churned.

Was it too early for a pregnancy test?

Once out of sight of the construction, she pulled to the curb and set the car in Park. Still holding on to the steering wheel for all she was worth, Moira let the fear wash over her. It sensitized her skin, set her to rocking, made her pant.

How could this *be?* He'd used the condom. She knew he had, saw him put it on.

Yes, but condoms had a failure rate a whole lot higher than birth-control pills. Which she wasn't on. Hadn't wanted to start until she was sure her relationship with Bruce was moving to that point.

She'd had sex once. Once! *And* they'd used a condom. Even if it had failed—had a hole, or leaked, or whatever went wrong—a woman shouldn't get pregnant the one and only time she'd had sex in over ten years. Wasn't there some justice, somewhere, that would keep her from being punished so severely for her foolish need to prove she was desirable?

And to make matters worse, she wasn't even convinced she'd proved that much. Yes, he'd made passionate love to her. He'd said the right things. He'd touched her with such care, such longing, and his eyes had darkened to near black when he thrust into her. But…he had also left the minute she fell asleep, simply stole away.

And even though he'd said it would be only the one night… A part of her couldn't help wondering why. Why, in the three weeks that had passed since then, he hadn't made the effort to find out who she was, hadn't called. She would have been easy to find, Moira knew, with her flaming red hair and freckled face. They'd known people in common; all he would have had to do was make a phone call or two.

But he hadn't done that.

Please don't let him be married, she prayed. *Don't let him have lied. I'd hate to have to live with that. Especially now, especially if…*

If she was pregnant. Moira bit her lip so hard she tasted blood.

What would she do if she was pregnant? Would she track him down and tell him?

Still rocking herself, she thought, *No.* If this was anyone's fault, it was hers. She'd asked him to make love to her. The condom was hers, so she couldn't even blame him for using a defective one. He'd warned her that the one night was all he could offer, and she'd agreed. How could she now contact him and say, "Hate to tell you, but you're going to be a father, so how do you feel about paying child support for, oh, say, the next eighteen years?"

That wasn't the deal they'd made.

My fault, my risk.

And—oh, Lord—she didn't know if she could face him anyway. Maybe the standards she'd grown up with in Montana were dated, but the closest she'd come to shaking them was sleeping with her college boyfriend. Having too much to drink followed by a one-night stand... She shivered. She'd all but *begged* him to have sex with her.

Moira was whimpering now, the fear swamping her. She felt like a drowning victim, going down for the last time, desperate for a hand to reach for her. But there wasn't one. Wouldn't be one. If she made Will Becker take responsibility, all she'd be doing was dragging him under with her.

It was a long time before she felt able to drive again. She'd made one decision: she would wait another week before she bought a home pregnancy test. Heck, maybe her anxiety was holding off her period. A watched pot never boils, after all. And...really, was there any advantage to knowing for sure this early? Abortion wasn't an option for her, she knew that. She *wanted* to have children. She'd always assumed she would be married by the time she had a baby, that there would be a father in the picture, too, but hard reality was that she was thirty-four years old. Maybe she should be grabbing at any chance to have a family, even if it wouldn't be the ideal one.

Moira wished she wasn't supposed to meet Gray and Charlotte. Hiding her distress would be hard. And the truth was, if she really was pregnant, carried the baby to term and kept him or her to raise, Gray would pay some of the price, too, however unfair that was.

When he got the idea of running for mayor of West Fork, they'd had a long talk. He wasn't married then, hadn't even met Charlotte, so it was only the two of them making the decision. The mayoral job wasn't full-time, or he wouldn't have considered it. But he'd have to cut back substantially on how many architectural commissions he took. Unless they wanted their revenue to decline substantially, Moira would be carrying more than her share of the work.

She'd liked what he wanted to accomplish for this town that was now home for both of them, and understood why it mattered to him. Understood more, probably, than he'd be comfortable realizing. Gray was usually closemouthed about his deepest motivations, but they had been best friends in college. There'd been a couple of times when he'd had too much to drink and had told her things he had probably regretted—assuming he'd remembered the next day.

She knew he had had a twin brother who died in an accident when the two boys were ten years old. They had been riding bikes together, racing down a hill. Garret had pulled ahead, just a little. He slammed into the side of a car passing on the street that intersected the foot of the hill. Gray shot past the rear bumper. A split second one way or the other and it would have been different. Garret might have been fine and Gray dead. Or both fine. Garret went into a coma and never came out before dying two days later. In their grief, Gray's parents pulled away from each other and ultimately divorced, his mother moving to Portland, his dad to Boise. They'd left behind the small-town life that in later years came to seem idyllic to Gray, who had also had to cope with the realization that he was a constant, aching reminder to both of his parents of the son they'd lost.

In coming to West Fork, Gray was trying to recapture everything *he* had lost. She knew that, and feared it was impossible, but had agreed to open their architectural firm here anyway. To her surprise, he seemed to have found what he was looking for. The satisfaction of shaping the town to suit himself, a woman to love, the start of a family.

But Moira wasn't going to be able to keep her end of the agreement. Would she even be able to work full-time when she got near the end of her pregnancy? Didn't most new mothers have to take some time off? And then, how many hours a day could she bear to leave her baby in day care? There was no way Gray would be able to continue serving as mayor, not if Van Dusen & Cullen, Architects, was to survive.

And that made her feel horribly guilty.

Fortunately, if she was quiet during lunch, neither Gray nor Charlotte seemed to notice. They talked some about their current projects, some about Charlotte's pregnancy, which was starting to show, and some about Charlotte's twin sister, Faith, who had recently married West Fork Police Chief Ben Wheeler and who was also thinking of starting a family.

Call her pathetic, but it made Moira feel even lonelier to imagine Charlotte and Faith both pregnant at the same time as she was, but the two of them having men who loved them and worried about them and hovered over them. While all Moira was doing by getting pregnant was screwing up her life.

Worry about it when you're sure, she told herself.

A WEEK LATER, MOIRA BOUGHT a pregnancy test at a pharmacy in Everett where nobody knew her, and decided to wait until after dinner to use it. She should be hungry, but wasn't. A part of her knew it wasn't only anxiety, that the lack of appetite and faint queasiness of the past few days shouldn't come as any surprise.

She peed on the stick, then sat on the edge of the bathtub waiting, staring at it. Maybe the watched pot *wouldn't* boil. If she didn't take her eyes off it, didn't blink….

But she couldn't help blinking, and the blue color first tinted the slot, then brightened.

Oh, God. Oh, God.

All of her fear poured back. She dropped the stick in the wastebasket and bent forward, holding herself as tight as she could as a hundred different emotions eddied and tumbled like flood waters, almost more than her body could contain.

In the end, all she could think was, *I'm pregnant.*

And now she had to live with it.

"Lunch?" Moira said. "Um…sure. Now?"

Oh, heavens. She'd done her best in the two months since she realized she was pregnant to…not avoid Gray, how could she when they were partners and friends? She saw him every day, and she had dinner with him and Charlotte at least once a week. But she had tried not to spend time alone with him, not to let conversation become really personal. It hadn't been as hard as she'd have thought. Mostly in the office they talked business, exchanged ideas, looked over each other's preliminary sketches and made suggestions, offered solutions to jobsite problems. Lunch for Gray was usually fast food or a deli sandwich, snatched between city hall and their architectural office or a job site.

But today, he'd appeared earlier than she had expected him, and now stood in the doorway waiting.

"If not now, when?" he asked with his usual good humor.

She saved her CADD drawing and closed out the program, then took her purse from the bottom drawer of her desk. Gray stood back to let her out the door, then flipped the sign to Closed.

"The Pea Patch?"

"Fine." Perfect, in fact. The small vegetarian restaurant used only organic, healthful ingredients, exactly what a pregnant woman should be eating. Gray had probably taken to eating there with Charlotte.

He didn't say much during the short drive and found parking right in front. The main street of West Fork probably hadn't changed much since the 1950s, with false-fronted buildings and small, locally owned businesses. The Pea Patch was relatively new, of course, as was the antiques store beside it, but the barbershop and hardware store could have starred in a Norman Rockwell painting. One of Gray's goals had been to maintain the old-fashioned atmosphere of downtown and keep people shopping here.

Moira ordered the day's special, a bowl of split-pea soup and a half sandwich, Gray a burrito. He glanced at her sidelong when she asked for a juice instead of the latte that had been her habit.

Once the waitress took the menus and left them alone, he contemplated Moira over the table. Gray was a handsome man with calm gray eyes and sun-streaked light brown hair. They had dated a time or two when they first met, then fell into friendship instead of romance. Gray wasn't the first or the last guy to see her as buddy material instead of potential girlfriend. In his case, she didn't regret it. He'd become family to her, a lot more important than the college boyfriend with whom she'd lost touch shortly after graduation.

"Something's off with you," he said bluntly. "Or maybe with us. Have I been unavailable when you needed to talk?"

Swallowing the lump in her throat, she shook her head.

"Then what, Moira?" His eyes were kind.

Her chest hurt. "Oh, Gray."

"What?" He leaned forward and reached for her hand.

"I've been dreading telling you."

"Telling me what?" His fingers tightened. "You're not leaving me, are you?"

Even in her misery, Moira giggled. "Do you know what that sounds like?"

A grin tugged at his mouth. "Yeah, someone who knows I'm married might wonder." The smile faded and he repeated, "What, Moira?"

She had to tell him eventually. Now was as good a time as ever.

"I'm pregnant."

He jerked. "Pregnant?"

"Jeez, tell the whole town, why don't you," she said indignantly.

He looked around. "There's nobody close enough to hear." He paused. "Is it a secret?"

"No." Damn it, she felt watery again. "I guess it'll be obvious anytime."

"How far along?"

"Um…three months."

He frowned. "You've lost weight instead of gaining, haven't you?"

"Didn't Charlotte?"

"You're sick, too?"

Moira nodded. "Well, not sick. Just…icky feeling. I don't dare do more than nibble at any one time."

He was staring at her. "Pregnant," he repeated. His expression hardened. "Who's the father?"

She gazed steadily back. "No one who is in the picture."

"It was that son of a bitch Girard wasn't it?"

Moira gave a choked laugh. "He is a son of a bitch, but no. It's not him, Gray."

"Then who?" This man, her best friend, sounded implacable, as if he intended to beat the crap out of the man who'd impregnated and abandoned her.

She swallowed, the backs of her eyelids burning again. "It really doesn't matter. He…used a condom. It's just one of those things. Not his fault. And we didn't have the kind of relationship that means I'm going to stick him with this."

The waitress appeared with their lunches, and Moira sat silent, head bowed, while Gray said the right things. The minute the waitress was gone, he said, "You're having the baby." It wasn't really a question.

"I'd have done something about it long ago if I wasn't."

He gave a one-sided shrug, as if to say, *Oh, yeah.* "Why did you dread telling me? You're not planning to move home?"

"Home?" She wished she could laugh. "Missoula? Are you kidding? I love my mother, but…no. I'm not going anywhere. It's just that…"

Neither of them had reached for a spoon or fork.

"You're trying to tell me I'm going to have to start carrying my fair share of the work, aren't you?"

"Probably more than your fair share," she said in a rush. "Gray, I'm sorry. We had a deal, and now I've blown it."

Suddenly he was smiling, so tenderly the tears she'd kept at bay filled her eyes. "Moira, falling in love and having babies are way more important than who does what share of work. You gave me my chance, I had fun. But I won't run for reelection. I can't even say I mind that much. It's been a lot tougher than I envisioned, trying to hold down both jobs. I didn't mind so much before Charlotte, but things are different now." He picked up a napkin and dabbed at her cheeks. "It's past time I take up the slack at work. It's you I'm worried about."

On the verge of major blubbering, she gulped and leaped to her feet. "I'm sorry, I—" She hurried to the bathroom, a small, unisex one where she could lock the door and sob without embarrassment.

It didn't take her long; heaven knows, she'd cried enough lately, and should have had it all out of her system. Even though she splashed cold water on her face, she was blotchy when she returned to the table.

Gray gave her a comprehensive look, but all he said was, "Eat. Your soup's getting cold."

She sniffed and picked up her spoon.

"Do you mind if I tell Charlotte?"

"Of course not. I'll be showing before I know it anyway."

He nodded, and they ate in silence for a few minutes. Moira was hungrier than usual, she was surprised to discover. Maybe something had loosened inside her, now that she'd told Gray.

As though his mind was following a similar path, he asked, "Does your mother know?"

Moira groaned. "No."

His mouth quirked. "Unless she's planning a visit, you have six months to work yourself up to it."

"She'll be supportive."

"Then…?"

"This isn't the way I ever imagined starting a family," she heard herself telling him. "I hated not having a father. It seemed like everyone else did. I always swore—" Her throat closed up.

Once again, his hand enveloped hers. "You know I'll be there for you as much as I can."

"Yeah." She felt her smile wobble. "I do know. Thank you, Gray. But we'll be fine." Unconsciously, she laid a hand on her belly. "Mom and I were fine. It's not as if I grew up unloved."

He was quiet for a moment, his gaze perceptive. "Your baby does have a father."

"I haven't told him."

"I'd have been pissed if a woman I was involved with kept that kind of secret from me."

Admitting something like this was hard, but… "It was a one-time thing, Gray. We weren't involved. He doesn't even know my last name."

His eyes narrowed. "But you know his."

After a moment she nodded.

"Damn, Moira."

Heat swept over her face. "I've never done anything like that. Doesn't it figure I'd get caught, big-time, when I did."

"You know I love you."

She nodded again. "I've cried enough, okay?"

Gray gave a low chuckle. "Okay. But let me say this again. Unless you know the guy's a creep, I think you should tell him. If I had a kid out there, I'd want to be part of his life. Give the man a chance."

She sighed. "I think…I've been trying to pretend it didn't happen."

His eyebrows rose. "An immaculate conception?"

Once again he'd managed to make her laugh despite everything. "Something like that." She folded her napkin, then folded it again. And again. "I'm embarrassed to talk to him," she mumbled. "And…it really doesn't seem fair to me to ask anything of him."

"He was there." Gray's voice was hard.

Yes. Will Becker definitely had been there.

"Give him a chance," Gray repeated.

After a moment, she nodded. "Okay. You're right. I know you are."

He smiled then, satisfied, and reached for her hand. One quick squeeze conveyed plenty. "Let me know what I can do, all right?"

There wasn't any point in saying more, not yet. She hated to think he wouldn't be able to finish his term in office, that he'd have to resign early, but they'd have a better idea later when she found out how she was affected by the pregnancy. His term ended the first of the year, and her due date was the middle of January, so they'd be okay as long as she could work until the end.

She should feel better, having gotten this out of the way. And in a way she did. He'd reacted exactly the way she had expected he would: with understanding and affection.

But she still felt guilty, and panic still whispered at the edges of her awareness, prepared to engulf her if she let it.

No matter what, her life would never be the same again.

And now she'd committed herself to calling Will and saying the unthinkable: "I'm pregnant with your baby."

CHAPTER FOUR

BY THE TIME HE REACHED the outskirts of Harare, Will was weary and grateful to be back. He'd spent the past two weeks in rural east Zimbabwe, negotiating with workers, suppliers, local officials, town leaders, hell, even the community *n'anga,* or healer, who seemed to be particularly influential in that district.

The job had turned out to be nothing like he'd envisioned. When he'd first arrived, it hadn't taken him two weeks to discover that the architectural renderings drawn by a firm in Providence, Rhode Island, were useless; that nothing near as elaborate as the original plans was required; that, if these community hospitals and medical clinics were to be useful, they needed to spring from local needs and with local approval. He'd made the mistake, too, of believing he could conduct most business in English, the official language. Zimbabwe had been, after all, a British colony when it was Southern Rhodesia. But, while road signs and the like were in English, it was mostly spoken in the cities. In the countryside where he was working it was another matter. He was now learning Shona, the language of the majority tribe. He still needed a translator, but was gaining confidence in his ability to understand discussions before they were sanitized and translated for his benefit. He was already adept enough to conduct the ritual conversations that preceded any real business.

"How is your mother? Your father? Your son? Good, good," he would say with grave nods. Then, in answer to the requisite polite questions for him, "I don't often speak to them, but my brothers and sister are well."

Nothing happened rapidly, and getting frustrated did no good.

He pulled his ancient Datsun pickup truck into a curbside parking spot in the block adjacent to the foundation offices. As he got out, his mouth quirked as he imagined what Clay would say about the irony of Will, the strong, silent member of the Becker clan, having to spend his days and weeks and months in seemingly never ending conversation. Or—most delicious irony of all—being good at it. But these first months, Will had realized, would build the bridge of friendships strong enough to see a dozen medical clinics and two community hospitals built in the next two years. Or it wouldn't happen.

Harare was Zimbabwe's largest city. It had a surprisingly European look, to his eye, and a population of over a million people. Every time he reached the outskirts of the city after days' or weeks' absence, tension melted away. He was American enough to feel most at home here. There were Western-style grocery stores. He could dine out on Italian food, Greek, Chinese. Hold conversations with American businessmen and women.

He felt rueful amusement when he thought of the last cocktail party he'd attended. He wasn't any better at that kind of socializing. Lurking in a dark corner, he'd wished for his mysterious redhead.

In the first week Will had rented a small house less than half a mile from the office. Even though he seemed to be away more than he was here, he needed a base. And he'd somehow acquired a full-time housekeeper-cook.

At home in the U.S., the closest thing to a servant

he'd ever had was a woman who came in to the Becker home weekly to clean. He'd seen her once in a blue moon; mostly they communicated by notes. *Please clean the refrigerator this week,* he'd write. *I'll be coming on Tuesday instead of Thursday next week, if that's okay,* her sticky note would inform him. But having someone *wait* on him…well, that was different. He'd intended to take care of himself. But he'd barely moved in when women began knocking on his back door asking for work. He was met with blank astonishment when he said he didn't need anyone, thank you. And it wasn't totally true, he discovered; buying food in the unfamiliar markets where English often wasn't spoken was a hassle, and he'd come to Africa with the intention of immersing himself in the culture, not living in a bubble like a tourist admiring the scenery. Yeah, sometimes he appreciated seeing familiar brands on grocery-store shelves, but he didn't want to shop only in the Western-style supermarkets. God knows, he wasn't much of a cook. He had no microwave here. And unemployment was sky-high. He could afford to give someone a job.

So now, when he was in town, he came home to *sadza* ready when he sat at the table. *Sadza* was the word commonly used for any meal, but also for the staple of the diet: a sort of stew served on cooked grain. Jendaya, his housekeeper, most often used chicken in the stew, although she was scandalized that he preferred it to goat, which his relative wealth would have permitted. He liked the stew without meat at all, and she obliged with scandalized shakes of the head. Only the poor didn't put meat in their *sadza,* she made sure he knew. When he was in Harare, he usually ate lunch out, so Will was content with the traditional evening meal even though it varied little.

Jendaya had expected him back today, so he assumed

dinner at home would be ready at the usual seven o'clock. That gave him time to stop at the office and check email. He hadn't even seen an internet café the past two weeks— to find one, he'd have had to drive into Mutare, the city closest to the Mozambique border, and it hadn't seemed worth the bother. One of the pleasures of getting home was anticipating email: responses to questions he'd asked of the foundation headquarters, and especially to hearing from Clay, Sophie and Jack. Will missed them more than he'd expected.

The early evening was cool enough to remind him of home as he walked the half a block to the two-story stucco-fronted office building. He'd become accustomed to the rich scent of the air: diesel fuel, wood smoke, ripe fruit and the heady scent of flowers in bloom. September was spring here, south of the equator, still dry, the reverse of seasons in the Pacific Northwest. The hard rains, he was told, fell during the summer in Zimbabwe, therefore at the same time as they would be falling in Washington State.

The front door to the foundation headquarters was still unlocked, although he was greeted with silence inside. He'd started up the stairs when a light went out in an office at the top and Perry Marshall rushed out. Another American, he'd arrived only a few weeks before, and would be acquiring the equipment, furniture and supplies for the clinics as they were built.

"Will!" He paused on the stairs. "Good trip?"

"Yeah, I think so."

"Can we talk in the morning? We're having a dinner party, and Rachel's going to kill me if I'm late. You'd be welcome to join us," he added.

Will smiled. "Thanks, but I suspect Jendaya will have dinner ready. And I've got to tell you, I'm beat."

The other American's bushy gray eyebrows rose. "Then what are you doing here?"

"Just wanted to check email."

"Internet's slow today," Perry warned him, and kept going.

It was, but Will got on eventually and relaxed in his chair, glad the building seemed otherwise empty, as he watched a dozen messages load. Good, a couple from each of his siblings. He liked hearing from them so often. There was one from an unfamiliar address and he clicked on it first, figuring it would be a quick delete. But it wasn't the junk he expected. It was short, only a paragraph, and ended with *Moira*. His pulse quickened.

His mysterious redhead. What the hell? His thoughts had turned to her with disturbing frequency, but if she hadn't tried to get in touch in four months, why now?

Will, I've hesitated over contacting you at all, but I think you deserve to know that I'm pregnant. I don't know what happened; I suppose the condom tore or something. You need to know that I don't hold you responsible. I invited you to stay, I knew you weren't offering anything but the one night. Heck, I was the one who provided the condom. But…I am pregnant. I intend to have the baby, and am well able to afford to raise him or her. I have friends and family. I'm not asking for help from you, or any involvement. I'll be honest. I'm not even sure I would *welcome* either. Since you don't know me, you may not even believe the baby is yours. That's okay, too. I thought I should tell you, and now I've done that.

Moira

Stunned, he stared at the computer monitor, rereading the email a second time, a third time.

She was pregnant.

The first wave of anger took him aback, because it was a stupid thing that pissed him off. Did she really think he wouldn't believe her when she said the baby was his? He'd have had to be an idiot not to recognize her essential innocence. His redhead didn't sleep around.

"I haven't done this in an awfully long time," she'd said. He'd wondered then how long that actually was. A year? Five years? She'd been incredibly sexy but also… awkward. Unpracticed. No, if she was pregnant, it was his baby she was carrying.

Not *if*. After four months, she might even be showing.

He shook his head in…not disbelief, not shock, but something related. He was going to be a father.

A sound escaped his throat. A father was the last thing in the world he'd wanted to become, at least for the next few years. He'd already raised a family. The idea of starting over appalled him. And yet…that was *his* baby she was carrying.

He shoved his fingers into his hair. As things stood, his son or daughter would grow up without him, and it sounded as though that was what she'd prefer.

He should be grateful. *Glad* she wasn't demanding he be an every-other-weekend father, or that he send child-support checks. She was right; they didn't know each other.

Numbly, Will sat back in his chair. It would be worse if he hadn't liked her, if it really had been a typical one-night stand. A chance-met stranger encountered in a bar, say.

Wasn't that what it was?

He found himself scowling. No. No, he'd been drawn to her from the minute he set eyes on her. He'd ached the next morning to call her. The temptation to see her in the few days left to him had been acute. Now…hell. Now he wished he had. At least then they *would* know each other better.

He felt another surge of anger. She wouldn't welcome his involvement? Did that mean she hadn't liked him nearly as much as he had her? That he really was nothing but an available sub for the jackass?

Had it occurred to her that, if she'd had sex with *him,* using that same condom, she might still be pregnant? Would she prefer that, even given the way the creep had treated her?

I have friends and family, she said. Will gritted his teeth. A mother. She had a mother. Had she forgotten that she'd told him it was just her and her mom? Okay, she probably did have friends, but friends had their own families. With the best will in the world, how much good was a friend going to be to her, caring for a baby by herself?

He swore aloud, his voice hoarse. He didn't know what to tell her. How to respond. Damn. He looked again and saw that her email was dated almost two weeks ago, in fact the day after he'd left Harare. She had probably already concluded that he wasn't going to reply at all.

Maybe she was relieved. That idea pissed him off yet again.

One more day wouldn't matter. He had to think about this.

At last he made himself read the emails from his brothers and Sophie. None had any real news. Clay had met a woman shortly after Will left and sounded as if he might be serious about her. Jack had had a minor accident in a company pickup, and Clay was ragging him. Sophie was renting a room in a house with other grad students in L.A., where she'd be attending UCLA, classes to start next week. She'd met with her faculty advisor, and told a few amusing stories about her roommates, two guys and two girls.

Will responded to their emails with a general one telling them about this latest trip. He tried to draw word pictures, so they could see the general meeting held under a baobab tree, with him in a metal folding chair facing the sixteen men who'd sat comfortably on the dusty ground despite Western business attire that made him suspect they'd dressed up for his benefit. He described the tea plantations, with leaves as big as elephant ears, and the kraals of round mud huts with thatch roofs, women wearing Western garb cooking on open fires outside. He made fun of his more ludicrous language mistakes.

He didn't say, "Hey, the real news is that I'm going to be a father." Although he'd have to tell them eventually, wouldn't he? After years of lecturing them on safe sex.

Yes, but he'd used the damn condom. He'd come close to forgetting it; closer than he'd ever come in his life. But he'd remembered in time, so he couldn't blame himself now for carelessness. He hadn't seen any obvious tear when he disposed of it, although now he wasn't sure he'd even really looked. He'd been wishing he had another condom, wishing he wasn't leaving his redhead to awaken alone in the hotel room.

Will sent the email, figuring he'd write shorter, more personal ones to each of them individually tomorrow. Then he read Moira's one more time, as incredulous and confused as he was the first time. Finally he closed the internet and turned off the computer.

What was he going to say to her?

IT WAS FIFTEEN DAYS AFTER she'd made herself write that hideous email and send it before she saw a reply in her in-box from Will Becker. The first week, Moira had compulsively checked her personal account at least twice a day while she was at work, something she rarely did, then a couple more times at home. When there was nothing from him, she'd…not given up, *relaxed*. A better choice of words. Since then, she'd gone back to reading personal email in the evening at home. Tonight, she'd sat at the computer while leftover casserole was heating in the microwave. At the sight of his address, her heart took an unpleasant bump and her hand was actually shaking when she reached for the mouse.

She distantly heard the microwave beep and ignored it.

Moira,

I'm sorrier than I can say that you've had to deal with this on your own. I should have told you that night why the one night was all I could offer. I suspect that, despite my denial, you still worried I might be married, engaged, whatever. It wasn't anything like that. I had just accepted a job from a nonprofit committed to build schools and medical clinics in sub-Saharan Africa. I've been in Zimbabwe for nearly four months now, and have made a two-year commitment. I often have no access to email for weeks at a time. I just read yours last night.

It would never have crossed my mind to think you'd tell me the baby was mine if it wasn't. Maybe you believe I don't know you, but I thought I did. Well enough to be sure you're honest, and that your invitation to me was out of the ordinary for you. I hope you know me well enough to guess what I'm going to say now.

No child of mine is going to grow up not knowing his father. I can't do much to help you right now, although I am more than willing to offer financial support if you find you can't continue to work all the way through your pregnancy. I ask that you stay in touch and let me know how you're doing. I'll be back in the states every few months, and we can talk the first time I am. Come up with a plan. But fair warning: I will be involved.

He gave her the website address of the foundation he worked for in case she was interested, and repeated that he wanted to hear from her. He closed by asking what she did for a living. *Tell me about yourself,* he said. *Please.*

Moira cried for the first time in months, and she didn't even know why. She *didn't* need him. She kept remembering the intense note in his voice when he told her about his worst nightmare. "Being trapped. Spending my life doing what I have to do." There was more, but she'd known what he meant.

This was what he'd been trying to say. Getting stuck with an obligation he hadn't willingly, wholeheartedly made. Having to accept responsibility for helping raise a child he couldn't possibly want.

Her email, she thought wretchedly, was his worst nightmare.

TWO DAYS LATER, MOIRA REPLIED.

Will,
Now I think I'm sorry I told you. I remember that you

said your worst nightmare was to get stuck, to spend your life fulfilling obligations. I don't want to be your nightmare. And please, please don't feel you have to be involved if you'll resent it. That would have to be awful for a kid, don't you think? I barely remember my father—did I tell you that?—but even though I often wished that he was around when I was growing up, I know it might have hurt worse if he'd been there because he felt he had to be. I really will be fine, you know. We won't starve without you.

If you want to look me up when you get home, that's fine, though. I live in West Fork, and work here, too. I'm an architect, in partnership with a friend. Van Dusen & Cullen. I'm Cullen. I guess you can tell that from my email address, huh? It's not a real physical job, which is good right now. And I'm hoping I can bring the baby to work some of the time. I know Gray, my partner, won't mind.

She went on to say that she'd looked at the foundation website and was impressed with what they were trying to accomplish. She'd taken the time to read some about Zimbabwe, too, and knew how high the rate of AIDS and HIV was and how desperately more accessible medical care was needed.

Will brooded some before he hit Reply, trying to get over being mad before he said something that would stiffen her resolve to keep him at a distance. And yeah, that made no sense when he didn't *want* to be a family guy, but, man, had she turned him into a mass of warring emotions. She could enrage him quicker than the most venal local bureaucrat, and he'd done his share of teeth grinding these past months dealing with them. She also had a way of zinging him with powerful protective impulses.

Did she really think so little of him, she believed he'd let any kid of his feel *resented?*

Damn it, damn it, damn it, he wished he couldn't so easily picture her as a freckle-faced kid herself who couldn't understand why she didn't have a daddy like everyone else did. He wished he hadn't seen that fleeting, wistful look in her eyes as she remembered.

Finally he sighed and started typing.

Moira, I can promise you I won't feel resentment. Someday I'll tell you why I said that, about my worst nightmare. It doesn't really matter now. You reminded me, as I recall, that life's made up of obligations. Not all kids are planned. They should all be loved. I never doubted that my parents loved me, and I was lucky enough to have a stepmother who did, too. Another promise: I'll love any child of mine.

Will hoped that was true. He wanted to believe it was. The idea of holding that baby was pretty abstract right now.

But he thought of himself as a decent man, and even though there'd been times he *had* felt resentment for getting stuck raising his siblings, he thought what they'd most been aware of was security and love. Yeah, they'd probably known on some level how he felt. No twenty-year-old kid was capable of completely hiding his shock and desperation. But he'd tried, they'd understood, and he was damn proud of how they had all turned out.

He went back to his email.

You don't say whether you're feeling okay. Aren't pregnant women supposed to be sick to their stomachs and tired? Or is that the exception?

You're right about the toll AIDS is costing here. It's painful to see. Unlike in South Africa, the majority of AIDS orphans are being raised by relatives, which is a testament to the power of family here. This is a country of astonishing contrasts. The literacy rate is quite high and schools good. Meantime, out in the countryside, medical care is close to nonexistent, and what itinerant medical clinics are held are often outside, with patients lined up waiting to see a nurse who sits at a folding table beneath a shade tree. Not much that nurse can do for the desperately ill. I'm often struck by the patience people here seem to have. I imagine Americans throwing a temper tantrum because the line for the drive-through window at McDonald's is four cars long.

My part in this project is less important than the care that will be provided—the nurses and doctors, the AIDS cocktails, the surgical supplies. I provide only the walls and roofs, and simple ones at that. We've finally broken ground on the first clinic, and it will have brick walls and a metal roof, like the store in the village. The homes are crude, with thatched roofs.

He told her about the architectural drawings he'd scrapped and why, about his need to build structures that belonged, that people would be comfortable going to. In fact, when he reread his email a few minutes later, it was to find he'd waxed eloquent, revealing more of the passion quietly building in him than he'd intended. He frowned, finally, and left what he'd written. She was an architect herself; she might be interested. And anyway…he wanted to know her. To be fair, he had to reveal something of himself in return.

By the next day, he had an email back from her. *She waxed eloquent on her belief that structures should meld with their surroundings. Her partner, apparently, teased her about emphasizing function over form, although Gray, too, she said, preferred to design buildings that didn't immediately command attention. She told him about her partner's house, which appeared to be part of the river-bank so that a fisherman casting his line below might not even notice it was there atop the bluff. She thought many of the more admired homes featured in magazines were hideous. Original, yes, interesting, but jarring.*

I'm content to design staid but dignified office build-ings that have grace and pleasing proportions but do not startle. If I were to plan a medical clinic for a small town in the African savannah, I'd go with mud brick and a metal roof, too. Good for you.

Will found himself smiling.

I was sick to my stomach for a couple of months, al-though not as miserable as some women are—Gray's wife, Charlotte, could hardly keep any food down—but it's passed, thank heavens. Now I'm starved all the time, making up for the weight I lost. I dread my next monthly weigh-in and the lecture I'm bound to get from the doctor. I'm trying *very hard* not to gain too much. I am a little more tired than usual, but all it means is that I go to bed earlier than I used to. No big deal. So you see, I really am fine.

Without you, was what she meant. Will suppressed his irritation.

He wrote an email in response longer than the ones he'd sent Clay and the others. He felt a strange tension, sitting here digging into himself for what was most important to tell her about his life and values. It was as if they were connected by a thread so delicate, he could snap it with the wrong word, but perhaps with the right ones he could lend it strength. He was hungry to hear back from her. Half an hour ago, when his messages had been loading, it was *hers* he'd hoped for with eagerness that embarrassed him.

He felt, Will realized after he'd sent his response, like a boy with his first crush. Ridiculous, maybe, when they'd already made love and now he longed for so little: the equivalent of a shy glance.

This time she didn't write back right away. Stuck in Harare meeting with government officials, Will was therefore able to obsessively check his email in any stray minutes, which made the three days before he did get a reply from her seem endless. But her response was long and satisfying. She'd read more about Zimbabwe and wondered whether he was in any danger, a white man in a country where white-owned land was still being violently snatched by black mobs.

She was worried about him. He felt a warm glow to realize it.

She told him about a movie that had recently been released about South Africa and talking to a woman whose daughter was currently in Ghana with the Peace Corps.

Several people I know who've been to Africa tell me they'd give anything to go back. They always have this look in their eyes, as though there's some kind of magnetic pull. Although that's silly, isn't it? Africa is an enormous continent. I'm sure Zimbabwe is nothing like... I don't know, the Ivory Coast or Kenya. See, I've revealed typical American ignorance about a huge swath of the world.

He assured her that, as a foreigner, he felt safe and that people were warm and friendly. He told her more about what he'd seen, about the astonishing sight of elephants ambling across the road in front of his Datsun, about seeing so many hippos in a river he could have walked across, stepping on their backs. About Victoria Falls where water plummeted into a canyon and raised a cloud of spray so vast, it created a rain forest for miles about. He told her that he hoped soon to go see the Great Zimbabwe, the granite ruins of the greatest city in ancient Africa. About the rock art, more faint traces of people long gone, that could be found everywhere.

For all my wonder, I feel an astonishing pang of homesickness every so often. I didn't expect that. To miss my brothers and sister, yes, but not the mundane realities of everyday life at home. For all the beauty here, I sometimes feel a strange sense of not-belonging. As if I never could, even if I lived here for the rest of my life. It works both ways, though. I met a white couple a few weeks ago who fled the country some years back, when it was obvious what was happening, but after staying for two years in England—where their daughter and her family live—they came home even though there was no way they could recover their farm. That was how they put it: they came home. It was too late for them to really belong anywhere else.

Four days later, without having heard from her again, he left Harare, this time for the eastern lowveld near the Sanyati River. He sent Moira a quick email before he left, telling her he'd be out of touch for two to three weeks.

Then he worried. Had he said something wrong in his last, long email? Or did she not want to continue exchanging long, chatty communications with the man who'd fathered her baby but whose involvement in their child's life she didn't *welcome?* Was she not feeling good?

God. Had she lost the baby? Will thought most miscarriages were earlier in the pregnancy, but he didn't know. He was astonished at how sick he felt at the idea. Did women die when they miscarried? Surely not anymore, not at home, anyway, with modern medical care readily available.

If anything was wrong, would she let him know? Would anyone else?

Had she told anyone he was the father of her baby? He bounced irrationally from the cold sweat of fear at the idea of her sick or hurt or grieving to sharp anger because she might not want her mother or her friends to know who he was.

Checking email wasn't an option; he hadn't even driven on this trip, but had been flown along with Chionesu, his translator, into a dusty bush airstrip in a thinly populated region where the roads, he'd been told, were abysmal.

He evaluated, he met with local leaders, he chose a site. He slept in thatch-roofed huts and dined with host families, sitting cross-legged to eat *sadza* out of a communal pot. Will had become adept at molding the thick millet or corn cereal into a shape he could use to dip stew.

And the whole damn time, all he could think about was Moira. By the time he was on a small bush plane taking off from the same dirt airstrip, he'd made up his mind he would take a trip home to the States. He had to see her.

CHAPTER FIVE

"I'M GOING TO GRAB some lunch on my way to city hall," Gray said. "You want me to get you something and drop it off here?"

Moira straightened on the tall stool in front of her drafting table and rolled her shoulders with a groan she hoped Gray didn't hear.

"Thanks, but I brought a sandwich." She smiled at him. "Come on, when have you ever known me to let myself go hungry?"

He grinned. "Well…you were looking a little peaked there for a while."

"I'm making up for it," she said ruefully. "I swear, I'm ravenous all the time. It's awful."

He laughed, a warm rumble. She expected him to head for the door, but instead he leaned a hip against his desk and kept looking at her. Finally he said, "I haven't wanted to push, but curiosity is getting to me. Have you contacted your baby's father yet?"

Heat rose in her cheeks. "Yes. I sent him an email…"

His eyebrows rose.

"I tried calling first!" Moira snapped. "It's not my fault I had to email instead. Turns out he's moved to Africa for two years."

"Good God."

"He's, um, actually been really nice. We've exchanged half a dozen emails. I told him he was off the hook, but he insists he doesn't want to be, that no kid of his is growing up without a father."

"Told you so."

She rolled her eyes. "It was a one-night stand. I might have picked a scumbag to sleep with."

"Nah. Not you." He straightened, came to her and kissed her cheek. "I know you better than that, Moira."

They hugged, and for a moment she closed her eyes at the pleasure of his solid embrace. Then he stepped back. "What's the guy doing in Africa?"

She told him, and Gray nodded. "Would I know him?"

Moira hesitated.

Gray looked sardonic. "Aren't you planning to put his name on the birth certificate?"

She grimaced. "Yes, of course I am. Uh…his name's Will Becker."

Her partner's eyes narrowed. "Of Becker Construction?"

"Yes, but his brother Clay has taken it over now, with Will gone."

"Huh."

"Do you know him?" she felt compelled to ask. Oh, Lord—was she wrong about Will?

But Gray shook his head. "I hear they do good work. Mostly stuff that wouldn't interest me. Shopping centers, grocery stores, that kind of thing."

"I don't think it interested Will, either. There's some reason he threw it over to build mud-brick medical clinics in Africa."

Gray laughed. "Yeah, I guess so. Okay. Is he planning to help financially? See the baby?"

"He says he'll be back in the States every so often, and the next time he is we'll talk." Moira bit her lip. "He did say he'd be glad to help financially if I can't work all the way through the pregnancy, so I guess he probably will offer child support at least."

"Good. Not as good as his being here, but better than nothing." Gray jiggled his keys in his pocket as if to make sure they were still there. "I've got to run. See you tomorrow?"

She nodded. "Except I'll be out at the Fletcher house first thing in the morning."

They exchanged a few words about the project that had turned into a huge trial for her, with the clients changing their minds about what they wanted at least weekly.

"Don't worry about the cost," Jennifer Fletcher would say blithely. "It's important to get it right. Tearing it out at this point is better than living with a layout that isn't perfect."

Jennifer would undoubtedly want something else torn out this week. The contractor, Dave Hendricks, was getting even more aggravated than Moira was. During most of their meetings, she played peacemaker.

Waiting until the door had shut behind Gray, she strolled to her desk and took out her sandwich. She might as well have lunch now, too. She'd intended to make herself wait another hour, but...damn it, she was hungry. And anyway... She peeked out the window at the parking lot to be sure Gray wasn't coming back for something he'd forgotten, then, when she saw his car gone, sat in front of her computer and went on the Internet. There hadn't been one word from Will in three full weeks. He'd said it might be that long, but she couldn't help worrying. He'd dismissed her concerns, but from what she'd read, Zimbabwe under Mugabe *wasn't* a safe place. Not many nonprofits were working there right now, and she suspected the potential danger was why.

There was no email from him today, either, she was disappointed to see. She'd send him another one tonight, Moira decided, something chatty and casual. She could tell him about the Fletchers. He'd undoubtedly had difficult clients and would sympathize.

She ate quickly, drinking cranberry juice with her ham sandwich and longing for her usual iced tea. She missed caffeine. She *craved* caffeine. Especially these days, when she tended to get drowsy right after lunch. Her body really, really wanted her to take a nap. Even the nine hours she'd slept last night apparently didn't cut it.

Ruefully she laid her splayed hands on her belly and gently rubbed. For Pete's sake, she was only halfway through this pregnancy, and she was so blasted *big*. Didn't it figure? Of course, Will was an exceptionally large man, which meant his child probably wouldn't be petite. She thought he was at least six foot three and maybe taller, with shoulders so broad he'd alarmed her at first sight. His enormous hands had dwarfed hers. She imagined what his hand would look like on her rounded stomach, and felt a disturbingly sexual twinge at the image. No one had ever touched her the way he had, so gently even though she could feel the power he kept curbed. She wondered if, as big as he was, he often felt like the classic bull in a china shop.

With a sigh, Moira managed to get herself back to work.

Jennifer Fletcher *did* want something else torn out when they met the next morning.

Bright eyed, her dark hair artfully disheveled, she swept in and said, "I keep worrying that there won't be enough storage here in the kitchen. And last night it came to me. What if we bump out the dining area here with a bay window instead—" she waved one hand toward the large, small-paned window she'd been measuring for blinds last week "—and then we could squeeze in a sort of butler's pantry on the other side of the doorway?" She gave first Moira, then Dave, a limpid look and waited expectantly.

Moira heard a rumble rising from the middle-aged contractor and interceded hastily. "Let me do some measuring and we'll see, Jennifer. Did you consult with Stella?" The kitchen designer, Moira suspected, had long since thrown up her hands, or maybe thrown in the towel was more accurate, but she might be a voice of reason.

"Oh, I know Stella will agree with me. Absolutely she will." Jennifer's smile was radiant. "With Ron and I entertaining so often, we can't live without enough storage for serving pieces. And I have four different sets of china, you know."

Moira knew. Normally this would be Dave's problem and Stella's problem, not hers, but if they were to knock out this wall...

She made no promises, but soothed Jennifer, who made a whirlwind tour of the unfinished house, pronounced herself delighted and left. Another fifteen minutes, and Moira had Dave settled down, too.

As she walked to her car, the faint flutters she'd been feeling in her stomach intensified, as if the baby had decided to take up swimming the butterfly.

"Just wait'll you're in the last month and the kid weighs thirteen pounds. And *then* discovers the trampoline," Charlotte had warned darkly. She was eight months along now and could hardly get out of a chair. Moira had heard Gray clearing his throat to suppress his laugh at the idea of a thirteen-pound fetus, but he'd had the wisdom to have noticed that Charlotte's sense of humor seemed to have waned recently. Moira was beginning to see why.

She settled with relief behind the wheel of her car and carefully arranged the seat belt around herself. Everything took longer these days, and it was going to get worse, not better.

She treated herself to the guilty pleasure of a burger and fries on her way back to the office, even though it was awfully early for lunch. She'd probably put on a pound with the one meal.

"I'll have a salad for dinner," she said aloud, and knew she lied. Maybe a salad and a grilled cheese sandwich. And frozen yogurt after. She'd developed a sweet tooth lately.

At the office she told Gray about the latest hitch at the Fletcher house, he commiserated then grumbled in turn about the city council. He swore they'd gotten less cooperative now that they knew he was on his way out. Moira felt even guiltier about that than she did about the sinful lunch. She was glad when he left for city hall.

She determined that yes, they probably could install a bay window and find room for Jennifer Fletcher's new pantry, called Dave who ranted for a few minutes, then went back to the drawing she'd begun yesterday of a building that would house a new real estate office. She used her computer at a certain point, but liked to rough out ideas with pen and paper, and found that clients liked a drawing, too.

A client popped in at one point and looked at preliminary sketches, after which Moira checked email for the second time today. Still nothing from Will.

It wasn't like they were best friends, she reminded herself. She hadn't even wanted to tell him about the baby, for heaven's sake. But she was honest enough with herself to admit that, somehow, in the past six weeks he'd become important to her. Only because knowing she had some support from him made her feel a little less scared about the future, she tried to convince herself. She knew it was more than that, though.

When she read his emails, she could almost hear his voice, as if he were talking to her instead. He had a good voice, deep and relaxed, laced with amusement that she sensed was often directed at himself instead of at other people. The emails reminded her why she'd trusted him enough to make love with him. She'd freaked the next morning, but the truth was she couldn't remember ever liking anyone as much so quickly. She guessed in some ways he'd reminded her of Gray. There was something rock solid about him. She'd be surprised if he had one-night stands with women he barely knew very often.

Her mind wandered; her hand stilled.

Had he really thought she was beautiful? she wondered wistfully. He said he'd been watching her for quite a while through the glass. That might have been a line, one of those things he'd have said to any woman who joined him out there. But she thought maybe he'd meant it. He didn't seem...slick. The way, she had belatedly realized, Bruce was.

When the door opened, Moira turned in surprise, her hand pressing her lower back as she summoned a polite smile. They didn't get that much drop-in traffic. Who...?

She gaped. Will Becker, who was supposed to be in Africa, had just walked into Van Dusen & Cullen, Architects.

"Will?" she whispered.

He'd been dreaming of Moira for months, and still she looked better than he remembered. Although...different. He took in the sight of her freckled face and astonished green eyes, the copper bright curls escaping the knot she'd fashioned at the back of her head, then lowered his gaze to the unmistakable swell of her belly. The knowledge that she was pregnant suddenly became a whole hell of a lot more visceral.

"Can you feel the baby moving?" he heard himself ask.

She nodded and stared at him from her perch on a tall stool in front of a slanted drawing table that stood before one of the large windows.

He wound his way past desks until he was only a couple of feet from her. Made a little uneasy by her obvious shock, he cleared his throat. "I should have told you I was coming."

She blinked a couple of times in quick succession. "I thought...you were still out, um, wherever you went."

"I got back to Harare a few days ago, and caught a flight as soon as I could. I, uh, needed to clear some decisions with people back here." That was a flat-out lie; sure, he wouldn't waste his time here, but he'd endured the twenty-five-hour flight to see her.

Will still wasn't sure why that had been so important. There'd been a couple of emails from her waiting for him when he got back to Harare. He'd known she was fine, the baby was fine. But once he'd let himself formulate the desire to see her, he couldn't seem to let go of it. He *had* to see her.

And there she was, right in front of him, lush, curvaceous and pregnant with *his* baby.

"How are you, Moira?" he asked quietly.

"You didn't believe me when I said I was fine?"

"You have a backache."

She hastily withdrew her hand from the small of her

back and clasped her fingers together in front of her. "I've been bending over all afternoon."

"What are you working on?"

She seemed to hesitate, then swiveled toward the drafting table. "You can take a look, if you want."

It was a typical architect's rendering, but skillfully done. He liked the look of the bungalow-style building with a deep front porch.

"A real estate office," she told him.

"I like it," he said simply.

"I can't believe you're here."

"I kept thinking about you," he admitted. She was even prettier close up, with the sunlight slanting in the window turning her freckles to pale cinnamon. This was the first time he'd seen her in daylight. He wished he could tell better what she was thinking. She was surprised, certainly, maybe even stunned, but beyond that... Was she glad to see him, or unhappy?

His mysterious redhead, he thought, was still mysterious.

"I was a little worried," she admitted. "When I didn't hear from you, I mean."

Chagrined, he said, "I should have emailed. Once I realized I had a chance to come home, I wanted to surprise you. I don't know why."

And that was no lie. He didn't understand a damn thing he'd felt since he'd gotten that first email from her.

I think you deserve to know that I'm pregnant.

She'd thrown him for a loop from that moment on.

No, he thought, she'd done that from the moment she walked onto the terrace and straight to his dark corner.

"Well." She took a deep breath. "You can see what I mean about the weight gain."

"Actually…" Will frowned. "Your cheeks look thinner. Are you sure you're eating enough?"

Moira laughed, a flash of genuine humor that relaxed him. "You're kidding, right? Nobody has ever accused me of being skinny."

"You have a perfect body." And, damn, he was getting aroused.

She laughed again, but less happily, and looked down at her stomach. "Right."

"I love the way you look."

Her cheeks flushed, and he saw the shyness in her eyes. She mumbled. "Um…thank you."

Why was she so determined to believe herself to be unattractive? Will wondered, puzzled. It couldn't be only the scumbag. Her doubts had to be more ingrained than that. Someday he'd find out, he promised himself. But that kind of question wasn't exactly the ideal opening salvo today.

"Will you have dinner with me?" he asked.

She looked around as if she'd find an excuse floating in the air like a dust mote, but finally took a deep breath. "Yes. Sure. I suppose we should talk."

Gee, thanks. He'd only flown halfway around the damn world to see her.

Hiding his frustration, Will asked calmly, "What time do you close?"

"Five. I don't have any more appointments today."

"All right. I'll be back at five."

More color flowed into her cheeks, but she nodded. "Okay."

"If you don't mind eating that early."

"I could eat six times a day," she told him ruefully.

He smiled at her, said, "You decide what sounds good," and left.

He didn't go far, only to the parking lot. He'd brought a book, but thought he might close his eyes. He could set his cell phone to wake him up. At this point, Will's sense of time was so screwed up, he had no idea whether his body thought it should be the middle of the night or what. Mostly, he was disoriented. He'd gotten into SeaTac early this morning and surprised Clay and Jack, too, at the breakfast table. Scared the daylights out of them, actually, when he'd strolled in the door as if he'd been out getting the newspaper. Will grinned at the memory.

He got in his truck—not really his anymore, but Jack had let him drive it today—and pushed the seat back. He could tell the minute he closed his eyes that he wouldn't actually be able to sleep.

He was buzzing, in that irritating state where tiredness kept him awake. And simply being here felt strange, to put it mildly. Everything looked wrong, from the trees to the cars to the people driving them, all white. The smells were wrong. Even this morning, when he'd walked into the house where he had lived for most of his life, he'd almost felt as if he existed in two different dimensions. In one, he was where he belonged; he'd reached for his mug in the kitchen cupboard without thinking about it, poured coffee, known which shelf in the refrigerator the milk would be on. All the while, on another plane he had thought, *I'm not really here. I don't belong.*

The weirdness of international travel, of being hurtled by an airplane that chased the setting sun from one continent to another, so that you had breakfast one morning in Africa and the next morning in Lynnwood, Washington, was partly to blame. But Will knew that it was more, that he *didn't* belong. He would never move back into that house, no matter what. Right now, not much would have drawn him home to Washington at all.

Only his redhead.

Even with his eyes shut, he saw her. Actually seeing her was as weird as being here. He knew her and yet he didn't. He'd had the best damn sex of his life with her, he'd sucked on her bare breasts, touched her everywhere, been *inside* her, and now he wondered nervously how she'd react if he kissed her.

Will gave a grunt that wasn't quite a laugh. With outrage, is how she'd react. They'd never even been out on a date. What they had done was meant by both of them to be something not quite real, remembered later as if it might have been a dream.

The most erotic dream in the world didn't result in pregnancy, however. Fate had apparently grinned wickedly and said, "Gotcha!"

He returned to her office at five on the nose to find Moira plucking a purse from a drawer and holding keys in her hand.

"Your partner's not around?" he asked.

She glanced his way. "No, Gray's at city hall. Or on city business, anyway. Did I tell you he's mayor?"

"No." He frowned, not liking the implications. "You mean, you're the whole firm right now?"

"No, the mayoral gig, as he calls it, is part-time. He's putting in really long hours keeping up at least half his usual workload here, sometimes more, *and* being mayor."

He stood aside as she locked the door. "Leaving you, almost five months pregnant, to keep your firm alive."

"It's not Gray's fault I'm pregnant," she said sharply.

Will winced.

They walked together outside, where the chill of evening was making itself felt as the sun dropped low on the horizon. A row of small hybrid maple trees marched along the sidewalk, their leaves—a vivid orange—beginning to fall. One crunched under his foot.

"He isn't running for reelection." Moira's head was bowed and her voice had become more subdued. "Because of me." She touched her stomach. "He'll be out of office in January, about the time I'm due."

I have family and friends, she'd told him, and this was partly what she'd meant, Will realized. How good friends were she and this Gray?

"Why don't I drive?" he suggested. "I'll bring you back to your car later."

"Fine."

She hoisted herself into the cab of the pickup without too much trouble. Will reached to help her but she didn't see his hand and he let it fall as she settled into the seat. She was doing fine without him. She'd said that enough times.

When he got in, she suggested a restaurant right there in West Fork, and directed him. "It's mostly a steak house," she said a little apologetically. "But I seem to be more of a carnivore these days than I used to be."

He glanced at her belly and smiled. "Do you suppose every baby has his own tastes?"

"You mean, the next one might be a vegetarian?" Quickly she added, "Assuming I have another one."

He ignored that. "Yeah, or be especially fond of…fish. Italian food. Nothing but Italian food."

Moira sounded more relaxed. "Pregnant women are famous for their cravings."

"Pickles."

"Right. Charlotte—Gray's wife, who is eight months pregnant right now—has a thing for lemon-meringue pie. And lemon bars. Lemon pudding." A dimple appeared in her cheek. "The pudding, she says, is for emergency fixes. Otherwise, she keeps baking."

Will laughed. "You?"

She sighed. "I don't dare. I put on weight if I take too deep a breath around fresh-baked goodies. Charlotte can afford the calories."

"What's with the obsession about weight?" he asked.

Moira leveled a look at him. "I see the obstetrician every month. I get weighed. Then I get lectured."

"Oh."

"See, there's this ideal. You have to gain enough, but not too much. And I don't want to gain too much, because then it would be hard to lose it. As if," she added gloomily, "it's not going to be hard enough to lose the weight anyway."

"How much are you likely to gain?"

Her face was cute scrunched up in a grimace. "Like, twenty-five to thirty-five pounds."

"And babies are, what, seven or eight pounds?"

"Right. You do the math."

He did, silently. The baby wasn't all that came out when a woman gave birth, though, he knew that much. There was the umbilical cord, and after-birth, and whatever fluid the baby had been swimming in. Still...

"Do you plan to nurse?" he asked.

Moira gave him another look, this one startled and rather shy. "Yes." Then, unnecessarily, she said, "This is it."

"I see." He pulled into the nearly empty parking lot of the River Fork Steakhouse. They were definitely beating the dinner crowd.

The place was nice in a casual way, the booths deeply padded, the lighting designed to give a sense of intimacy even when the restaurant was busier. Moira studied the menu with more care than she probably needed, given that Will assumed she'd eaten here often. They both ordered steaks, baked potatoes and salads. She asked for a glass of milk. He'd have liked a beer, but didn't dare. With his luck and lack of sleep, even a little alcohol would probably knock him out, and he did have a forty-five-minute drive home after he dropped Moira off.

He felt a strange ache. He'd wanted her to run into his arms today when he walked in. He wanted to be going home with her, to see her new curves, unclothed, to sleep wrapped around her.

Yeah, and he'd have been scared to death if she'd flung herself at him. He was offering the minimum a decent man would offer, and no more. Better if they maintained a relationship that was cordial, not sexually charged. If they both forgot—or at least pretended to forget—how she'd gotten pregnant with his baby.

The silence between them was beginning to seem stifling, alone as they were in this part of the dining room.

Will reached out and touched the back of her hand. "I'm sorry. I did wear the condom."

Beyond the faint quiver he'd felt beneath his fingertips, she didn't react. "I know. I saw." She hesitated. "Thank you, for believing me."

He nodded. After a minute, he said, "I'll expect to pay child support."

Her eyes searched his. "I meant it when I said you didn't have to."

"Yeah. I could tell. But I want to."

She dipped her head once, in acknowledgment.

"I really am committed in Africa for two years. Actually, for just over a year and a half, now. But after that, I'll want visitation."

Her lips compressed, but she nodded.

"You'd rather I ditched you?"

She couldn't hide her turmoil. "No. In some ways, it would be easier, but…" Her fingers drummed on the table. "I keep thinking about how much I wished my father cared at all." She focused briefly on him. "I remember telling you that I didn't know him."

"Yes."

In a near whisper, Moira said, "This isn't the way I wanted to start a family. But…I wouldn't undo it, either. I just turned thirty-five, Will. If I was going to have a baby at all, it was going to have to be soon. I'm sorry I stuck you with responsibility, but otherwise…I'm glad, now that I'm over the first shock."

"You knew for a long time before you emailed me," he said slowly.

She nodded. "I thought about not telling you at all. You'd made pretty clear that you didn't want any future involvement."

He closed his eyes. "If things had been different, I would have. I'd have called you the next day, Moira."

Her half laugh was disbelieving. "It doesn't matter," she said, although he suspected it did. "Gray chewed me out and said I had to tell you, that he'd be angry to find out he had a child he'd never been told about."

"Then I owe him one."

She didn't say anything; didn't believe he was grateful any more than she'd believed he actually liked her. Will wanted to shake her father and everyone else who'd ever made this woman feel unlovable.

The knowledge that he'd contributed curdled in his stomach. He'd screwed her then slipped away in the night. He couldn't quite convince himself that child-support checks and occasional weekend visitation made him in any way noble or good.

Anger came to his rescue, roaring through him like the blustering winds of winter. What the hell else was he supposed to do? Throw over his life again? He'd done it once. Wasn't that enough?

He stared at her averted face, and had no idea what to say to make any of this better.

CHAPTER SIX

AFTER THAT INCREDIBLY AWKWARD dinner, Moira couldn't believe she'd invited Will to go with her to her monthly checkup with the obstetrician. And poor Will— he was likely horrified, but what could he say?

What he *had* said was, "I'd like that."

Now she snorted. Probably he couldn't think of an excuse quick enough.

With a sigh, Moira got out of her car in front of the clinic, a block from the hospital. Thank goodness West Fork had a hospital. Otherwise she'd have had a half-hour drive to Everett when she was in labor. Even so, she was already worrying about getting to the delivery room when the time came. There had probably been pregnant women who'd had to drive themselves to the hospital. Hey, she could pull over to the shoulder every time a contraction hit.

Of course that was silly. She'd have a list of friends prepped to go. One of them was bound to be home.

Except, what if the baby decided to make an untimely appearance, when no one did expect to hear from her? Or—her new nightmare—what if a winter storm knocked out phone service and she *couldn't* call anyone?

She'd keep her cell phone charged.

But *their* phones might all be out.

Jeez, she thought, disgusted with herself. *Then I stag-*

ger over to a neighbor's house and hammer on the door. Do I need to find things to worry about?

Will had arrived at the clinic ahead of her. The minute she walked into the waiting room, he rose from one of the chairs. "Moira," he said, in that quiet, deep voice of his.

"You're here." Oh, brilliant.

Pretending she hadn't said anything so inane, she checked in at the front desk and then they sat next to each other. They weren't alone. A very pregnant woman was in the corner, flipping through a magazine, and a couple holding hands had come in behind Moira. Their warmth and intimacy were so obvious, she had to tear her gaze from them.

When she looked at Will, it was to find him watching her, his brown eyes unreadable but his expression gentle. "I'll really be able to hear the heartbeat?" he asked.

"I'm sure the doctor will let you."

His gaze lowered to her stomach. A couple of lines between his dark eyebrows had deepened, not quite in a frown, but as if… Moira wasn't sure. As if he was unsettled, maybe.

"Moira Cullen?"

Moira stood automatically and turned toward the smiling nurse who held her chart. She was aware that Will had risen also and was following her.

The nurse said, "Oh, good. You brought the father today."

"Uh…yes."

She produced a small cup and handed it to Moira. "Why don't you give us your sample first, and then we'll weigh you."

Will looked so horrified, Moira had to swallow a giggle even though she was probably blushing, too. She'd had *sex* with the man, for Pete's sake. Why should she be embarrassed to talk about peeing in front of him?

She was relieved when she came out of the bathroom to find the nurse, a comfortable woman in her fifties, had shown him to the exam room so that he didn't see her step on the scale. She had gained four pounds this month, which horrified her even though she knew it was normal. After spending a lifetime battling her weight, though, it was killing her to watch it climb.

The nurse led her to an exam room, which had never looked so small. Will really was a very large man, Moira realized afresh. He backed out of the way and wedged himself into the V between the table and the cabinet so that she could sit in the one visitor's chair to have her blood pressure and pulse taken. He seemed unwillingly fascinated, she thought, by the whole process.

The nurse finished up then. She told them the doctor would be a few minutes and left, closing the door behind her.

"I'll hop up on the exam table," Moira said. "Then you can sit."

"You don't have to get undressed?"

She shook her head and muttered, "Thank goodness."

"You have to pee in a cup every month?"

"They're looking for protein in the urine and things like that. That's how they know if something's going wrong."

"Huh."

Having him sit didn't reduce the way he dominated the room. The effect was partly physical, partly just presence. It was funny, she thought, because Will didn't give the impression of arrogance, but she also couldn't imagine anyone not assuming that he was in charge on sight. He was simply that kind of man. She doubted he ever had to raise his voice.

The door opened then, and Dr. Engel darted in. A tiny woman, she'd reminded Moira from the beginning of a hummingbird constantly hovering rather than settling in place. She listened, though, when Moira had questions, and answered without any impatience, her head tilted in a way that was birdlike, too.

"Marcia Engel," she said, thrusting out her hand at Will.

"Will Becker. I'm the father."

"Ah. I'm glad to see you here." She took him in with one sweep of her bright blue eyes. "How much did you weigh at birth?"

He looked startled. "Almost ten pounds. My two brothers, too. My sister was eight and a half pounds."

"Then chances are we can expect the same for this one, Moira. Well." She set the open chart on the small counter and skimmed the newest information. "Things are looking good. I'm glad to see you putting on weight now."

Moira made a face.

"She wasn't?" Will asked.

"Nausea," the doctor said. "Not unusual, but always a concern." She gave him a sharp look. "You didn't know?"

"I've been away."

"Will and I don't live together," Moira said. "He's being good enough to share responsibility for the baby, that's all."

His mouth tightened, but he said nothing.

After one more appraising look, Dr. Engel ignored him and smiled at Moira. "Lie back now, please." When Moira did, she raised her shirt and pushed down the waistband of her maternity pants, exposing the freckled mound of her belly. Moira knew she was blushing, which seemed to be a redhead's curse. It was dumb. He'd seen her stomach before, and a whole lot more, but she couldn't make herself look at him.

Even so, from her peripheral vision she knew he was staring.

The doctor manipulated gently, then blew on the bell of her stethoscope to warm it before placing it on Moira. Listening intently, she moved it several times, and smiled. After a minute, she glanced at Will. "Would you like to listen?"

"Please." He stepped forward, bent and slipped the earpieces of the stethoscope in place. He frowned. "I don't hear anything."

Dr. Engel moved the bell half an inch, then, after a pause, another half inch. The expression on Will's face transformed. Now Moira couldn't help watching him, seeing what wonder did to the hard lines of his face.

"It's so fast," he whispered.

"Normal for a baby."

"I guess I knew that, but…" He kept listening, and when at last he removed the earpieces and handed the stethoscope back to the doctor, Moira could see his reluctance. "Amazing." His eyes met hers. "You've heard it?"

She nodded.

"Have you felt the baby move?" Dr. Engel asked him.

He shook his head and looked again at Moira's belly.

"Let's see." The doctor gently pressed, sliding her fingertips around. Finally she reached for his hand and laid it where hers had been. Will's was so very large, it covered much of Moira's stomach. A movement came inside, the flutter and swirl. Will stood very still, concentrating, then cleared his throat. "Thank you," he said, sounding hoarse. "Wow."

Dr. Engel pulled up the waistband of Moira's pants, drew down her shirt, said briskly, "One month," and breezed out.

Moira shifted her weight to an elbow to lever herself up. Without a word, Will wrapped an arm around her and helped her to a sitting position.

"That's only going to get harder, isn't it?" He sounded amused.

"I've perfected the art of rolling out of bed."

The amusement left his face. He was silent as they walked out and she scheduled her next appointment. Still quiet until they were in the parking lot.

"If you have an emergency, do you have someone to call?"

"Of course I do," she said. "But I don't expect an emergency."

"No." He had that look on his face, the not-quite-a-frown one. "Four more months."

Moira nodded, unlocked her car door and opened it.

He gripped the top of the door and watched as she got in and put on the seat belt. "I'd like to see you again," he said quietly. "Before I go."

Her throat felt clogged, as if she wanted to cry.

When she didn't say anything immediately, his hand tightened until his knuckles turned white. But his voice stayed calm. "You're not comfortable with me, are you?"

Breathe in, breathe out. A chance to practice her Lamaze techniques, Moira thought a little hysterically.

"I don't know why you're here," she said. "You can't possibly want this baby."

"You don't know what I want." The timbre of his voice had roughened.

She stared at him fiercely. "Be honest. You were horrified when you got my email."

"Shocked," Will admitted after a moment. "Yeah, I was. I'll bet you were, too, when you first suspected."

"Yes." She had to be honest. Not just shocked: terrified. She wasn't going to tell him that. "But I do want the baby now. What I don't want is to…oh, count on you in any way then have you back out. Do you understand? It's not money, it's…everything." She hardly knew what she meant herself. It was dumb to feel so distraught when she didn't even know why she did. "I don't want her to count on you if you're not going to stick it out."

His gaze flicked to her belly. "Her? Do you know it's a girl?"

"No." Oh, damn, damn. Her voice was thick, and she *would not* cry. "I was just…"

"Talking about yourself," he said softly.

They stared at each other.

"Maybe," she whispered.

Will circled the car door and squatted close to her. "Have you told your mother yet?"

Moira bowed her head and saw a tear splash onto her maternity top and soak in. She took an angry swipe at her face. "No. I don't know why. I…keep putting it off."

"Like you put off telling me."

"I'm used to doing things for myself. I'm *good* at taking care of myself." It seemed important that she convince him. She didn't want him feeling guilty in some way. "I'm not telling you that I need you," she said, looking fully at him despite a nose that had probably resembled Rudolph's. "I just want to know. If you're going to send support checks, that's great, but then…then don't come and see me, and be nice, and…" Crap. Her vision was blurring again and she hated herself. She was doing the absolute last thing in the world she wanted to do, which was laying a guilt trip on him. "No," she said suddenly. "No, I don't want to see you again. All right? My hormones are going crazy, and I'm up and down, and I'm confused about you, and I don't want to see you tomorrow or the next day when you won't be around again for another six months."

Something happened to his face, although she couldn't see clearly and didn't want to. She thought it contorted briefly. Then he stood so she couldn't see it at all.

"All right." His voice was low and scratchy. "Thank you for this. For today. Please keep letting me know how you are. Will you?"

She swallowed and nodded.

After a moment, he said, "Goodbye," closed her door and walked away.

Moira sat with tears running down her face until she saw his pickup drive out of the parking lot and knew he was gone. And she didn't even know why she felt like her heart was breaking.

FOUR DAYS LATER, Will got on the goddamn airplane and felt like scum. Worse than scum. All he could see was her face, all he heard was the way her voice broke when she said, "Then don't come and see me, and be nice, and…"

Every time he thought about her, he felt as if his guts were spilling out, and it *hurt*.

He shouldn't have come at all. She was right. They *didn't* mean anything to each other, and he'd let himself start thinking they did, as if there must be a connection between them if they were having a baby together. He'd never imagined having a child with a woman who wasn't his wife, a woman he didn't love. Somehow he'd turned things around in his head and gotten to believing he felt things he didn't. That was all this was.

He closed his eyes and ignored his seatmates, who seemed to be ignoring each other, too. Three strangers, compelled by circumstances to sit shoulder to shoulder, thigh to thigh, for hours.

It was all Will could do not to jump up, grab his carry-on and bulldoze his way off the airplane before the door was shut. But he sat where he was, muscles locked with the effort not to move, and thought, *What the hell's wrong with me?*

Torturing himself this way was stupid. Moira had a mother, she had friends. Single women had babies all the time. He could tell she meant it when she said she really wanted this child. There wasn't a reason in the world she wouldn't do fine without him.

So why was it killing him to know that he wouldn't be in the States for another five or six months? That she'd already have had the baby by then? That at best he'd have a brief visit before he was off again?

The expressions on his brothers' faces when he told them hadn't helped. He'd done it last night at the dinner table.

"This woman," Clay had said slowly, as though to be sure he understood, "is having your baby while you're off in Africa."

"I didn't know her well. We had sex. I used a condom, but it apparently failed."

Jack had offered a profanity. Clay never took his eyes from Will's face.

"You came back to make sure she's all right."

He unclenched his jaw. "Yes."

"Is she?" Clay might be young, but he had the

implacable expression Dad had done so well. Funny, until that moment Will hadn't realized how much his brother had come to look like their father. More so than Will did.

"Yes," he said. "I, uh, went to the doctor with her. Heard the baby's heartbeat."

They were all quiet for a moment. "Well, damn," Clay said at last.

"I don't like it," Will had told them finally. "I don't like anything about this. The only thing that would have been worse is if she'd aborted my baby. Okay?"

"The timing is piss-poor," Jack said thoughtfully.

Will turned on him almost savagely. "You don't have to tell me. I should have kept it zipped. Do you think I don't know that?"

Goddamn it, right now Jack looked like Dad, too. Dad had believed there was right, and there was wrong, and not one hell of a lot in between. He'd taught his children his unbending rules. Will couldn't remember even hesitating about whether he'd come home and take Dad's place after he died. That was the right thing to do.

The plane was accelerating down the runway, then lifting off, tilting upward to climb. It was too late now to sprint down the aisle and beg to be let off. Sitting here, his body still rigid, Will thought, *This is wrong.*

But, for one of the first times in his life, he had no idea what the right thing to do was. He'd believed he was doing the right thing. Maybe this was one of those hellish situations where there was no right.

What stayed with him all the way to New York then across the Atlantic was the knowledge it wasn't the baby he was worrying about. He didn't doubt that Moira would be a good mother. The best. No, what was tearing him up inside was Moira herself, the woman whose vulnerability he'd seen from the beginning. No matter how beautiful he'd thought she was, he wouldn't have stayed talking to her so long that night if he hadn't seen that someone had hurt her. Yes, he'd wanted her, but even more, he had wanted to be the one man who would make her feel good about herself.

And look what he'd done instead.

He'd known grief twice in his life, once when he was a boy and his mother died, then again when his father and stepmother were killed. This shouldn't have been as bad. Nobody had died. Nothing was unfixable. But by the time he got off the plane in Harare, his heart felt like a rock in his chest, and not one that had been tumbled smooth. This stone was so rough, it scraped his sternum and ribs every time he took a breath.

THE HOSPITAL HELD REGULAR cycles of childbirth classes. The sessions were eight weeks long, and it was recommended that expectant mothers not wait until the very end. After all, the online description pointed out, not all pregnancies went full-term.

Charlotte would have been her first choice for a partner, but Gray had woken Moira at 4:00 a.m. five days ago to let her know their baby had been born. A little girl, Emily Faith Van Dusen. Moira didn't think she'd ever heard him sound so exhausted and so happy. And all at the same time.

He hadn't looked or sounded any more rested since, and Charlotte, who was breastfeeding, was probably even more tired. Obviously, she was out as a labor partner for Moira.

And even if Gray had been willing to leave Charlotte and Emily for the weekly class, Moira didn't want him. The fact that he was a man and she was a woman didn't usually seem to matter. For heaven's sake, he'd even had her stand up for him at his wedding. She'd always thought, if she got married, she would ask him to do the same for her. But she wasn't asking him to coach her in childbirth the same way he had his wife, the woman he loved.

Sheila Daniels would be her next choice, but Sheila lived in Mukilteo. Only a forty-minute drive from West Fork, but Moira suspected she'd want someone *now* once labor started. Bonnie Pappas was another possibility, or Jill Shore... Moira's brow wrinkled. No, with two young kids of her own, Jill might have a hard time getting away for the weekly classes, never mind at whatever hour of the night or day Moira went into labor. Bonnie, then. But Moira didn't call her. She had time. She didn't have to start childbirth classes quite yet.

What she did have to do was call her mother. Admitting to Will that she hadn't told her had made Moira shrivel inside, knowing how Mom was going to feel about her having kept this secret. Will hadn't looked too happy himself when he did a mental count and realized how long she'd known she was pregnant before she'd told him. And Moira had even less excuse where her mother was concerned. Worse yet, she and Mom talked every couple of weeks, so she'd been lying by omission for months now.

Filled with resolve, she called that evening.

"Sweetie," her mom said with pleasure. "How nice to hear from you."

Moira gulped. "I have something to tell you. I've been putting it off for ages."

During the ensuing pause, she could all but see her mother's eyebrows arch. "Oh?"

Deep breath. Bald words. "I'm pregnant."

This silence was even longer. "Pregnant?" Mom whispered.

"It was, um, an accident. The guy isn't anyone I was seriously dating… He wore a condom, but…" She stumbled to a stop.

"Oh, honey."

Moira squeezed her eyes shut. "I'm sorry, Mom."

"Please tell me you're not apologizing to me," her mother said tartly. "Are you sorry in the sense you wish you weren't pregnant?"

"No." She took a deep breath. "No, actually I've become reconciled to that. I want to be a mother. I'd even given thought these past couple years to… I don't know, adopting, or looking into a sperm donor bank. No. I'm excited about having a baby. I just wish I'd fallen in love and gotten married first. I know raising a child alone wasn't easy for you."

"It was also the greatest joy of my life," her mother said.

Moira sniffed. "Oh, Mom."

Her mother's laugh was warm and familiar, almost as good as an embrace. "When are you due, honey?"

"Oh, uh, January. My official due date is January 14."

This silence fairly crackled. "You're six months pregnant."

"Yes." She closed her eyes and said again, "I'm sorry. I guess I've been ashamed to tell you. Which I know is dumb. It's not like I'm sixteen. Or that you wouldn't have guessed I'm not a virgin."

"No, although I've wondered… Well." Mom cleared her throat. "I'd like to be there when the baby comes, or whenever you need me most." She hesitated. "Is the baby's father going to be involved at all?"

Moira found herself telling her mother about Will, including his visit and her own bewilderment. It felt like it had when she was a confused teenager who'd been able to cuddle up to her mommy on the sofa and confide all her troubles. She'd been the envy of her friends because she *could* talk to her mom. Of course Mom wouldn't be ashamed of her or ever have anything but faith in her. She didn't know why she'd ever feared otherwise.

She was the one who didn't have faith in herself. Who'd been ashamed of herself.

Moira swallowed a few lumps in her throat, told her mother she loved her, and finally hung up the phone feeling both better and terribly, inexplicably sad.

Until she'd felt the first movements inside her, she hadn't realized how lonely she was. She had friends; Gray, especially, would do almost anything for her, she thought. But Mom was the only person in the world for whom she, Moira, came first. And…it wasn't supposed to be that way. By her age, she should have found someone else to love her completely, so much that she never had to doubt it. Instead, she would turn the fierceness of her love on her child. She could see herself replicating her mother's experience, her own experience, and it scared her to wonder if she hadn't somehow made this happen because it was the only kind of family she knew. Maybe she wasn't capable of loving a man and being loved by him, of forming a true family circle.

She sat in the quiet of her house and thought, with a kind of chill but also the knowledge of her own strength, *If that's the way it is, so be it.*

There were worse fates. She was lucky enough to have the chance to be a mother. Mom had talked about joy, and she'd have that. The man-woman thing…so, it hadn't happened. She'd have a rich, satisfying life anyway.

To heck with Will Becker. Who needed him?

CHAPTER SEVEN

"YOU UNDERSTAND," THE SMALL, balding man told Will, "that I will need to get permission from higher up for these plans."

The government office looked like those the world over, although the desktop computer was an antique by American standards. Will had had to wait for over an hour for admittance to see this official, who had then, of course, been extremely cordial. Now, twenty minutes later, they were getting down to the nitty-gritty.

Which, as expected, was that this particular man couldn't make that decision. Nobody, Will had long since discovered, ever admitted to being able to make a final decision about anything. The buck was always passed upward. No one ever wanted to look him in the eye and say, "Sorry, no can do." Or even, "Sure, no problem."

He'd been a model of patience until these past few weeks. Become damn good, if he did say so, at these protracted negotiations, all seemingly friendly.

Today, he seethed, even as he said with hard-won civility, "Indeed, these matters are complex. It's my hope that a man in your high position can get the needed permissions. It would be unfortunate if we couldn't proceed before the heavy rains. Building might not be possible until fall, if we don't start soon."

Yes, yes, summer was not the season to build, indeed it

was not. Ten minutes of amiable, time-killing conversation later, Will escaped.

Just for the day, he was in Mutare, Zimbabwe's fourth largest city and very close to the Mozambique border. Also European in looks, Mutare was beautiful, surrounded on all sides by mountains, green on the slopes and crowned by tumbles of granite. He was working toward building two clinics in the area, one to the south in the rich, agricultural valley below the Vumba Mountains, one not far north in the Nyanga region. Yesterday he'd taken the time to wander the ancient remains of Nyangwe Fort, a stone enclosure built of granite blocks and slabs that wouldn't have looked out of place in the Peruvian Andes. He'd driven through the Nyanga Mountain National Park and seen tumbling rivers and wildlife.

And all he could think about was Moira. He'd been back in Zimbabwe for four weeks, during which time she'd sent exactly three emails letting him know that she was fine and commenting pleasantly on the humorous stories he'd shared of his adventures. The tone of her missives enraged Will, even though he knew damn well he didn't have a right to expect anything different.

She was now seven months along. He'd close his eyes and picture her pressing a hand to her lower back, or climbing awkwardly onto that exam table. He saw her sitting in her car, not looking at him, tears thick in her voice as she told him to get lost.

Will had emailed Clay last week and asked him to check on her. She'd probably be ticked, but he didn't care. He'd noticed an internet café earlier, and now decided he could walk to it rather than move his truck. A row of red blooming poinciana trees arched overhead, and he passed pedestrians: men in business suits, some teenage boys with a scrawny dog, a pair of women in bright colored western sundresses. Both women had babies slung in equally bright slings on their backs, while one balanced a full duffel bag on her head, the other a tote bag topped with a bulging white plastic grocery sack. Their arms were free, their gaits graceful despite the burdens. Their burst of chatter didn't register as words with him; although his Shona became more fluent by the day, he still had to concentrate and hope the speaker talked slowly.

He bought a tea in the café and waited for a computer to become available, then waited longer to get online and finally for his email to load. He immediately sought Moira's email address; nothing. But Clay had replied.

I met your Moira. Damn it, Will! She wasn't in the office, but a man was. Gray Van Dusen, the partner. I had the feeling he was real glad to be able to send me to a new development out by Lake Stevens, built on a hill. Said he'd offered to go in her place and she wouldn't let him.

Will's gut knotted. He wasn't going to like any of this.

I've gotta tell you, it's done nothing but rain buckets all week. I've had to idle a couple of crews, if that gives you an idea. The house I found her at was down a *lo-ong* steep driveway. The ground is ankle deep in mud. I mean, sucking-your-feet deep. The walls were up, the inside rough. She's in there, pissed about the grade of plywood, the foreman is yelling at her, she backs up and damn near falls over an exposed pipe. I flung myself forward to catch her. I don't know much about pregnancy, but man, her belly is sticking out there. As imbalanced as she is, I don't know how the hell she got down the driveway. I know how she got up, because I waited around to walk with her. Slowly, me hovering to grab her although I didn't have to. She's sturdy, I'll give her that, but I had to boost her into the SUV she was driving, with it tilted off the road the way it was. She went on to a second house in the development, and I let her go when I saw that the driveway wasn't as long or as steep, but, crap, she has no business being there in her shape.

She was friendly enough, but looked surprised when I told her you were worried about her. I half expected her to say, "Will who?"

So okay. I checked. She's alive, maybe not big as a house but holy shit she's getting there, and apparently not willing to cut herself any slack because of it.

Damn, I wish you hadn't sent me.

Clay

Will felt sick. What was she thinking? But he knew—what she was thinking was that she had to be independent. She couldn't start letting herself lean on her partner because she might keep leaning. She wouldn't take any more help than absolutely necessary, because she didn't feel entitled to it.

Didn't she believe that any of them cared?

He closed the program without reading any of the other messages. He stood and walked out, started down the street toward his Datsun, otherwise oblivious to his surroundings and passersby. He churned inside: stomach, mind, heart. With ruthless honesty, Will admitted to himself that he'd wanted Clay to say, "Yeah, we met. Nice lady, she seems to be doing great." His anxiety would be quieted, if temporarily. He'd be able to keep justifying having left her.

Left? Abandoned. That's what he'd done. Will reached his pickup and laid both hands flat on the rusting roof, bowing his head and surprised to discover he was panting. No, they hadn't had a relationship, not really; he hadn't promised her anything, she didn't expect anything of him. But no matter how it happened, she was carrying his baby, and he had goddamn abandoned her to do it alone. He'd heard the heartbeat, felt his child move beneath the hand he'd spread over the firm swell of Moira's belly. He'd seen fear on her face and taken it as a ticket to go. Nope, she didn't need or want him.

But she did, whether she knew it or not. And while the commitment he'd made here could be fulfilled by someone else, the one he owed her couldn't be.

Will was scared as he hadn't been since Sophie fell off the monkey bars during recess at school and remained unconscious for three terrifying hours. He had the sudden, unreasoning conviction that Moira *would* fall, that she'd lose the baby if she kept plodding on alone. Maybe just as bad, he couldn't imagine that she'd ever believe in any man again. The scumbag hadn't dealt the deathblow; Will had. And yeah, he knew that was irrational, too, but he still believed it.

There might be a blurry gray area between right and wrong, something like the eternal drizzle of a November back home, but he wasn't standing in it. Will knew what was right, and he knew he'd been wrong.

No, he didn't love Moira Cullen. He didn't know her well enough to feel anything like that for her. But the possibility had been there from the moment he first saw her in that ballroom, dancing with another man. There was a reason he hadn't been able to forget her, even before he learned she was pregnant.

Will straightened at last, clearheaded for the first time in months. His choice made, he wished he could head straight to Harare this minute, but it was too late in the day for the drive over mountainous country. He'd find a room here instead of going back to Nyanga as he'd intended. Tomorrow morning, Harare. He could be home in the U.S. within the week.

Whether his redhead liked it or not, she'd have him beside her as long as she needed him.

Because he couldn't live with himself if he wasn't there.

"No, I'm great, Clay." Moira managed a chuckle into the phone. "I'm pregnant, not disabled." She was trying, damn, she was trying, not to sound sharp, but she was getting awfully tired of everyone fussing. For Will to have sicced his brother on her was the last straw.

"I just don't like the idea of you taking a tumble," he said. For the second time. "That driveway was steep and slick."

Yes, it was. And, unfortunately, he'd seen her struggle up it. By now he'd probably reported back to his big brother, who would likely then send his *other* brother to check on her, too, and maybe his sister and an aunt and who knew who else. And it wasn't as if she didn't already have Gray on her case.

"You can reassure Will," she said, "that I'll be careful. I have every intention of cutting back on anything physical these last couple of months. Okay?"

Eventually she had him soothed. She was just banging the phone down when the office door opened and Gray walked in. Her glower honed in on him and had him pausing.

"Problem?"

"I'm mad at you all over again. I didn't need another nursemaid."

He grinned. She'd torn a layer of skin off him last week because he'd had the nerve to tell Becker's brother where to find her. "That was Clay Becker on the phone?"

"Yes!"

"Good. Seemed like a nice guy."

"*Seemed* is the word for it. Neither of us knows him. I don't want to know him. I resent Will making him come here. I've told Will repeatedly that I'm fine, and he refuses to believe me." She was shouting, Moira realized in surprise. She never shouted. But frustration and, yes, fear had swelled in her chest until she felt like she could burst with it.

She didn't want to admit that Gray might be right, that Will's brother might be right, and that she shouldn't have gone out to Lake View Heights last week. It was her job. What good was she if she couldn't do the follow-up work on her own plans?

But she'd been scared when she parked and walked to the top of that damn driveway, when she'd teetered there on the edge of the drop-off and wondered how she could get down. She'd felt a sharp kick in her belly, as though her anxiety had awakened the baby, and she'd gulped as she took the first couple of steps, figuring out how her ungainly weight should be balanced over feet that were trying to skid out from under her despite the deep tread of her work boots.

Maybe next time she'd accept Gray's offer to go in her stead. But how could he do that very often and keep up with his own schedule? They were both hoping he could hang on until his term of office expired in January. It was bad enough that he hadn't been able to run for reelection, but if he had to quit early because of her, she didn't know how she could live with it.

Gray dropped his briefcase on his desk and strolled over to hers, where he half sat on a corner she kept clear for him. Smiling, he said, "You're a stubborn woman, Moira Cullen. Must go with the red hair." He reached out and fingered an escaped curl.

She slapped his hand. "That's a stereotype."

His smile widened. "Maybe."

"Once upon a time, a woman would work in the fields until the baby dropped out, then sling it on her back and keep working."

"Now, why do I suspect that's apocryphal? Probably no more true than claiming all redheads have tempers and a tendency to dig in their heels."

She felt like tearing at her hair. "I have two more months to go. What do you suggest I do, take a lot of bubble baths and watch soap operas?" Moira let out an annoyed puff of air. "No, forget the bubble baths. I'm not allowed to take a hot one, and who wants a tepid bath?"

Gray listened to her indignation with clear amusement, but his gray eyes held a glint she recognized as serious. "Will is right to worry about you," he said bluntly. "Nobody has suggested you sit around and watch *Days of Our Lives.* All I'm asking is that you use some common sense."

Interestingly, his voice had begun to rise there toward the end. What temper Gray had most often came out in quiet, steely orders.

"Men," she muttered.

"If women worked the fields until they gave birth in the good old days, it was because they did it every day.

They had the muscles for it. They didn't sit in front of a computer four days a week, then spend the fifth scrambling over concrete foundations with exposed rebars and pipes just waiting to trip them up." Now he was definitely yelling, too. "Especially not when they reach the point where they can't see their feet!"

Moira blinked. "You're really worried about me."

He sucked in a huge breath and closed his eyes when he exhaled. "Damn it, Moira, yes."

"Oh." She looked down to see her stomach take a bounce. When she laid a calming hand on it, a knob bumped into her palm. An elbow, a knee, the heel of a foot, she didn't know, but felt awe every time she came that close to touching her unborn baby. Her shouting had upset him.

She almost snorted. *Him*. If it was a him, he was probably anticipating the chance to do his own yelling. Yee-haw.

"How on earth," she wondered aloud, "did I ever become best friends with a *guy?*"

"The same way I became best friends with a redhead."

She grinned at him. Then her smile vanished and her eyes narrowed as what he'd said sank in. "So, you're telling me women in the good old days had muscle, but me, I'm in such lousy shape I'm not safe to let out of the house."

"Oh, for God's sake," he snarled. "You're making me crazy."

"You've already made me crazy."

They glared at each other.

He sighed. His shoulders relaxed. "I've got to tell you, until recently I thought Charlotte was the most difficult woman in the world."

"I'm telling her you said that."

Gray only laughed. "She knows." He hesitated. "Why won't you let me do anything for you?"

"I will. When I need you," she said, knowing perfectly well that she *was* being stubborn, but not why.

He stood, shaking his head and muttering something under his breath that she suspected was an obscenity.

"I got a call yesterday," he told her. "From Reynolds."

Sam Reynolds was the contractor building both houses in Lake View Heights that she'd drawn the plans for. Moira stiffened.

"He doesn't want you out there again. Says the homeowner won't accept the liability."

Her eyes widened. "It was Curtis Tate. That creep," she stormed. "I caught him using lower grade materials than I called for, and he's getting back at me. I'm going to call Sam right this minute—"

"You ever think maybe you scared Curtis?"

"No."

They were back to glaring at each other. Moira was too mad and too upset, too tangled up altogether, to talk about this as if it was an everyday problem. And she was afraid that if she let Gray have a glimpse of her confusion, all she'd be doing was confirming to him that she was too weak to do her job.

"I'm going home," she snapped, shooting to her feet. Too fast—her belly bumped the desk and the chair scooted backward several feet. She ignored it, didn't care that her computer was still on or that she had a couple more calls she should make. She grabbed her purse, said goodbye and stomped out.

She thought she was doing well, out of respect for the attorneys across the hall, not to slam the door behind her.

WILL WALKED INTO Van Dusen & Cullen, braced to see Moira, but her corner of the big space was unoccupied. There was a guy sitting at the second drafting table, although he wasn't working; he was frowning into space until he heard the sound of the door opening. This must be the partner.

He was good-looking, gray-eyed, with shaggy hair that was almost light enough to be called blond. The minute he saw Will, those eyes narrowed.

"Will Becker," Gray said slowly.

"Have we met?"

"I found a picture of you on the Becker Construction website."

Will winced. It was a crappy photo, almost ten years old, and should have been replaced with Clay's by now.

"Met your brother last week, too." Van Dusen seemed to be musing aloud. "There's a resemblance, although I might not have recognized you just from that."

"He's better looking."

"Yeah, he is."

The other man was bristling, Will could feel it. Could even understand it. Van Dusen and Moira were close. Best buddies, and maybe more. Sister-brother, on a level that had nothing to do with genetics? Will wouldn't have felt real cordial, either, toward a man who'd screwed Sophie then walked away, leaving her pregnant.

But reassuring Gray Van Dusen wasn't Will's priority right now. "Where is she?" he asked.

"She went home."

Worry speared him. "Is something wrong?"

Gray clasped his hands comfortably behind his head and leaned back in his leather desk chair. Surveying Will, he began to relax.

"She's mad at me," Gray said. "I was coming down hard on her, probably for the same reason you're here."

Will's mouth tightened. "Clay emailed me."

"She's been banned from the Lake View Heights development by the contractor, who claims the homeowner doesn't want the liability for a pregnant woman scrambling around a half-built house on a steep hillside."

"She could scream sex discrimination."

"Oh, I'm sure Moira will think about that," Gray said drily. "Once she cools down a little."

Will felt the first stir of humor in days, although it didn't last long. "She scared the crap out of Clay."

"So I gathered. He just called. That's what set her off in the first place."

Eyebrows rising, Will said, "Clay called?" Apparently his little brother shared Will's overdeveloped sense of responsibility more than he'd realized.

"Had the gall to ask how she was, apparently. Moira's not about to tell anyone that, about midafternoon, it's all she can do to keep from falling asleep across her keyboard." Gray's expression hardened. "Or that her back aches whether she's been sitting too long or on her feet too long."

Will sat abruptly in one of the upholstered chairs in their small conference area. He hadn't had any choice; his knees had given out on him. "She swears she's fine. Doesn't need me. Doesn't want me."

"And you? What do you think?" Gray still lounged in his own chair, but the posture, Will guessed, was all show. Probably he wanted to ram his fist into Will's face. He had to have been seething for long months because Moira was pregnant and alone, and now the guy to blame was right there, in front of him.

It was understanding that allowed Will to meet Gray's

eyes steadily. "I think she's wrong," he said quietly. "I'm back to stay."

Moira's partner began to smile. He straightened in the chair, then stood and walked over to Will, who rose at his approach.

Gray held out his hand. "Glad to meet you, Will. I'm Gray Van Dusen."

Will didn't smile, but shook his hand with a strong clasp. "You going to give me her home address?"

MOIRA HAD JUST LAY DOWN on her sofa, cozily warm beneath a throw, when her cell phone rang. She'd set it on the coffee table within reach, in case someone needed to contact her. She'd been hoping nobody would—a nap sounded really, really good, even though she'd be sorry come bedtime if she took one. When she saw the number, she almost didn't answer. But on the fourth ring, she sighed and did.

"Gray."

"What made you think I'd let you get the last word?"

How was she supposed to stay mad at him? But she pretended she was. "Now what?"

"Your doorbell's going to be ringing in about five minutes. Thought you deserved a warning."

Her eyes widened and she sat up. "What? Who?"

"Will himself. We met, we talked, he persuaded me to tell him how to find you."

"Will?" she repeated numbly. "He's *here?*"

"Yep."

"But…why?" she all but wailed.

"Seems he's been worrying about you."

The undercurrent of amusement in Gray's voice made her grit her teeth. "He wasn't satisfied by his brother's report? He had to come and see for himself? I told him—"

She bit off the rest and closed her eyes. *Breathe. Deep and slow.* Hyperventilating wouldn't help. "Why did you tell him where I live?"

"You're in the phone book, Moira," he said patiently.

"Without my first name."

"Hmm. M. Cullen, with a West Fork address. You think he couldn't have figured that out?"

A car pulled into her driveway. No. She stood and peeked. A pickup truck that she recognized. "Oh, God. He's here. Damn it, Gray."

"Do you want me to come over, Moira? I can be there in a minute."

"No." She was being silly. She could handle Will. "No, of course not. He's a nice guy. Just…"

"Stubborn?" Gray suggested, and she knew—*knew*—he was smiling.

With a growl, she disconnected then thought, *Oh, my God, my hair!* Bathroom… No, there wasn't time. Her purse. Where had she put her purse? There, on the kitchen table. She hurried around the sofa to it and groped frantically in the depths until her hand closed on the bristles of her brush. Even as the doorbell rang, she ran the brush through the hair she'd released from a bun the minute she got home.

Then, steeling herself, she opened the front door.

Neither of them said anything for a long moment. He made no attempt to hide his thorough appraisal. She couldn't help feeling a moment of weakness, of—heaven help her—longing, to be wrapped in his arms for a minute. He was so big and solid, and from the moment she'd met him she'd heard something in his deep, slow voice, seen something in his brown eyes, that made her feel as if she'd be safe with him.

Get real. All she had to do was look down at her belly

to see how deceptive appearances were. *Safe* was the last thing she'd been with him.

"Will," she said, finally.

His gaze met hers. "You're not surprised I'm here."

"Gray called."

"Ah. May I come in?"

"I suppose," she said, embarrassed at how ungracious she sounded. Okay, she *felt* ungracious, but still had this compulsion to be polite. She stood aside and let him past.

He stepped into her living room and glanced around in an appraisal as blatant as the one he'd given her all-too-ripe figure. "Nice," he said after a minute.

The interior of her house owed as much as she could afford to the Arts and Crafts movement of the late 1800s and early 1900s. She loved the combination of strong, clean lines and sophisticated sensuality. Mostly her furniture was reproduction, but she'd started collecting pottery from the period. Will went immediately to the glass-fronted case where she displayed her pieces.

"Genuine?" he asked.

"Yes." Reluctantly, Moira joined him. "That's a Grueby." She pointed at a particular favorite, a small vase with the classic stylized designs in a matte green glaze, then gestured to a second pot, this one cylindrical with hand-incised, extraordinarily delicate geometric designs drawn in brown, rust and pale orange glazes. "Do you know anything about pottery of the time? That one's from Marblehead Pottery. I like that it was started to teach ceramics as therapy to sanitarium patients."

"That's interesting," he said. "I know enough that I'd have snapped one of those up if I saw it at a garage sale, but not enough to identify the pottery." He turned to face her.

Her interest was caught despite herself. "Do you go to garage sales?"

"Weirdly enough," he admitted, "I can't resist a garage or yard sale sign. I've found some good stuff at 'em. Mostly tools, but a couple pieces of furniture, too."

What an odd thing to have learned about him.

"Do they have them in Zimbabwe?" she asked.

His mouth quirked. "Not that I've seen. They have street markets instead. They're as irresistible, in their own way."

So much for the niceties. She took a deep breath. "Will…why aren't you *in* Zimbabwe?"

"I didn't like how we left it between us," he said bluntly.

Moira's heart began to hammer. "That's it? You flew home so we could…what? Have a heart-to-heart chat?"

She couldn't be sure, but she thought his expression had become wary.

"No," he said. "I came home to ask you to marry me."

CHAPTER EIGHT

MOIRA COULD ONLY GAPE at him. "You have got to be kidding."

Marry him? Was he nuts?

Dark color streaked Will's cheekbones. "No. I'm serious, Moira. We're having a baby together."

She backed up to the sofa and sank onto it. "Will... this is the twenty-first century. The word *illegitimate* has pretty much disappeared from our vocabulary."

He shoved his hands into the pockets of his trousers. In dark pants and a rather wrinkled, button-down gray shirt, he was dressed more formally than she'd seen him since the night of the gala. If he'd worn a tie, he'd shed it at some point and rolled up the cuffs of his shirt to expose wrists that had to be twice the size of hers. He looked as if he might have come from a daylong meeting. Or, it occurred to her, straight from the airport. If so, he must be exhausted.

"I'd rather my child have my name," he admitted, "but I'm more concerned that he knows his parents were both committed."

Stunned beyond belief, Moira said, "We're not."

He considered her for a minute, expression unreadable, then said quietly, "I am."

"I don't understand," she whispered.

Will came to sit on the coffee table facing her, his knees touching hers. He reached out and took her hands, engulfing them in a warm, steadying clasp. "I don't want you to be in this alone. I'm not asking you to promise me forever, although I'd like us both to go into this with the idea that we'll try to make our marriage work. But even if it turns out to be temporary, I'd like to stay here with you. I intend to take you to the doctor, do any work that needs doing around the house, cook dinners, drive you to job sites. I want to be there when the baby is born. Take my turn at diaper duty. I want him to know my voice as well as yours. When he's a few months old, then we can talk."

All she could think to say was, "You're supposed to be in Zimbabwe."

The deep color of black coffee, Will's eyes held hers. "You're more important."

"You loved what you were doing."

"I did." His pause was awkward. They both knew he couldn't with any honesty say, *I love you more*. Of course he didn't. She'd become a responsibility to a man who took them seriously. "We're having a baby together," he repeated instead of claiming any feelings for her whatsoever.

"Oh, God." Moira wrenched her hands away and covered her face with them. "I should never have told you I was pregnant. I knew better. I knew you'd feel stuck."

"Moira." He gripped her upper arms, squeezing gently. "I don't feel stuck any more than you claim you do. I like the idea of being a father. It didn't hit me as soon as it did you, but…I can hardly wait."

Slowly she let her hands fall, her eyes searching his. "You're just saying that."

He let out a rough laugh. "No. I admit I've surprised myself. I'd have probably preferred to wait to start a family, but…" His gaze flicked to her belly. "I keep thinking about the baby moving inside of you. I want to put my hands on you and feel him move again."

"What if he's a she?"

His smile was curiously tender. "That's more than okay. I hope she has bright red hair and freckles."

"God forbid," Moira muttered.

Will lifted his eyebrows.

"I've always hated my freckles. And when I was a teenager I would have killed to have plain brown hair so I could blend in. I would have dyed it, except with the freckles that would have looked dumb."

He laughed again, more naturally this time. "Moira, honey, you have gorgeous hair and lovely skin. That night, I wished I'd had time to kiss every single freckle on your body."

Like an idiot, she blurted, "That would have taken—" She stopped before the last word could emerge. *Forever.* That's how long it would have taken.

"Weeks," he said softly. "Months, maybe."

Get a grip, Moira Cullen. "You're crazy," she told him.

"No. What I am is determined."

"You're already committed, and not to me."

Now his tone was completely inflexible. "I'm going to quit my job with the foundation. They can replace me."

"Midway through the job?"

"I've given them a good start. Someone else can take over."

He was serious, she realized. She couldn't tell at all from his face how he really felt about walking out on something that had meant so much to him. No, that was stupid; of course she knew how he felt. But Will Becker was made up of bedrock that was…traditional, maybe, but solid enough to be earthquake proof. The fact that the condom had failed was no one's fault, but he'd still feel responsible.

No. Her forehead crinkled as she kept studying him. That wasn't it. The thing was, this baby was his. It carried his genes. That was what he took so seriously.

"How old were you when your father and stepmother died?" she asked.

A ghost of some emotion passed through his eyes. "Twenty."

Her suspicion solidified. "Clay's a lot younger than you, I could tell. And he's the next oldest, right?"

"Yeah. Dad didn't remarry right away. Clay is seven years younger than I am."

"And you said Sophie just graduated from college. So she's...twenty-two?"

"Twenty-one, actually. She got a year of college credits while she was still in high school." He realized he'd never told her how old he was. "I'm thirty-five, in case you wondered."

She nodded acknowledgment, but stuck to the point. "Who raised them?"

Other than the flex of muscles in his jaws, Will was expressionless. "I did. I was an adult. There wasn't anyone else."

"Did you go to college?"

"I dropped out."

She pictured him, a shocked, grieving kid as immature as she and Gray had been their sophomore year in college, only Will had left behind dorm life and gone home to console three children who'd lost their parents. In the years to come, instead of studying and going to keggers, arguing all night with friends about American policy abroad, dating coeds and soaking up knowledge, he'd been making school lunches, attending parent-teacher conferences, taking his young brothers and sister shopping for new shoes. His sister for her first bra.

Moira ached for that boy.

"And the construction company. You took it over for your dad."

"Yes."

"You gave up everything for them." She sat looking at this big, kind, sexy man and said, despite the pain in every word, "That's what you meant, isn't it? When you said your worst nightmare was being trapped. Spending your whole life doing what you have to do."

He didn't respond.

"I can't do this to you, Will. No. No, I won't marry you."

"This isn't the same."

"It is."

"No. No, Moira. Leaving you and flying back to Africa was torture. Right now, all I want is to be with you. I want to hold our baby as soon as he's born. I *want*." His gaze bored into hers. He leaned forward, took her hands again, his grip tighter this time. "Listen to me. Don't think I'm making a sacrifice I'll regret. Life is full of choices, and I've made mine. I'm not going away, no matter what you say today."

She couldn't seem to speak. Emotions were rising in her like floodwaters, dark and tumultuous. She didn't know what she felt, only that it was too much. All she could do was shake her head hard.

"Don't say no, Moira." Like that day outside the obstetrician's clinic, Will's face spasmed with some emotion she couldn't read any more than she could understand her own. His voice was hoarse. "Please. Don't say no."

When she still failed to say anything at all, he let her hands go and leaned forward until he could draw her into his arms. Gently but inexorably, he tugged her forward until her brow rested against his broad chest and he could settle his chin on top of her head.

"Marry me, Moira," he said, so low she barely heard him. "Let me do this for both of us."

She could hear his heartbeat, as strong and steady as he was. Maybe the powerful rhythm was what allowed the floodwaters of her confusion to subside, the emotions to resettle into their places. She didn't ache anymore when she finally sat back, separating herself from Will.

"Are you sure?" she asked. "If this makes you miserable, I'll know eventually. That would be worse for both of us than being honest now."

"I've never been more honest in my life."

"Then..." Well, shoot, *now* she was going to cry. Didn't that figure. "Then yes," she managed to get out. "Yes, I'll marry you."

"Oh, sweetheart." He framed her face with his hands and caught the tears with his thumbs. "I'll try to make sure you're never sorry."

For some reason that struck her as funny, so that she laughed even as she wept. He kissed her forehead, then pulled her to him again, so that she got the front of his crumpled cotton shirt soggy.

"That's it. Let yourself cry," he told her, sounding so blasted *comforting* that she did, even though she couldn't help thinking of how often he must have cuddled his brothers and sister when they cried. When he was trapped, being a daddy whether he wanted to be one or not.

IT WAS ASTONISHINGLY EASY to get married, Will found. Easier than it ought to be, in his opinion. But then, divorce was easy these days, too.

He didn't want to think about that.

They got married in the church the Becker family had always attended. Will couldn't claim to be much of a believer—nothing had happened in his life to make him one—but his parents had insisted on Sunday attendance, and for their sake he'd done the same with Clay, Jack and Sophie. Moira resisted initially the idea of a church wedding, which annoyed Will. Was she trying to make sure she felt less guilt when she walked out on him a few months from now? But she eventually gave way, as most people did when Will dug in his heels. They were getting married, and they were going to do it right.

They did it on a Saturday so her mother could fly over from Missoula for the ceremony without missing any work. She was trying to save her vacation to be available when the baby was born if they needed her. Sophie came from L.A., too. There was no maid of honor. Instead, there were two best men—Gray for Moira, Clay for Will. There were only a handful of other attendees: a couple of friends of Moira's, Dennis Mattson, a good friend of Will's, Gray's wife, Charlotte, and her twin sister, Faith, who'd also brought her husband, Ben, the police chief of West Fork. Jack and Sophie, of course.

Moira had refused to make a big deal out of walking up the aisle, which was fairly short anyway in a church that was in temporary quarters while the congregation was remodeling and expanding the original building. Instead of preceding her, Gray walked her the short distance, her hand resting on his arm.

Will was stunned by how much he felt at the sight of her. She hadn't worn white, which annoyed him in one way, but he suspected the rich shade of cream was a better color on her anyway, setting off her fiery hair and redhead's skin. She was so gorgeously rounded with pregnancy, full with his baby, he found himself both choked up and aroused as he held out a hand to her. Then she looked at him, her green eyes scared and worried and vulnerable, and damned if it wasn't like being shot by a nail gun in the chest.

Somehow, from somewhere, he found a smile for her as she searched his face anxiously for that brief moment when it seemed as though they were the only two people there. He didn't know if the smile reassured her, but she did take a deep breath, square her shoulders and turn to face the pastor. Will did the same.

The church might be modern, but the promises they made were the same ones their grandparents and great-grandparents would have made. That's the way Will wanted it.

When Pastor James said, "You may kiss the bride," and Will drew Moira gently to him, her stomach lurched and bumped against him. Startled, he looked down, and Moira laughed. He liked kissing her when her lips were curved with pleasure. His lingered, and she didn't object. She was breathless and startled by the time he eased back.

My wife, he thought, undecided whether this felt unreal or more astonishingly real than anything else he'd ever done.

Clay hugged Will, giving his back a good, firm whack, then kissed Moira's cheek. Jack followed suit, and Sophie, tears in her eyes, rose on tiptoe to kiss Will then turned to embrace Moira. Moira's mother—good God, his mother-in-law—kissed them both, too. Moira all but disappeared in the bevy of women, leaving Will at Gray's side.

"I'm still stunned you were able to talk her into this," Gray said softly.

Will grinned. "I'm a persuasive man."

The other man's eyes met his. "Don't hurt her."

I won't, snagged in his throat. He had even less idea

what was to come than most grooms did. The best he could do was a quiet "I'll try not to."

"Good," Gray said. "Moira is…" He seemed to be searching for the right word.

Thinking of everything he'd seen in her eyes when she was distressed, Will said, "I didn't marry her just because she's pregnant. I'm not stupid enough to do that. It's…Moira," he finally finished, unable to find the right thing to say himself but hoping Gray understood.

A smile warmed the face of Moira's best man. "Good."

Will knew the minute she turned, looking for him. He went right to her side. Taking her hand, he said to the small crowd, "Everyone knows where we're going?"

Everyone did. Mom was riding with Moira; Will would be following in his pickup truck. The others were taking their own cars to the restaurant where they'd reserved a private room for lunch.

He had barely met her mother before the ceremony. Will had half expected her to be a redhead, too, but she wasn't. She had short, brown hair frosted with gray she hadn't bothered to color. She was a pretty, slender woman whose blue eyes had filled with tears when she embraced Moira after the ceremony. Sitting side by side at the restaurant, their heads bent together as they talked quietly, there was a palpable warmth and closeness between them that didn't surprise Will. They'd had only each other. He couldn't help wondering why a woman as attractive as Sylvia Cullen had never remarried. He supposed she'd kept her ex-husband's name because of her daughter.

"Aren't you curious whether you're having a girl or a boy?" Sophie asked at one point during lunch. She was seated halfway down the table, but didn't mind talking around several other people. Sophie wasn't shy.

Moira smiled. "Of course I'm curious, but I like the suspense."

"Do you have a preference?" Clay asked, from Will's other side. Apparently nosiness ran in Will's family.

She glanced down at her stomach. Will thought he caught something on her face, but he couldn't pin it down. "No," she said, after a moment. "No."

Was that true? She might feel more comfortable if she had a little girl. She would know better how to raise one, especially if she were on her own. Will clenched his jaw at the idea, then deliberately relaxed it. At this speed, his dentist would notice he was grinding his molars down. And he had no right to feel irritated because Moira felt emotions that were surely natural. She had no reason to trust he was in this for the long haul, no matter what he said.

He'd count his blessings. She'd said, "I do." He was going home with her tonight.

Actually, he and her mom both were going home with Moira tonight. He'd overheard her mother at the church earlier saying, "Moira, honey, I really wouldn't mind at all getting a hotel room. For heaven's sake, it's your wedding night." Clearly, they'd already had this argument.

"Don't be silly," Moira said. "You know our marriage isn't like that." He'd ground his teeth at that point, too. She had continued, "Besides, I want to see you while you're here. I wish you were staying longer."

Conversation became general again. Will was a little surprised at how well this mixed group of people seemed to get along. His gaze moved down the table. Dennis, an electrical contractor, was having an animated discussion with one of Moira's friends, while Sophie was listening, seemingly rapt, to some story Charlotte's sister, Faith, was telling. Jack was quizzing Ben Wheeler, the police chief;

no surprise there, Jack had briefly considered a career in law enforcement.

The wedding cake the waiter brought in was a surprise to Will and Moira both. A couple of people pulled out cameras and took pictures while the newly married couple cut the cake together. Moira's cheeks flamed.

Will and Clay wrangled briefly over the bill for the meal, Clay winning. Little brother was coming into his own, which apparently included the familial stubbornness.

"You didn't give us time to think of decent gifts," he said. "I'd like to give you at least this much."

In lieu of a gift, Jack had given Will back his pickup truck. With a grin, he'd said, "Clay's paying me slave wages, but, you know, I can afford to buy my own."

More hugs and kisses were exchanged in the restaurant then in the parking lot as the crowd broke up. Will walked Sylvia and Moira to her car. His pickup was loaded with his suitcases and a few of the boxes he'd stored seven months ago at the house. He had spent his last night in his old bedroom, but this time, closing the door behind him, he'd felt none of the pang he had the night before he left for Africa. This house where he'd grown up didn't feel like home anymore, not the way it had. He hoped like hell Moira let him feel at home with her and didn't treat him like an inconveniently lingering guest.

As she drove out of the parking lot, he turned to his own vehicle to find Clay leaning against the bumper. His brother rose to meet him. Clay looked good. Unfamiliar, but good in a dark suit and red tie.

"So, you're a married man," he remarked.

"Yeah." Will looked down at his hand. For the first time in his life, he wore a ring, a simple gold band. The sight of it induced something between panic and satisfaction in him. "Guess so."

"You quit officially with the foundation?"

"Yeah," he said again.

They'd professed to understand, but had to be disappointed in him. During the interview process, they'd heavily stressed that he was making a minimum two-year commitment. "No problem," he'd said. Uh-huh.

"Your old job is waiting for you," Clay said. "I figured you might want a week or two to settle in with Moira before you pick up the reins, but…"

Will shook his head. He should have foreseen this conversation and headed it off. "No. I'm not coming back, Clay. I told you before I left that I wasn't. I meant it."

His brother frowned. "Then what the hell do you plan to do?"

"For now, take care of my pregnant wife."

"You really think she's going to let you trail behind her all day, every day?"

"I'm assuming there are days she doesn't leave the office and I won't have to hang around. If she goes out on a construction site, I'll be with her."

"Then what?" Clay asked.

This was the part Will didn't like to think about. Funny, when he'd spent years craving his freedom like a sober alcoholic did the drink he wouldn't allow himself. But now that he was free in a way he'd never intended, Will felt like as if he'd stepped out of an airplane without knowing whether he'd be able to reach the ripcord. It was unsettling.

"I don't know," he admitted. "I've got time to think, and I intend to use it."

"Have you considered going back to college?" Clay asked, his tone tentative.

"I'm too old." Will moved his shoulders uncomfortably. "No, that's not true. I'd do it if I was sure where I was going. Say, I hankered to be a lawyer. But right now, if I went back to school I'd be taking classes like any eighteen-year-old with no idea what I wanted to be doing with my life."

"Would that be so bad?"

"I like building," Will said slowly. "More than I realized all those years. I want to build something that matters. And...I discovered over there that I was better at persuading people to do what I wanted them to do than I expected to be."

Clay grinned. "I could have told you that. You're the original immovable object. People *always* do what you want them to. You didn't notice?"

"Being bullheaded is one thing. Patient and diplomatic is another."

"Hell, maybe you *should* think about law school."

"Maybe so." Will shrugged. "Like I said...I've got time."

Ignoring the uneasiness that rose at the idea of so much unstructured time and an uncertain future, he reached for his brother and gave him a hard hug.

"Thanks."

Clay hugged him back, just as hard. "We've missed you."

Stepping back finally, Will said, "I missed all of you, too. Those first weeks were a little like going off to college. Caught me by surprise, but I was homesick as hell."

"See? You could be eighteen again."

A reluctant laugh escaped Will. "Got to tell you, I don't feel that young. Thank God. No eighteen-year-old should be a father."

"Man, I'm going to be an uncle." Clay shook his head. "That day I went out to meet Moira, I kept feeling weirded out when I thought about how it was your kid in there."

They said their goodbyes and Will started, at last, for West Fork. He'd expected to be right behind Moira, although he doubted that she was watching her rearview mirror. She didn't need him when she had her mother with her.

Clay, he thought as he merged onto the freeway, wasn't the only one occasionally weirded out by the stunning realization that Moira was carrying his baby. It amused Will to realize that he also felt a whole lot of satisfaction and some primitive, male triumph.

Maybe that was even okay now. After all, Moira was his wife. She and the baby both were his.

Temporarily.

His hands were rhythmically squeezing the steering wheel. He heard it creak.

What a time to discover that he hated a state of uncertainty. He'd married a woman who'd agreed only because she'd grudgingly conceded she could use some help. For now. And, oh yeah, he was unemployed.

It didn't make him happy to realize that he was a hell of a lot more nervous now than he'd been the day he got on the airplane to start a new life in Africa.

CHAPTER NINE

WILL HADN'T ARGUED AT ALL when Moira had informed him, the day he asked her to marry him, that she wasn't ready to share a bed with him.

"I don't know you well enough," she'd whispered, knowing how dumb that sounded under the circumstances. "And with me so pregnant…"

Watching her, seeing the distress on her face, he'd only nodded calmly and said, "We'll have time."

She hadn't been able to tell if he minded her ultimatum. Probably not. Just because he'd had sex with her once—at her invitation—didn't mean he really lusted for her.

And things were different now anyway. She'd wondered ruefully whether men ever genuinely lusted for a woman who was starting to waddle from pregnancy. She hadn't quite worked up the nerve to ask any of her friends whether their husbands had found them sexy this far along.

Now it was not only Moira's wedding day, Will was moving in with her.

He had arrived twenty minutes after she and her mother got home. He rang the doorbell, probably for the last time. She had a small burst of panic. She'd have to give him a key. From now on, he would simply walk in. It would be *home* for him. Wow.

Leading him down the hall, she explained, "I'm going to pull out the couch in the living room tonight for Mom.

She slept in the bedroom last night, but I've already changed the sheets."

"You didn't have to displace her," Will said mildly. He was close behind her, a big plastic tub in his arms. "I'd have been okay on the couch."

"You have all your stuff." Which he'd refused to allow her to help carry. "It makes sense for you to go ahead and settle in now."

Her mother came out of the bathroom as they passed. "Oh, I thought I heard voices. Will, can I help?"

"No, I can get it all."

Gee, of course he didn't want a woman carrying anything when he—a man—was around to do it. Moira was beginning to wonder—oh, shoot, why kid herself? she'd wondered all along—what she'd gotten herself into. Will Becker, she suspected, was sexist and overbearing, even if he mostly disguised those tendencies behind a relentlessly pleasant manner.

Mom laughed and said, "I can certainly pull a suitcase," and went out to his truck.

His eyebrows drew together as he watched her. After a minute, evidently resigned, he passed Moira and walked across the guest room to set the tub on top of the dresser.

"The drawers are empty and the closet is mostly," she told him hastily. "I have some extra bedding in there up on the shelf…"

"I don't need that much space." He glanced around, his gaze finally settling on the open doorway beside her. "Is that your room across the hall?"

"Yes. I have a second bathroom in there. You can put your stuff in the one out here."

His expression told her she sounded like a bellhop unnecessarily pointing out features of a hotel room. She couldn't seem to help herself. This was so bizarre. A man she hardly knew was moving in with all his worldly possessions.

She was wearing a wedding ring that he'd put on her finger.

Ulp.

"Uh…let me check that there are clean towels in the bathroom."

With a nod, he left. Moira still hadn't moved when her mother pulled a giant suitcase in, said, "I'll go back for another load," and disappeared again. Moira hurried to the bathroom before Will could catch her still standing there like a dolt. She already knew there were clean towels in here because she'd hung them on the rack not ten minutes ago, but this was a good place to hide briefly. And heck, while she was here she had to pee anyway. That was pretty much a given these days. She was awfully glad the master bedroom had a separate bath, or else he'd hear her getting up all night long.

She made a face. Not that he could live with her for long without noticing she needed the bathroom constantly. Gray hadn't commented, but that was probably only because he was used to his pregnant wife doing the same.

Thank heavens Mom was here tonight. Her presence made Will's feel less strange. More as if Moira simply had houseguests, two of them instead of one. Of course, one of them was going to be staying a whole lot longer than the other.

Marriage might have been an even bigger mistake than sleeping with him had been in the first place. Moira stared at herself in the mirror and saw how dilated her eyes were, how shell-shocked she looked. And how not married. The first thing she'd done when she got home was change out of her wedding dress into a denim jumper over a forest-green turtleneck. Nicer than she probably would have put on if she'd been by herself, but comfortable. And a contrast to Will in his well-cut dark suit.

Seeing him today at the church, she'd wondered whether it was the same suit he had worn that night at the gala. When she'd approached him at the altar and he held out his hand to her, the moment had felt eerily familiar. As if the two scenes had layered one over the other, she'd seen him stepping into the hotel room, his eyes devouring her face. His expression had been similar—intense, maybe hungry, and yet also tender.

It was the tenderness, she admitted to herself, that got to her.

She slipped out of the bathroom after hearing his footsteps going down the hall. She lurked in the kitchen pretending to be thinking about what she'd make for dinner even though she already knew. What was she going to *do* all afternoon?

Will appeared in the kitchen. "What are you up to?"

"Um...making sure I took the chicken out of the freezer."

"You look tired." His voice was gentle. "Why don't you lie down for a bit?"

The minute he suggested it, Moira wanted that nap with all the desperation of a chocoholic grubbing for a hidden stash of Hershey's Kisses. She needed sleep. More, she needed oblivion. A chance to recharge.

"You know, I think I will. If you don't mind."

"No." He smiled at her. "You'll feel better."

"Where's Mom?"

"She's as determined as her daughter. She's out getting another load."

"Oh. Will you tell her...?"

"Yeah."

He didn't touch her as she went by, but she felt his gaze following her all the way to her room.

As overwhelmingly sleepy as she suddenly felt, Moira expected when she lay down to spend some time thinking about Will and the fact that they were married now and what that meant, but it didn't work that way. She kicked off her shoes, slipped under the covers and conked out.

THIS OUGHT TO FEEL SIMILAR to living at home, Will thought a week later. Somehow it didn't, even though he was used to sharing his home with a woman.

But Moira wasn't Sophie. He didn't feel about her the same way he did about his sister.

The two women had things in common, though. Neither of them took direction well. They were both smart, too, and curious. And they both had smiles that warmed his heart.

In some ways, of course, Moira was the more confident of the two. She was in her thirties, not twenty-one. She had a successful career. She'd won recognition as an architect, had homes and commercial buildings she'd designed featured in Sunday supplements of the *Seattle Times* and *The Herald*. She was more of an artist than most architects were, Will had seen; her sketches weren't only clear, they had grace and deserved to hang framed on the wall.

What he couldn't figure out was why she also had a quality of vulnerability that Sophie, who'd lost her parents early, didn't. Why that trace of sadness clung to Moira, why he'd been able to tell that she wasn't surprised at all when Bruce Girard treated her the way he did. Moira maybe wasn't beautiful by the standards set by fashion magazines, but Will was a hell of a lot more attracted to her generous curves than he would have been to any skeletal runway model. She was vibrant and sweet and yet had a quality of innocence that made him think of Botticelli's Venus, or maybe a Renaissance Madonna. Pregnant, she embodied fertility, but he never saw even a hint that she was aware of herself as a sensual woman.

He found he wanted to know badly whether she'd had her heart broken. Who had hurt her and why. Why she'd never married and had reached the point of being grateful to have become pregnant during a one-night stand.

Since their wedding day, she'd been as skittish with him as the dainty impala he had startled once at the edge of a Zimbabwe woodland. A patient man, Will was smart enough to bide his time. It was easy to talk about work, about clients and friends, to draw her out. He waited several days even to ask how she and Gray had gotten to be so close.

They were eating a dinner he'd cooked—grilled salmon and baby potatoes sautéed in butter and dill. Moira wrinkled her nose at the broccoli, but took a decent helping. He'd noticed that she wasn't fond of most green veggies, but Will was trying to make sure she ate right.

"How'd you and Gray get to be friends?" he asked, helping himself to another serving of potatoes, his tone deliberately casual.

"Our freshman year we were in the same dorm, same hall." Moira's smile was soft as she remembered. "We flirted a little, went out a couple of times and had a really great time. He kept coming by my room to hang out. We talked and talked, and somehow never got around to seriously making out or anything like that. Even then, Gray was always totally upfront. One day he said, 'You're, like, the best friend I've made here, but I sort of get the feeling neither of us has the hots for each other,' and I realized he was right."

Had she really felt the same? Will couldn't help wondering. Or had she fallen in love and, given her lack of experience, was waiting for Gray to make a move?

Sounding breezy, she went on, "He told me about the girls he was seeing, I talked about guys. I ended up getting pretty serious about this one guy my junior year, and even so there's stuff I'd have never in a million years have told him that I'd already told Gray. When we graduated, we promised each other that someday we'd open a firm together."

"Promises like that are easy to make," he observed.

"And unlikely to be kept? That's what I thought. I went home to Missoula. I'd worked summers there for this firm and they offered me a job. Gray took one in Portland. I figured we'd drift apart."

"So what happened?" Will asked.

"It was Gray more than me. More than anyone I've ever met, when he says something he means it. He had a goal, and he never let himself forget it. We talked often, emailed all the time and we both saved money. When we thought we had enough, Gray told me he'd found the perfect town. Aside from nixing a few places—with my skin, I don't do well at all in hot climates—I didn't care so much where we opened our firm. Gray, though, had this ideal town in mind, and as far as he was concerned West Fork was it. Small town, but close enough to Everett and even Seattle that we're not dependent on a strictly local clientele. And he was right. It's worked great."

"Was he already married when you moved here?"

She shook her head. "No, Charlotte had grown up on a farm here, but she came back to town again only last year when her dad needed her. She got pregnant pretty soon after the wedding. I don't think she and Gray planned it. Which I think is funny, because Gray plans *everything*."

Will nodded. There was no reason for him to be jealous of her relationship with Gray Van Dusen, but he felt a jab now and then anyway. There was a sense of intimacy between the two of them that made him wonder whether Moira would have liked her *friend* to feel more for her. Will knew she wouldn't admit it even if he asked, though, so he didn't.

"What happened with the college boyfriend?"

One shoulder lifted in a dismissive, who-knows shrug. "It wasn't the romance of the century. He met someone the summer between our junior and senior years and I didn't actually care."

Yet another guy who'd ditched her. Or was he reading entirely too much into normal stories of youthful romance? He'd had a girlfriend himself his freshman year, and he couldn't remember her last name or quite picture her face.

"Anybody serious since?"

She didn't quite meet his eyes. "Not really."

He wasn't buying that; she was thirty-five, not twenty-five. Most people their age had had a few near misses, at least.

Suddenly stunned, he thought, good God, what if it was true? What if she hadn't had the high of knowing a man she liked was falling for her? What if that college boyfriend had been the last? Was it possible?

After a moment, she said, "You?"

Surprised and pleased, since up to this point she'd avoided asking him anything very personal, Will said, "I've had a couple of relationships that lasted a year or more, but…" He frowned, mulling it over. "Truth is, I was pretty tied up, between the business and my sister and brothers. I was doing well to sneak away for a date once a week." His mouth tilted in a rueful smile. "Plus, I made a house rule that none of us could have overnight guests of the opposite sex. I was the one who suffered the most from it in the early years, but I didn't want home to degenerate into a frat-house atmosphere. Especially with my sister being the youngest. The rule broke down eventually, when each of them had college friends stay, but the friend always had a bed made up in the family room. If anybody sneaked down the hall..." He laughed. "I pretended not to notice."

She was smiling, too. "Even when it was Sophie's boyfriend doing the sneaking?"

"I might have been a little stricter with her. I guess you've noticed that I'm an old-fashioned kind of guy."

Quietly, Moira said, "We wouldn't be married if you weren't."

He couldn't read much with her eyes downcast. "No," he said after a moment. "I guess we wouldn't be."

"Dinner was good." She gave him a bright, artificial smile. "Thank you."

Right now, he was the original house-husband. What else did he have to do but grocery shop and cook on days when she didn't need him? A week into it, he'd have thought he would be bored to death, but strangely he wasn't yet. He'd been reading voraciously, a pleasure he hadn't been able to make much time for even once Sophie was off to college. Will had found he enjoyed accompanying Moira to job sites, too, seeing her in her element demonstrating a quickness of mind and creativity he admired. The contractors, electricians and plumbers she dealt with were almost universally men, but aside from a certain nervousness when their gazes strayed to her protuberant belly, they treated her straightforwardly and with respect. Will knew some of them, and he'd been careful to deflect any attempt on their parts to include him in discussions.

"This isn't my job," he'd say briefly. He wouldn't blame Moira for getting her back up if anyone tried to defer to him instead of her. Will did stay close to her from the minute they got out of her car or his pickup. If she so much as stumbled, he'd grab her or wrap his arm around her waist.

He thought she was starting to get used to having him touch her, progress of a kind. The first few times he'd laid a hand on her lower back as they walked, or reached for her to help her out of a vehicle, she'd been obviously startled. Today, she had walked in the front door looking exhausted, and when he pulled her to him she'd simply leaned, as if she had waited all day to do just that.

"No," he said now when she stood and started clearing plates. "I'll clean the kitchen. You sit."

"If you cook, I should clean."

"You worked today. I didn't." He took the empty serving bowl and plate out of her hands. "Want me to put hot water on for tea?"

She followed him to the kitchen but settled on a stool at the breakfast bar. At his question, she sighed. "No, it'll only make me have to, um…"

It amused him that she should be shy about something like that.

"Get up at night?" He raised an eyebrow at her. "According to the book about pregnancy I've been reading, that's pretty normal."

"You've been reading a book about pregnancy?" Moira looked aghast. "Why?"

"I want to know what to expect," he said simply.

"Speaking of which…" Color tinted her cheeks. "I need

to start a childbirth class. Actually, I should have started a couple of weeks ago. And, well, I need a labor coach." She was talking faster and faster. "I wondered if you wanted to go with me. Except it would mean you being there. I mean, when I have the baby."

He'd opened the dishwasher, but now he straightened. What the hell? Had she been thinking of asking someone else? "I told you I intended to be there. Of course I want to be your labor coach."

"Oh. Well." Moira rubbed her fingertips on the tile counter. "Okay. Then I'll sign us up. It's only once a week."

He nodded, willing himself not to get pissed off. He felt more married than she did, but he couldn't blame her. He'd pushed her into this.

He was getting damn tired of repeating that to himself, but he'd keep doing it as long as he had to.

"We can practice the breathing at home," he said.

Moira nodded, then said a little tentatively, "I was thinking we might get a Christmas tree pretty soon. Unless you want to go to your brother's, or…"

"You mean, do *we* want to go to my brother's?"

He must have sounded ticked, because she looked wary. "I did assume you wouldn't take off Christmas Day and leave me behind. Although I spent last year with Charlotte and Gray and Faith and…oh, everyone. I'm sure we'd be welcome if we'd like to do that."

Damn it, this wasn't a minefield. She shouldn't have to watch her every word.

"What do you want to do?" he asked. "Can your mother come for the holidays? Or would she rather wait until you have the baby?"

"I think that's what she has in mind." She hesitated.

"We should have Christmas with your family. Maybe have them here."

He reached across the counter and took her hand. "Yeah, I'd like to do that. Maybe just us Christmas Eve, unless you want to do something with Gray and Charlotte."

"They're having a party the Saturday before." Her smile was a little tremulous. "I'd like to get a tree. And maybe put up lights. If you don't mind climbing the ladder."

"I'd rather you keep both feet on the ground." He grinned at her. "I like Christmas. Bring it on."

Her smile brightened and he saw a glow of excitement in her eyes. "Have you shopped yet? I mean, for Sophie and everybody?"

"For a change, yeah." He laughed at her expression. "What did you think? I'm a guy. But in this case I brought presents from Africa." For her, too, but he didn't mention that. "I even have a few extra things. A basket your mom might like, for example." He'd packed a whole suitcase full of things that had caught his eye.

Moira gave a happy wriggle. "Let's get a tree next weekend."

Will felt a glow of his own, centered right under his breastbone. "Works for me."

Their first Christmas.

She might assume it would also be their last, but Will was finding that he liked being married to Moira. Failure wasn't an option. Starting a few traditions together spiced by Christmas spirit might be just the thing to convince her that they could be happy together.

"OH, MY," THE CHILDBIRTH instructor said when she saw Moira. "When are you due, dear?"

She must be enormous. Everyone who set eyes on her

thought she should be ready to go into labor. "Not as soon as I look," Moira said. "My doctor wondered earlier on about twins, but my husband was a big baby and she thinks this one is going to be good-sized too."

The instructor's assessment was practiced. "You may not make it full-term. Well." She smiled at Moira then at Will, who stood behind her. "Welcome. Why don't you take a seat on one of the mats?"

Moira glanced around. There were six other couples and one very pregnant woman whose labor coach was likely her mother, given the resemblance between the two women. Will stood over Moira while she clumsily got to her hands and knees then sat with a groan.

"I feel like a...a hippopotamus," she mumbled to Will.

She loved his smile.

"They're actually graceful in water, you know," he told her. "It's when they lumber *out* of the water that they, uh..."

"Resemble me?"

His laugh was a low, husky rumble. "Something like that."

He sat behind her, spread his legs to each side of her and said, "Lean back against me."

With a sigh, she did. In theory, she still had a month to go, which made her wonder if she'd be able to get out of a chair by the last week. She was more grateful than she wanted to admit for Will's frequent helping hand. In fact, she was beginning to wonder how she'd have managed at all without him. And that made her uneasy. When was the last time she'd actually *needed* someone?

The class started off with breathing exercises. Moira felt silly lying on the mat panting and blowing, but the other women were doing it and Will had listened to the explanation with a seriousness that Moira found touching. Not that she would have expected anything different. He wouldn't be here with her if he didn't take *all* his responsibilities seriously.

And clearly, she was number one these days.

Kneeling beside her, he counted for her until the instructor had the women roll onto their sides.

"Coaches, now we're going to practice massage techniques. Touch is important at keeping your partner relaxed. Some women feel their contractions in their lower backs. Others gather tension in their necks or between their shoulder blades. They might suffer from cramps in their calves. You'll learn to feel when the muscles knot and take advantage of the breaks between contractions."

She walked around the room, pausing to give suggestions. Moira had been embarrassed at the idea of Will giving her a back massage, but, honestly, it felt so good from the minute he laid his big hands on her shoulders that she only closed her eyes and sank into bliss.

He seemed to know how much pressure to bring to bear, working his way from her shoulders down her spine to her incessantly aching lower back.

"We'll do this at home, too," he murmured, kneading more firmly down there.

Moira couldn't help letting a groan escape her.

His hands momentarily went still. "Did I hurt you?"

"No. It felt really good," she admitted.

"Ah." After a noticeable pause, he resumed the massage.

The instructor stopped, watched for a moment and said, "Excellent."

She had already set up a projector, and she gave them the option of sitting on folding chairs or staying on their mats to watch a short film on the progression of labor.

Will looked at Moira, and when she said, "I'm so relaxed now I don't think I *can* get up," he smiled, helped her sit up and drew her back to lean against him again.

At first she had trouble concentrating on the film. With the lights dimmed, she was even more conscious of being wrapped in his embrace. He held her so securely, one hand splayed on her belly. The baby must like the feeling of his hand there, because he got active. After feeling the movement, Will chuckled quietly and began to rub her stomach. The gentle motion of his hand was astonishingly seductive.

But the film got more and more explicit. Moira found herself tensing up and gaping. When the credits rolled, she whispered, "Oh, my God."

"*That* was supposed to reassure us?" he said.

"I guess we're supposed to go into this knowing what to expect."

"I'd rather not, thanks."

His obvious shock lessened hers to the point where she could laugh. "Too late."

Will gave her a dark look, then hoisted her to her feet. Moira staggered on legs that felt as if they'd gone to sleep, and tipped against him. Once again, he enfolded her in his arms as if that's where she belonged.

Increasingly, she wished that was true. Wished they hadn't gotten married only because they'd accidentally made a baby together.

But it could be more. Couldn't it? Will had thrown himself wholeheartedly into the marriage as well as into impending fatherhood. If she did the same, they might make something of this. Maybe their marriage would never be the love match Charlotte and Gray had, but they could be happy. Moira wanted to believe it was possible.

They were both quiet walking out to the car. They

were halfway home when Will said thoughtfully, "Do you suppose the baby will come early?"

"Dr. Engel didn't say anything."

"No." He'd accompanied her to her appointment today. "I just can't imagine you, a month from now..."

She couldn't, either. "If I'm a hippopotamus now, what will I be then?"

He chuckled and reached out to take her hand. "To tell you the truth, I've been thinking pygmy goat."

Moira faked indignation. "Wow, that's flattering!"

Will laughed again. "I happen to think they're cute."

When he said things like that, she got this warm flutter inside. She hoped, so much, that he meant it. If he really did like her, if he really *was* attracted to her, then maybe there was hope.

He was going to work with her tomorrow, as she had a couple of construction sites to visit. Both were on flat ground and were nearby, but he had insisted anyway, and Moira wasn't going to argue. His presence was reassuring in a way she didn't want to examine too closely. On the way into the house, they talked about her schedule. Then she said, "I think I'm going straight to bed."

Will nodded. "I'll probably read for a while."

The most awkward part of this whole marriage business was saying good-night. Tonight was no different. She wondered if he ever thought about kissing her. She knew that he always had the same expression on his face when he watched her turn to go down the hall, or when they parted outside their bedroom doors. It was...pensive. He was thinking really hard about something. He always stood where he was until she went into her room. A couple of times this week, she'd glanced back, to find his eyes on her.

Tonight she couldn't resist. One hand on the doorknob,

she looked back. He was standing by the kitchen, one shoulder propped against the wall, his hands in his pockets. When their gazes met, Will didn't move, not a muscle, but although he gave the impression of being relaxed she somehow knew he wasn't at all. She'd have sworn his eyes had darkened. The air between them all but shimmered with tension. Moira found she was breathing hard when she slipped inside her room and closed the door behind her.

Maybe a man *could* lust after a very pregnant woman. Or maybe she only wished Will could. Was.

It took her longer than usual to fall asleep. She kept listening for his footsteps or the bathroom door opening or closing and not hearing either. The baby decided this was an excellent time for some gymnastics.

She hadn't looked at the clock and didn't know how long it was before she had to go to the bathroom again. A half hour at least. She was getting back into bed when she finally heard Will's footsteps in the hall.

Sleep kept eluding her. Fifteen minutes later, sighing, she got up again. She hadn't had anything to drink all evening. She couldn't possibly have to pee again! But once she started thinking maybe she did, she couldn't get the idea out of her mind until she gave up and went to the bathroom.

As she was pulling up her nightgown, she thought she felt a damp spot in back. Alarm quickened in her. That was bizarre. She couldn't have wet herself in bed without realizing it, could she?

But she felt dampness between her legs, too. Really scared now, she sank down on the toilet and looked down at herself. Blood streaked her thighs.

CHAPTER TEN

WILL HAD JUST TURNED OUT his bedside lamp when he heard the soft snick of Moira's bedroom door opening. He didn't like it that she closed it at all; he had been leaving his open at night in case she ever called out for him. He lay rigid, waiting. She might be going to the kitchen, she might not need him at all….

"Will?"

He sat up and reached for the lamp. "Moira? What's wrong?"

The light came on, and he saw that she had taken only a couple of steps into his room. A long flannel nightgown enveloped her from neck to ankle. But it was her face he focused on, and the fear he saw.

"Will, I'm bleeding." Her voice was tremulous. "I think…I think I'd better go to the emergency room."

"God." He surged from bed and crossed the room to her. "Should I call 911?"

She bit her lip. "No, it's not that heavy. It's just…well, not quite spotting, a little more than that, but…" She drew a shuddery breath. "I don't think I should be bleeding at all."

Will gripped her upper arms and squeezed. "Even if they have to do a C-section right now, the baby should be mature enough to survive." He sounded one hell of a lot calmer than he felt. "Let's get to the hospital, okay?"

"Okay. Um…let me get dressed."

"I'll help. No. Hell. Let me throw on some clothes first." He'd worn only pajama bottoms to bed. "Go lie down."

Moira nodded and disappeared, ghostlike, from his room.

He'd never gotten dressed so fast. Will didn't bother with socks, simply shoved his feet into his running shoes. Then he went to her room. She'd actually curled up on the bed rather than ignore him and dress herself.

"All right. Tell me what you need."

"I already put on panties. A top and bottoms. There are some in the closet."

He grabbed the first ones his hands touched. Gently he helped her struggle out of her gown. Trying not to focus on her naked breasts, larger than they'd been, he tugged a knit shirt over her head then helped her slide on loose pants.

Moira insisted on walking, and he let her, although he kept an arm around her the whole way. Outside *was* cold, frost sparkling on the grass beneath the streetlight. Despite her parka, Moira shivered as he backed the pickup out of the driveway.

Will broke speed limits all the way to the hospital. She sat silent and tense beside him. Not until he braked in front of the brightly lit emergency entrance to the hospital did she say very softly, "I'm scared, Will."

"Oh, sweetheart." He hugged her, quick. "Let's not worry too much until we know there's reason to. Okay?"

She pressed her lips together and nodded, but her eyes were huge, her gaze clinging to his.

A couple of people in scrubs had come out, and within moments had her in a wheelchair. He had to park the pickup before he could sprint in.

The next two hours were hellish, even though the emergency-room doctor found the baby's heartbeat immediately. The doc seemed okay, although he was younger than Will liked. He had a million questions. How much bleeding? When did it start? What color was the blood? Was she cramping? Had she had sexual intercourse this evening?

Moira flushed at that question and cast Will an agonized look before shaking her head.

Had she fallen? When had she last seen her doctor?

It seemed to Will that the level of tension in the room dropped noticeably after Moira told them that she'd seen her doctor today and that yes, she'd had a pelvic exam.

Nonetheless, they took her away for an ultrasound, and when they brought her back he still wasn't allowed into the curtained exam cubicle because now the doctor was doing yet another pelvic exam and cervical culture. Will hated like hell that he was out here and she was alone with her fear, staring at the ceiling while some strange doctor had his hand inside her.

Sitting in a plastic chair in the hall, Will prayed as he hadn't in years. Amazing how much more faith a man *wanted* to have at a moment like this. He'd read about some of the things that could go wrong in late-term pregnancy, including placental abruption, when the placenta separated from the uterine wall. If she started to hemorrhage, it could kill her as well as the baby.

Will groaned. He rubbed the back of his neck, wishing he hadn't educated himself, that he didn't know how serious the trouble Moira might be in.

"Mr. Becker?"

He looked up to see the green-garbed nurse, who said, "You can come in."

Will followed her through the gap in the curtains, his

broad shoulders causing them to rattle on their rings. Lying on the narrow bed, Moira was covered now by a white blanket. The nurse had been bringing her warmed ones because Moira kept shivering as if she were cold. Cold, or in shock.

The moment he stepped into the cubicle, her eyes fastened desperately onto his face. A lump in his throat, he went to her side and took her hand in his, then looked at the doctor.

"At this point," the doctor said straight-out, "I'm not very concerned. The bleeding was minor, and it seems to have stopped. The fetus shows no signs of distress. I think this was likely triggered by the exam Mrs. Becker had earlier today. Minor instances of bleeding are most often associated with a pelvic exam or sexual intercourse. I have some question about the possibility of placenta previa—which means that the placenta is implanted over or near the opening to the birth canal. If it's the case at all, however, my guess is that it's resolving itself, as most often happens. Your doctor will want to keep an eye on it, however. And I'm sure it goes without saying that you need to let her know about any further bleeding."

Moira nodded. She looked drained, almost numb.

"I would certainly speak to Dr. Engel before you consider resuming sexual intercourse—"

"Fine," Will interrupted. "Should Moira be on her feet at all?"

"Assuming there are no further episodes of spotting, I see no reason she can't resume normal activity. No dancing." He chuckled, uttered a few pleasantries and went away.

Will breathed an almost-silent profanity and sank onto the chair beside the bed. "Damn. Does that mean we can go home?"

"I think so." Moira sounded uncertain. "I guess you were right that I panicked unnecessarily."

"You weren't the only one panicking," Will admitted. "I just tried to hide it."

Her smile trembled, but it was a smile. "I'd never have known. You're always so…steady."

"Practice," he told her. "Clay mostly avoided hurting himself, but I had to rush Jack and Sophie to Emergency way too often. You get inured." Which was a lie. Yes, he'd gotten so he barely rolled his eyes at a broken finger or even a broken arm—Sophie in particular had been an adventurer. But tonight, he'd been more scared than he could remember being in years. At least.

The nurse came in with discharge papers, and Will went to get the truck. They wheeled Moira out, helped her in, and not many minutes later he pulled into the driveway at home once again.

"Wow." Moira fumbled to unbuckle the seat belt. "I think I'll reschedule the stuff I was supposed to do tomorrow." She focused on the dashboard clock. "Not tomorrow. Today."

"How about you sleep in? Maybe even take the day off."

She must be shaken, because she nodded. "I think maybe I will. I'll set the alarm and call Gray—"

"I'll do it." When she opened her door, he said, "Wait until I get around there."

Wonder of wonders, she was docile again, waiting for his hand to take hers. She climbed the few steps to the front porch slowly, leaning a little as she went. When he helped her out of her coat right inside the front door, Will couldn't help thinking about how fragile she was. Generous curves or no, her bones were almost delicate. With the bulk of her pregnancy, it was easy to forget that.

"Let's see if I need to change any of your bedding," he said.

She went to the bathroom while he checked and found that her nightgown had apparently soaked up any blood and the sheet was fine. He pulled open drawers in her dresser until he found a clean nightgown. When she came back, she didn't argue when he reached for the hem of her top and drew it over her head. Moira did cover her breasts protectively, though. Again he tried not to look, but couldn't help himself. God help him. She had the most beautiful breasts he'd ever seen, ripe and full, creamy skin dusted with freckles paler than the ones on her face and shoulders. He regretted letting the gown drop to cover her body.

When he eased her back on the pillows, Moira said, "I'm not helpless."

"Tonight, let's pretend you are. For my sake."

She looked up at him, her eyes very green, and finally gave one small nod.

Bracing himself for argument, he said, "I'm going to sleep with you. I want to be right here, and know you're okay."

Her lips parted, then, after a perceptible pause, closed. She swallowed. "All right."

"Give me a minute to get undressed."

Will went back to his room and shed his clothes as quickly as he'd put them on. He thought about leaving on the T-shirt but decided not to. He'd always worn pajama bottoms because he'd had to get up often enough during the night with one of his brothers or his sister. That was as far as he was willing to go.

Moira watched warily when he returned to her room. He was grateful she had a queen-size bed, at least. They'd want a king-size eventually, he thought, but this would do for now. He slipped in on the far side from her, then rolled toward her.

"Do you sleep on your back?"

She shot him a glance that made him think of a spooked horse. "No. I was, um, waiting to turn out the light."

"Okay," he said agreeably.

Moira reached for the lamp and plunged them into darkness. After a moment, he felt her moving, settling. He reached out a hand and found she'd turned on her side facing away from him. Probably on the very edge of the mattress. No surprise. He gently rubbed her back. "Sleep tight, sweetheart."

After a moment of silence, she whispered, "Good night, Will." Yet another pause. "Thank you. For…being here tonight. For…I guess for being here at all."

He smiled. "You're welcome."

Then he waited. Waited until she relaxed, until he heard her breathing deepen and slow. Only when he was sure she was asleep did he move the last foot closer to her, slide his arm under her head, and spoon their bodies together. He went still when her breathing hitched, but she sighed and, it seemed to him, snuggled against him.

He lay there in the dark, her springy hair tickling his chin and throat as it hadn't since that first night, and smiled again. Very carefully, so as not to awaken her, he splayed his hand on the large mound of her belly. Then, his wife and child held safe and close, Will let himself welcome sleep.

WILL HOVERED THE NEXT DAY. There was no other word for it.

At first it was kind of nice. But nice wore off, and after a while, his edginess made hers worse. She'd stand up to go to the bathroom, and he'd automatically rise with her, as if she was bound to collapse going ten feet. She'd look up and discover he wasn't reading at all, he was watching her.

In case she didn't notice gallons of blood gushing forth.

By midafternoon, she was snapping at him. When all he did was raise an eyebrow, she huffed out a breath. "Maybe I should go into the office."

"No, you shouldn't."

Moira's eyes narrowed. "You know, I'm usually pretty competent at taking care of myself."

Will was sprawled in her easy chair, leaving the couch to her. He smiled. "I imagine you are."

"Last night excepted."

"Uh-huh."

"I freaked. I admit it. Today, I'm fine."

"Good."

"You're looking at me like you expect the worst."

"Maybe you should go take a nap," he said gently.

"Are you going to come in and stare at me while I sleep?"

He fiddled with the book he so obviously wasn't reading. "Can I check on you a time or two?"

"No." Moira rose from the couch and marched out of the living room. He was smart enough not to follow her.

She closed her bedroom door behind her with a satisfying click. Not quite a slam because that wasn't justified. But firm enough to make a statement.

She didn't even know why she was mad. Maybe it wasn't at Will at all. Maybe she was upset about her own predicament, for which God knows she bore almost all the responsibility, whatever Will said to the contrary. Yes, it took two to make a baby, but she'd practically shanghaied him. And now he was being so damn *kind,* and she was all mixed up because it felt so good to have someone to lean on, but it was also scary and unsettling because she'd gotten so used to not having anyone. All these emotions seemed to tangle inside her, like a knot that got tighter and more complicated the more she picked at it trying to separate one strand from another.

She would never in her life forget how it had felt this morning to surface and find her head pillowed on his biceps, his warm, strong body touching hers from neck to calves. His breath had tickled her hair and raised goose bumps on her nape. His other arm enclosed her firmly and his hand lay open on her belly. One of *her* hands had clutched his arm as if to make sure he didn't get away. And she had loved waking up that way. She couldn't help thinking about the night she met him, the night they made this baby, and how much she had wished he'd still been there the next morning. How maybe everything would be different if he'd hung around. This awful, almost painful longing swelled in her chest.

And, damn it, she had to pee! So instead of lying there quietly savoring the experience of being snuggled by this man, or at least trying to deal with all these complicated feelings he brought to life in her, what she did was wriggle out from under his arm and rush to the bathroom. And by the time she came out he was awake, and his eyes on her embarrassed her, so she collected clothes and went back in the bathroom to shower—aka to hide out.

The rest of the day so far, nothing had felt quite right. She both wanted and didn't want him to fuss. All this emotional tumult annoyed her, it was so unlike her prepregnancy self.

Hormones. And the aftereffects of last night's scare.

I'm fine. Lying in bed so that she faced the side Will

had slept on last night, she stroked her stomach and turned inward. *You're fine. Oh, baby, I was so afraid.*

If Will hadn't been here...

She'd have managed. As it turned out, she could have driven herself. Or called Gray, or 911. Or even Joan Phillips next door. She didn't *need* Will.

Eyes wide, she stared unseeing at the wall. Tonight he'd return to her guest room across the hall, and she wished that wasn't so. If they were really married... But she didn't know whether they were or not.

He said he was committed, he said she was more important than his project in Africa, but...he'd also said that when the baby was a few months old, they'd talk.

And *that's* why panic swirled among all her other emotions, because it would be much, much worse to let herself believe he was really hers if he was only here on loan, so to speak.

She didn't know if she could bear it if that's all this was, all he was offering.

Oh, God, Moira thought, *I'm falling in love with Will.*

She was all but hyperventilating.

I'm already in *love with him.*

And he was so totally not in love with her, or he wouldn't have screwed her then slipped away into the night the way he did, not bothering to get in touch until he found out she was pregnant with his baby.

He was a good man doing the right thing, and how could she let him know she was starting to feel things that would tie him to her even more tightly? Her love would probably feel like ropes of guilt on top of his sense of responsibility. He probably thought they were becoming friends; wasn't that what always happened to her? And friends didn't want to wake up every morning for the rest of their lives with each other.

Instead of agonizing in silence she could ask if he saw himself going back to Africa in a couple of months. She lay staring at the ceiling knowing she didn't dare. What if he said yes? Think how miserable she'd be having to depend on him then, once he'd confirmed her fear that her need was all that held him here!

But if he didn't—if he said of course not…would she believe him?

Moira closed her eyes. No. No, she wouldn't.

WILL COULDN'T FIGURE OUT what was going on with Moira, but he was damned if he was going to give her the space she clearly wanted. What had she thought? He'd go snowboarding up at Stevens Pass and leave her alone for the day after she'd spent two hours in the emergency room the night before?

He kept getting this cold feeling. He had been wildly attracted to her from the minute he set eyes on her, but maybe for Moira he really had been nothing but a substitute. A bird in the hand, and she was tipsy enough not to be too particular, but now to her horror she was stuck with him.

God. What would he do if that's how she felt?

His throat almost closed up. Let her go. What else?

In a fit of frustration and something that might have been anger but was probably wounded feelings, he threw the paperback book across the living room, then winced when it thudded against the wall. Way to go. Throw a tantrum. What if she came out to see what the noise was?

Will made himself pick up the damn book and toss it on the coffee table. Then he went out on the front porch, needing the bite of fresh air. The neighborhood was quiet at this time of day, with most people at work and kids in school.

Half the houses or more already had Christmas lights up. Maybe he'd finally put up Moira's tomorrow, if he could get her to agree to stay put at Van Dusen & Cullen. She'd like to see the lights up. That might make her smile.

Shit. What did it mean that he was still thinking of them as *Moira's* lights?

A sound escaped his throat, one he couldn't even identify. Despair, disgruntlement, who knew? For only a moment, Will had a longing vision of the highveld in Zimbabwe, vivid green fields of tea leaves, a kraal of round, thatch-roofed huts housing the workers, tumbled slabs of granite topping a ridge. Some uniquely African baobab trees that would look so alien if they were transported here. His nostrils flared, trying to catch smells nothing like the sharp, cold air of winter here in the Northwest, air that carried a whiff of wood smoke. And that probably illegal, with the frequent burn bans aimed at reducing smog.

Then he remembered the way Moira had looked at him last night as if he was her everything, as if she did need him, and the angry tension left him. Just like that.

What an idiot he was. He was expecting too much, too soon. He had his own mixed feelings, of course she did, too. There must be times he felt like an intruder to a woman who had indeed taken care of herself just fine for…years. Had she ever lived with anyone else after she'd left home at eighteen?

Yeah, she was probably wrestling with the adjustment, the same as he was. He'd been careful not to let her see any of his regrets, and he needed to keep it that way.

Will shivered. It hadn't gotten above freezing today.

Ice still glittered on the lawn. And he was standing out here in his stocking feet and shirtsleeves.

Feeling like an idiot, he went inside.

Yeah, Christmas lights along the eaves tomorrow. That would be good. Right now, he'd think about dinner. One thing Moira hadn't objected to was his cooking. Evidently, she wasn't real fond of cooking. So that was something he could do for her.

But give her space? No, Will decided. With her so wary, it was up to him, if he really wanted this marriage to amount to anything. And maybe he was still a little stunned over the right turn his life had taken, maybe he still wrestled with some doubts and some regrets, but he also knew he'd never walk away from Moira and his baby, not of his own volition.

A big empty pit opened in his stomach when he thought of having to walk away because she sent him, because she didn't want him.

She was a complicated woman with secrets he hadn't yet plumbed, but he had to believe she could come to trust him and maybe even love him.

They were married. Last night, they'd shared a bed. And as far as he was concerned, continuing to share a bed was a step in the right direction. Actions were what counted, not words.

HE WAS A BULLDOZER. A steamroller. Moira already knew that, but wasn't thinking it when, at nine o'clock, she said good-night.

Will stood. "I think I'll go to bed, too."

Feeling him practically breathing down her neck as they went down the hall, she was glad to turn into her room.

"Leave your door open," he said.

She hesitated. Was that an order? A request? But truth was, the closed door was more symbolic than anything, and maybe she would feel better knowing he'd hear her if she called out. So she nodded. "All right."

She plucked her nightgown from under the pillow and went to her bathroom. She'd corralled her hair in a loose braid that morning, and now she decided to leave it. Who cared what it looked like? She dutifully flossed and brushed her teeth, dropped her dirty clothes in the hamper, and, after taking one alarmed look at her naked self in the tall mirror on the back of the door, hurriedly put on the gown.

I'm pregnant. Not fat.

She had to tell herself that ten times a day. She'd once been fat, and she wasn't going to be again. She tried really hard not to think about the way her weight had climbed. Even more with Will cooking. According to the doctor, she was doing fine, so she shouldn't recoil every time she caught a glimpse of herself.

But…wow. She *looked* fat.

Feeling more hippopotamuslike than ever, she got herself settled in bed and was reaching for the lamp switch when Will strolled into her bedroom as if she was supposed to be expecting him. Last night, she'd been too shaken up to notice how sexy he was wearing nothing but a pair of flannel pajama pants hanging low on his hips. Those shoulders were so broad and powerful. Dark hair dusted a wonderfully muscular chest and narrowed into a line that disappeared beneath the waistband of the pajama bottoms. Despite herself, her gaze lowered, taking in the whole length of him. It didn't help that she *knew* what was below that waistband.

"What are you doing here?" Her voice squeaked.

He stopped at the foot of the bed. "I'll sleep better here with you."

She felt silly, sitting up and clutching the covers to her like some Victorian maiden afraid of being defiled. Even so, she heard herself say, "Well, maybe I won't."

"Moira, we're married."

"You agreed we wouldn't—"

"I'm not trying to seduce you. I only want to sleep with you. You scared me last night. I like being here where I can touch you. Hear you breathing." He paused. "Didn't you find it a little bit comforting to have my arms around you last night?"

Oh, God. Yes. *Yes.*

Moira opened her mouth and nothing came out. She closed it, opened it again. Every instinct screamed, *Don't let him this close or you won't be able to save yourself,* but the truth was, she wanted him here. The idea of his hand spread protectively over her belly made her feel warm and weak enough in the knees it was lucky she wasn't standing up.

"Okay," she finally said, in a small gruff voice, and lay down.

Will didn't smile or say anything. He simply climbed into bed. He didn't reach for her the way she half expected.

Hoped.

Moira turned out the light. She lay completely still, excruciatingly conscious of Will beside her.

After a minute, she whispered, "I'm sorry."

The pause was so long, she wasn't sure he was going to respond. "For what?" he asked.

"I've been awful today. I know I have. I just, uh…" She just what? Was scared to death, not of losing the baby but of losing Will?

As if he had known right where her hand was, his closed over it. "It's okay," he said, his voice low, rough. "Believe it or not, I understood. Sometimes I should back off, but…"

A bubble of laughter rose, warming her chest and catching her by surprise. "You're a bulldozer. I've noticed."

"Sometimes ground needs clearing." Now there was a smile in his voice.

"Sometimes it does," she admitted, and realized she was smiling even though he wouldn't be able to see.

"I like being here with you."

"I, uh, kind of like it with you here, too," Moira said shyly. "I'm…not used to it."

"I'm not, either." He squeezed her hand. "We can get used to it together."

"Okay," she whispered.

"Would you mind if I cuddle you?"

She shook her head, realized he couldn't see her. "No-o. Except I do get up several times a night, you know."

"I know." She heard his amusement. "Even with the door shut, I can hear water running in the pipes after you flush the toilet."

"Great," she muttered.

He laughed, let her hand go, then gathered her firmly into his arms. She found her head right where it had been when she woke up this morning, and had the fleeting wish that she wasn't wearing a nightgown. She would have liked to feel his skin against hers. But despite the strangeness of being held like this, it felt so good that a soft, whispery sound of pleasure escaped her lips.

Will's chest vibrated with a silent chuckle. His hand on her distended belly moved in a soothing, circular pattern.

Moira was smiling as her eyes drifted closed.

CHAPTER ELEVEN

Four days before Christmas, Moira had scheduled a site inspection. The client was mad because he'd carried a tape measure on a walk-through of his framed-in house and found that the downstairs powder room was six inches narrower than the plans showed. If he was right, she wasn't going to be happy, either. What she specified was what got built. Now, by God, she and the contractor were going to measure every room, wall and door opening.

Well, probably Will would find a place to tenderly deposit her while *he* and the contractor measured. He was a bully that way.

He'd left her alone for the morning, but came into the office at noon, several white bags dangling from one hand, a plastic grocery sack from the other. In jeans, heavy sweater and down vest, he looked even bigger and more imposing than usual. He brought in a rush of cold and the scent of winter. White flakes dusted his dark hair.

"It's snowing?" she said in surprise, turning to look out the window.

"Yep. Just a skiff, nothing to worry about." He smiled and set the bags on her desk. "Lunch, as promised."

"I suppose it's wholesome," Moira said gloomily.

She liked salads, mostly. Or the veggie wraps from The Pea Patch. Just, once in a while… Her nostrils flared and she snatched at the first sack. "Do I smell…?"

"I thought you deserved a treat." He sat on the same

corner of her desk Gray had made his own. "Burgers and fries."

Moira moaned and took out a small carton of French fries.

Will laughed, but something flared in his eyes as she popped the first deliciously salty fry into her mouth.

"Damn, woman," he muttered.

She swallowed and reached for more. "Better eat, or there won't be any left."

He shook his head, still laughing. "Want a drink?"

"Please, please tell me it has caffeine in it," she begged.

"Apple juice or milk."

"Well, damn." She waffled briefly. "I guess I'll forgive you. Given how very, very grateful I am for the cheeseburger. It does have cheese on it?"

"Would I leave it off? You've got to get your calcium."

This was absolutely the best lunch she'd had in weeks. The worst for her, but he was right: she did deserve a treat, and she wouldn't feel guilty.

"Milk," she decided. "Unless you'd prefer…?"

"Juice is fine by me." He unscrewed the lid from the bottle and took a long swallow. "I got something else you'll like, too."

Moira paused with a burger halfway to her mouth. "A present?"

"Not exactly, but it's Christmassy." He shook his head before she could say a word. "Patience, patience. You have to wait to see."

He entertained her while they ate by telling her about all the children he'd seen that morning, from what he swore was a brawl being conducted on an elementary-school bus he'd followed for blocks—the driver oblivious in front—to a baby that screamed nonstop the entire time Will was in the grocery store.

"Man, it was like a fire engine," he reminisced. "Undulating. When that kid hit the high notes, the glass on the freezer cases shivered."

"It did not."

"Cross my heart." He did just that. "The glass wasn't all that shivered. I did, too. What are we in for, Moira?"

"Sleepless nights?" She wadded up her lunch wrappings and dropped them in the trash can, then heaved herself out of her desk chair. "I suppose we'd better go."

Gray arrived and stood there smirking as Will bundled Moira into her parka and checked to be sure she had gloves and a knit hat.

"My mommy used to do that for me." He paused. "When I was four."

Moira made a rude face. "Will's being a gentleman."

Her partner's chuckle followed her and Will out.

A very few flakes of snow still floated lazily down from a sky that was pearly gray. Maybe they'd have a white Christmas. The moment she saw Will's pickup, she smiled with delight. He'd affixed a big evergreen wreath decorated with holly leaves and berries as well as a fat red bow onto the hood so that it hung above the license plate. It was an unexpectedly frivolous note on his utilitarian, slush- and mud-splattered, black vehicle.

"It is Christmassy. Thank you."

"I deserve a kiss, don't you think?" her husband suggested.

Wow. As always when she thought of him that way, Moira felt a punch of surprise. *Her husband.*

When he bent down, she brushed her lips over his. His tongue took a lazy swipe inside her lips before he lifted his head. "Milk," he murmured.

Tingling from the pleasure of a too brief kiss, she ran her own tongue where his had sampled. "Apple juice."

Will opened the passenger door for her and boosted her in. "We live wild."

"Right." Moira groaned.

On the verge of shutting the door, he yanked it back open. "What? *What?*"

"I just remembered we have the childbirth class tonight."

"God." Will pressed a gloved hand to his chest. "Don't scare me that way."

"Wimp."

He snorted and slammed her door. Once he'd gotten in behind the wheel, he said, "So, where are we going?"

The development was on the west side of the freeway, just north of Lake Ki. She told him, saw him nod and make mental calculations, then put on the turn signal. She'd been impressed by how quickly he'd learned how to get around the north county, as if he'd drawn a mental map in his head. Moira got lost easily. She had to go someplace two or three times before she could reliably find it again without her GPS.

"Expect problems?" he asked.

She told him about the call from the homeowner and he grunted.

"Well, that sounds like fun."

"Yes, and it will get us all into the holiday spirit."

Their holiday spirits did lift when they arrived at the house-in-progress to find that Christmas lights were strung along the eaves and were plugged in. The lights, twinkling against unfinished wood, seemed to represent hope.

"Oh." Moira smiled, feeling suddenly more forgiving even if Ralph Jakes, the contractor, wasn't responsible.

Will parked behind three pickups, then came around to help her out. The raw, uneven ground was frozen solid and she had to pick her way. Moira had never been more grateful for Will's strong supporting arm.

She could hear the whine of a circular saw, the rhythmic punch of a nail gun at work, male laughter. The front door, still lacking knob and dead bolt, stood open.

"Hello," she called as soon as they were inside, and the saw paused.

Ralph appeared at the top of the roughed-in staircase. "Moira." He nodded resignedly. "I hear we screwed up."

"So Chuck says."

"Hell, we're already tearing it out."

She relaxed. She'd worked with Ralph before, and had believed him to be solid. "You checked other dimensions?"

"Yeah, but I'll bet you're going to do it again."

She grinned at him. "Yep. Will and I will. Have you met my husband, Will Becker?"

She *had* gotten almost used to introducing him that way. In fact, instead of uneasiness she'd begun to feel a small surge of proprietary pleasure in claiming him.

Unease tiptoed down her spine. What if by spring he was gone, and she had to tell all these same people that she was getting divorced?

She wouldn't think about that. Not now.

A flicker of interest showed in Ralph's eyes at the introduction. "Becker Construction?"

"My brother Clay is currently heading it."

"You're the one went off to…was it China? Something like that?"

"Africa." Will's voice was neutral. "That was me. I'm back." His hand moved in a seemingly unconscious yet reassuring way on the small of Moira's back, under the parka.

The contractor's attention switched to her. "Hell, Moira, you look like you're going to pop any minute. You sure you should be out here?"

She sighed. "My design, my job, Ralph. Though Gray will be stepping in for a few weeks."

He left them alone. She heard him yelling at someone upstairs.

Moira unrolled plans on a sheet of plywood atop two sawhorses that was being used as an impromptu table. Then she held one length of the metal measuring tape and let Will do most of the work. He referred frequently to the plans. It took them an hour to be confident the powder room was the only foul-up. She was pleased with how the house was going up otherwise. On a cold, clear day like this she could appreciate the way the sweep of windows took advantage of a view of the lake, the privacy gained by her having angled the house slightly to tuck it behind a mature stand of fir and cedar. She still thought the kitchen would have worked better without quite so much floor space, but the client had insisted.

Ralph walked them out so that he could discuss a couple of minor problems, one of which was going to necessitate her tweaking plans. With electrical in, he reminded her, an inspector would be out after the new year.

"We're winding up tomorrow," Ralph told her, "then taking the week between Christmas and New Year's off."

"Makes sense," she agreed. "You can't get wallboard up until we clear the inspection."

As she and Will started the drive back, he said, "Something I've been wondering."

Still thinking about the tweak she'd be making, she made an absentminded, questioning noise.

"Your house. Looks like it's, what, 1940s?"

She started paying attention. "Uh-huh. Postwar."

"You're an architect. Why buy an older place? Why haven't you designed your own?"

She asked herself that once in a while. The stock answer was easy enough, though. "When I first came to West Fork, I was focused on the building that houses our office."

Will glanced at her with interest. "You designed that?"

"Yes. We own it. Gray and I."

"So you're landlords."

Moira smiled. "We have trouble-free tenants. No one has trashed an office yet." She shrugged. "As for my house…I thought about renting for a while, then building like Gray was doing, but I didn't like the idea of having to move twice in a short time. So I went ahead and bought. I guess…" The snow had quit falling and barely dusted the pasture beside the road. A promise, like the Christmas lights on an unfinished house. She concluded, "I wasn't ready."

"Because you didn't have a family to share it with?"

"Maybe," she admitted.

"But Gray did build his own place right away, and he wasn't married, either."

Will and she had been to Gray and Charlotte's for dinner a couple of times already, and she'd been able to tell how much he admired the house.

"He's different. I've told you what Gray's like. He had a plan."

"A plan?"

"Choose town. Check. Establish firm. Check. Build

house. Check. Get married. Took him a *lo-ong* time to put a check there. I think he was a little disconcerted that his perfect woman didn't appear on schedule. Everything was supposed to fall into place." She found herself smiling as she remembered. "And when she did appear, Charlotte wasn't so sure she *wanted* to cooperate. Gray isn't used to being thwarted."

"But he got his way in the end." Will sounded reflective. It occurred to Moira, not for the first time, that the two men had quite a bit in common. In their own, equally agreeable ways, they were both bulldozers. Steamrollers.

"Gray usually does," she said simply.

Will drove with effortless competence. She suspected he was being particularly careful for her sake not to take corners sharply or stop too abruptly. She noticed that he never got in that first thing he didn't glance at how she'd positioned the two straps of the seat belt around the increasingly gigantic swell of her belly. It was probably a surprise that he didn't minutely adjust the belt before he was willing to start out.

From her peripheral vision she caught Will's quick glance. His tone, though, betrayed nothing but mild curiosity. "So he had a plan, and you didn't."

"Didn't I say Gray always has a plan?"

Will's hands flexed lightly on the wheel. "Because he's an optimist."

She frowned a little. "I suppose that's it."

"And you? You're a pessimist?"

Disconcerted, she took a moment before she answered. "Not in some ways."

"But your personal life. Hard not to tell that you have trouble expecting the best for yourself."

Maybe that's because she'd never gotten it.

The whisper came from deep inside. It wasn't so much bitter as sad. And it shocked her.

She hadn't had a terrible life. She'd had a happy childhood. She loved her mother. They'd stayed close, even when other kids her age were all rebelling against their mothers. And Gray. She'd been so lucky to find him. His friendship had changed her life.

Still stunned, staring blindly ahead, Moira thought, *Yes, but...*

There had always, in her mind, been a *but*. Maybe rooted in the fact that her father hadn't wanted her, maybe not. Deepened by those painful years when she'd been overweight and therefore self-conscious, when she hadn't been so much teased as friendless. Then later, even after she'd lost the weight, she hadn't really known how to flirt, and the boys she'd grown up with had gotten used to seeing her in a certain way so she didn't date. She didn't get invited to her senior prom.

She had felt such hope when she went off to college. It would be her new start. And it had been, in some ways. There was Gray, and she did date, and eventually she'd had a serious boyfriend for most of a school year.

But—yet another *but*—even that romance had fizzled, and though she'd dated off and on in the years since, the relationships never passed casual. Men didn't fall in love with her. They didn't want her passionately. And knowing that hurt.

For the very first time, Moira wondered if it was possible that *she* hadn't seen herself as lovable, as desirable. Whether other people might have if she had. Was she inadequate, or did she just think she was?

The very idea shook her. She didn't know which was worse: to *be* undesirable, or to have wasted years of her life because she was so screwed up.

God. I'm pathetic.

Self-pity was not an attractive quality.

She suddenly became aware that Will had parked in front of Van Dusen & Cullen, Architects, and had even turned off the engine. He'd half turned in his seat, his forearm laid across the top of the steering wheel, and was watching her sit frozen with her unwelcome self-revelation.

"Wow," she said, trying for a laugh that was such a failure it was—oh, God—pathetic. "You set me off. And not in a good way. You're right. I'm doom and gloom, and I didn't even realize it."

"Not doom and gloom." He had a way, even with that deep, sometimes rumbly voice, of sounding so gentle her defenses crumbled. "That's not you at all, Moira. But I feel a sadness in you sometimes that I don't understand."

"I don't understand it, either," she whispered. "I didn't know."

He reached out and squeezed the back of her neck with a big, warm hand. His fingers had become practiced at easing muscle tension even in a brief caress. This one wasn't brief; he worked her neck until she bowed her head, closed her eyes and let go of her bout of bewilderment and unhappiness.

Eventually she managed to clear her throat and lift her head. She met his steady, dark gaze with the flicker of a genuine smile. "Man, you should change professions. A Will Becker massage fixes all problems."

He laughed for her sake. She knew it was for her, because his eyes remained dark and worried.

"I'm just trying to understand you," he told her.

I'm trying to understand me, too.

And why, she had to ask herself, *is this suddenly all about me?*

Wasn't *Will* the one who'd given up everything for his sister and brothers, then had to do so again for her? Did she understand *him?*

Had she tried?

"I know," she said, a little shakily. "I do know. I'm… really lucky to have you." She managed a smile. "And now I'd better get back to work."

"Okay." His knuckles brushed her cheek, then he released her seat belt and his. He issued his standard order, "Wait for me," and got out to help her down.

She was so lucky.

And hated the whisper, the pathetic whisper, that said, *Yeah, you're lucky right now, but how long will all this last, given that he only married you because he thought he had to?*

CHRISTMAS WAS…NICE. Will and Moira didn't do anything that special on Christmas Eve, their gifts to each other weren't extravagant, but they were right. He could tell she really did love the soapstone bowl and the wooden carving he'd brought her from Africa, and she'd bought him an unbelievably soft alpaca scarf the exact color of his eyes—she said—as well as a couple of books that he had trouble tearing himself away from once he flipped open the covers. Her choices told him she listened to him and paid attention to what he said and maybe even to some of his silences.

One of those books was about a project not so different from the one he'd taken on in Zimbabwe, this one in South Africa. He could hardly wait to read it, but even a glance inside at the photos gave him a pang. He tried to hide that, though, when he looked up to find Moira watching him.

"Looks interesting," he said, more casually than he felt, and set it aside.

He'd built a fire in the fireplace, and he and Moira snuggled on the sofa sipping hot chocolate and gazing dreamily at the lights on the Christmas tree they had put up two weeks before. The sharp scent of fir needles reminded him of Christmases past, of times before he'd lost his parents, of trembling in bed waiting for the first light of dawn before he could wake Mom and Dad to open presents. Of his first bike, of the year he'd itched like crazy from chicken pox and was mad as blazes because he'd gotten it over the holiday and wouldn't even have the benefit of missing school. His first car, a used clunker, had been a Christmas gift, too, the year he was sixteen. He thought about the effort he'd put into making sure Sophie, Jack and Clay had memories as good as his of the holidays.

He found himself talking about them, about how glad he'd been the first year that Sophie, then seven, had become disillusioned about Santa Claus.

"It was sort of sad," he said, "as if that one year all her illusions got shattered, but, man, it would have been hard to keep that one propped up if she'd been young enough to beg Santa to bring her mommy back." He fell silent, remembering that particular Christmas when they had all ached with loss and any celebration was more pretence than reality. Even then, though, it had never occurred to him to say, "Let's skip it this year."

Moira, tucked under his arm, was for once utterly relaxed. "I forget sometimes that you're an experienced dad."

He gave a short laugh. "Not with babies or diapers. When Clay was born, I was still pissed that my father remarried and had another kid to threaten my place. By the time Jack came along, I was too tough a guy to be talked into helping with any baby. And I was a teenager when Soph was born. I sure as hell didn't want anything to do with her bare bottom."

"And then you ended up daddy to all of them."

He grunted an agreement. "Fate does throw you a curve ball sometimes, doesn't it?"

"You must still get nightmares about that first year or so," she said quietly.

"You're back to me admitting I felt trapped," he realized. "I can't lie. I did at first, and I guess I never threw that belief away. I tucked it in my wallet like...damn, a Dear John letter. I could pull it out now and again even as the folds on it frayed and the ink became unreadable. And yeah, I still know what it said, but..." He shrugged, knowing she'd feel the motion. "Truth is, when I think back most of my memories are good ones. I didn't know how good until I went away and found out how much I missed them. It shouldn't have been such a surprise, because when each of them left for college I had this big hole inside." He touched his chest with his free hand. "But I'm stubborn. I guess you've noticed that."

She gave him a quick, amused grin.

He laughed. "The thing is, I'm stubborn enough not to always admit I was wrong even when I should. Or even to realize that I was. I saw myself as having to give up everything I'd ever wanted to fill in for my dad. I was mad at him for dying. But now I think...sure, I lost a lot of choices I might have made, but somehow the four of us cobbled together quite a family. And my life has been pretty damn rich to this point. I still don't know what I wanted to grow up and be. Who's to say it would have been any better than what I had?"

Moira was silent for a long time. "Do you mean that?"

Will could admit to himself that he'd started with the intention of reassuring her that taking on an unexpected family wasn't so bad the first time around, which meant he really didn't mind having his life derailed a second time by yet *another* unexpected family. The funny thing was, as he'd talked he had known he meant it. He was as proud of Sophie and his brothers as any father would have been. He *liked* all three of his siblings. When he looked back, he remembered doing a lot of laughing along with the quiet swearing when he was by himself.

Keeping the business in the black those first years had been the most hair-raising. He'd known the construction side, but not the business itself. He'd made a lot of mistakes, lost good employees, hired some lousy ones. But after a couple of shaky years, he had found his footing and made a success of Becker Construction, too. He'd built it into a bigger company than his father had left him, one with a solid gold reputation. He was proud of that, too. Proud he'd saved a legacy from Dad for Clay and Jack.

"I do mean it," he told Moira. "I'm a different man than I would have been if my dad and stepmom hadn't died when they did, but it's possible I'm a better one."

In a strange, gruff little voice, she said, "I think you're a very good man, Will Becker. I just wish I didn't think you're such a good man, you'd lie to me to keep me from believing I've taken advantage of you."

He had a fleeting and uncomfortable instance of wondering if he might be lying even to himself. He didn't think so, even though it was a little unsettling to realize he had been looking at his own life upside down all along. No matter what, it didn't seem like words were going to convince her that she could count on him. She wouldn't believe him if he said, "I love you." Time, he thought, might be his only hope.

What he did was lay a hand on her stomach and rub. "This is *our* baby, Moira. This time, I really will be Daddy. I wouldn't want to be anywhere but here."

And that *was* the truth, whether she wanted to believe it or not.

She took a sip of her now cooling cocoa and didn't say anything else. But her belly surged under Will's hand and a knob poked his palm.

"Amazing," he murmured.

"It is, isn't it?" Moira whispered.

He turned his face to nibble her earlobe. "Merry Christmas, Mama of my baby."

He felt more than saw her smile. "Merry Christmas, Daddy," she said softly.

THEY MADE TWO MORE CHILDBIRTH classes, one the week before New Year's, one the week after. Two more visits to her obstetrician, too. Her due date was the fifteenth, but at the last visit, Dr. Engel said, "You're *sure* about when you conceived this baby?"

Will and Moira exchanged a glance. Newly self-conscious, Moira nodded. "Very sure."

"I doubt you'll last another week." She smiled at them. "Daytime labor would be nice."

Apparently that was a joke. They both laughed dutifully.

Once the doctor had whisked out the door, Will helped Moira sit up. It wasn't easy. Chuckling, Will said, "Now you're a pregnant pygmy goat."

All she muttered was, "God."

On the way home, she made a few observations about how unlikely it was that this gigantic, linebacker kid of theirs would be able to exit her body in any approved manner. Under her breath, she said, "It's the *Invasion of the Body Snatchers*. No one else in the Lamaze class looks anything like me."

"Most of them aren't as close to due."

"Mindy is. Did you *see* her?" The tiny blonde was the hateful kind of woman who'd have her prepregnancy figure back two weeks after she delivered.

"Her baby'll probably be five pounds and have to spend two weeks in an incubator."

"While ours will come out crawling. At *least* rolling over. He sure does plenty of that now. Especially when I'm trying to sleep."

Will thought that was funny. He wasn't the one who was barely sleeping in brief snatches.

Moira sighed. "I am so ready." She brooded on that for a moment. "What if he's *late?* If I have *weeks* left?"

"You won't." Will patted her hand. "I promise."

Like he had any more idea than she did.

He parked in the driveway at home and turned to look at her. Abruptly, he said, "I don't want you going back to work."

She'd managed half days this week because four hours was as long as she could bear either to sit in her desk chair or perch on the stool at her drafting table. Gray and Will had, together, nixed any more site inspections for her, and she hadn't argued.

"Gray's got another—" she had to calculate "—week in office."

"He can call in absent to city hall," Will said in a hard voice. "Or you guys can hang up a closed sign for a week. This has to be a deadly slow time of year anyway."

"Not so much. A lot of people are planning for

spring." Moira hesitated. "I guess I'm pretty much done, though."

Will looked closely at her, but didn't gloat at her capitulation. He only nodded and got out to come around and help her. Once they were inside, he said, "Nap?"

"I might as well lie down." Her back was killing her.

"I'll give you a massage."

"I'd love that," she admitted.

He followed her into the bedroom and sat on the bed once she'd settled herself on her side, facing away from him. Then he lifted her shirt and went to work, those big strong hands unerringly finding every ache and kneading as if she were stiff bread dough. Pure bliss.

Eventually his touch became more gentle. He was soothing her to sleep, and it worked.

The backache returned more fiercely that night. By the following day an occasional contraction rippled across her stomach, turning it rigid beneath her touch. Moira didn't tell Will. He'd fuss worse than he already was.

One week exactly before her due date, Moira couldn't sleep at all. The contractions become more painful, more frequent. Will had sprawled onto his back beside her. If he'd had his arm around her, his hand settled in its usual place, he would have felt the waves of tension seizing her. But she waited and let him sleep, her gaze on the clock.

Finally, she groaned and had to pant when the sharpest one yet gripped her in bands of steel.

"Huh? What?" Will rolled toward her.

She could only keep panting.

"Oh, God," he said. "That's it, sweetheart. One, two, three, four. You can do this."

He got her dressed, got her to the hospital. He had to go park and she could tell he'd been running when he rejoined her. Moira fumbled for his hand and held on tight.

She needed him. She did. His voice, his touch, his eyes, became the center of her world.

Eight hours and forty-five minutes later, Caleb Graham Becker was born.

CHAPTER TWELVE

IT WAS ALL WILL COULD DO to tear himself away from Moira's side. The sight of his wife nursing his son was so stunning, he had a giant lump in his throat and wasn't sure he could have said a word. Caleb hadn't taken much urging to latch onto his mommy's breast. He was so small, so precious. And for all that Moira looked exhausted, her hair sweat-dampened and matted, she was also lit up from inside with a glow that made her beautiful. Will hadn't known he could feel so much.

But she finally said, "You'll call Mom?" and he reluctantly nodded.

"Yeah. Sure." He started toward the door. "I'll be right back."

For a moment he wasn't sure she'd even noticed he was leaving. He felt a sharp slice of pain. For all that he'd held Caleb first, had been the one to lay their baby in Moira's arms, Will had this momentary fear that she had what she needed now, and it wasn't him, that he was on the outside looking in.

Then she looked up and gave him a smile that started soft and grew radiant. "Oh, Will," she murmured, and he found himself grinning idiotically at her. How foolish to get his feelings hurt for nothing.

"I'll hurry," he repeated, and left.

He went downstairs and stepped outside, startled to realize it was daytime. A part of him felt it should still be the middle of the night. He glanced at his watch. 11:20 a.m. Almost lunchtime. He had the same sense of disorientation he did after an international flight. The last hours had seemed entirely apart from the normal flow of time.

Shaking his head, he stepped aside from the double doors as a family pushed an old woman in a wheelchair in. He took out his cell phone and called Moira's mom first.

"You have a grandson," he told her, smiling as she exclaimed and wept and begged for details.

"Quite a bit of hair, I think you'd call it auburn. Not as bright as Moira's, but there's some red in it. I couldn't tell with his eyes, they were kind of muddy. Maybe they're going to turn brown. Uh…he's eight pounds, nine ounces. Thank God he was a week early," he said fervently.

Her mother laughed. "Has he said his first word yet?"

Discovering his legs were a little shaky, Will leaned against the stucco wall and laughed, too. "No, and I don't think he's quite ready to crawl, either. Now, if he'd had another week…"

"Think what a grump his mother would have been by then."

He was still laughing when he called Becker Construction and told Clay the news. Clay didn't weep, but he sounded staggered.

"Man. Are you going to call Sophie?"

"Yeah. You'll tell Jack?"

"Hell, yes! Can we come up and see the kid in a couple of days?"

"Any time after we're home and Moira's rested."

He then called his sister, who predictably enough did cry. She also, if he was hearing right, was jumping up and down while screaming, "So cool!" But then she went quiet, and finally said softly, "And you named him after Dad. That was, um…"

Will had to clear his throat. "I'm glad Moira liked the name."

"Oh, Will."

She, too, promised a visit, although thought she'd probably wait a couple of weeks.

Then Will made one more call, to Gray. "Moira and I have a son," he said.

"A son. Well. Damn." The pause made Will wonder if Moira's best friend wasn't fighting some tears of his own. "Have you named him yet?"

"Caleb." Will smiled even though he was only looking at the parking lot. "Caleb Graham."

"For me." He made a choking sound. "Damn."

"We should be home by tonight if you'd like to run over."

"You're okay with that?"

"Why wouldn't I be? You know Moira will want to see you."

"Yeah. Damn." Gray's vocabulary seemed to have deserted him. Will hoped he didn't have any important meetings scheduled in the next few hours.

Him, all he wanted to do was get upstairs.

Once there, he found that Caleb had been taken away for further assessment and to give Moira a chance to rest. She was sound asleep. Knowing she'd expect it, he backtracked briefly to the nursery and stared through the glass at his son, bundled like a burrito in a thin, pale green blanket, his spiky dark red hair covered by a tiny blue knit cap. As Will watched, Caleb's mouth moved and his face momentarily scrunched up in a frown, then smoothed out as he relaxed into sleep. Will stood there for ten minutes or more, unable to tear his eyes from this small person he'd barely met and yet loved so much. Nature in all her mystery, he thought ruefully.

Realizing suddenly that he needed to be with Moira, he returned to her room. She lay on her back clutching the white cotton blankets to her neck, as if she'd been cold when she fell asleep. He pulled up a chair beside the bed and sat looking at her with much the same wonder he'd felt watching his newborn son. Between the books he'd read and the class, Will had thought he'd had a pretty good idea what childbirth involved, but he'd discovered that he hadn't known at all. Now, he was in awe of what Moira had endured. He flexed his hands—they still ached from the strength of her grip as she struggled to ride the ebb and flow of contractions too powerful to be mastered.

Her eyelids were near translucent and her copper lashes lay against purplish bruising beneath her eyes. He doubted she'd had a good night's sleep in weeks. But...they had their son. Will felt exultation so fierce, he couldn't remember why he'd even hesitated about changing his life so that he could be here with her and Caleb.

Her breasts rose and fell; her lips were softly parted. A great bubble of emotion swelled in him as he fought the hunger to touch her: to smooth back the damp strands of copper hair plastered to her high, curved forehead, or to caress her cheek. He could hardly wait until tonight, when he could hold her.

I love her, he thought, waiting for that painful, glorious pressure in his chest to ease, although he wondered if it ever would entirely. And if what he felt was really love, or only the by-product of what they'd gone through together. It was logical that nature would want to ensure that he stay to protect and raise his child. What he felt, maybe this was the male version of the hormones that had a pregnant woman at their mercy.

But he didn't think so. He was pretty sure he'd started falling in love with Moira Cullen one week shy of nine months ago, and had kept tumbling ever since.

And now that love was all tied up with what he'd felt the moment the nurse laid baby Caleb in his arms and he gazed into those unfocused, bewildered eyes and known that nothing would ever be the same.

This, he thought with bemusement, is what his father had felt when he was born. He wished like hell Dad could be here. Wanted to think Dad *was* here, in some sense.

Right this minute, it was almost impossible to imagine how Moira's father could have failed to feel this savage certainty that he would do anything for her, give anything at all to make her happy, to keep her safe. Did the son of a bitch ever give his daughter a passing thought? Would he give a damn if he knew how his absence had damaged her?

Maybe, Will thought, he was wrong in suspecting that half the turmoil he sensed in Moira had to do with a childhood devoid of a father. She wanted her own child to have one, but maybe on another level she didn't. Maybe she didn't believe in fathers at all, or at least not their staying power.

The hospital sounds outside this room hardly made an impression on him. Will only smiled an absent thanks when a nurse brought a freshly warmed blanket to cover Moira, who gave an unconscious sigh of pleasure when it settled over her. He just kept looking at her and wishing their marriage was different, that she felt any faith at all in him.

MOIRA WAS SITTING ON THE SOFA nursing Caleb when Will walked into the living room. Surreptitiously, she adjusted her blouse, knowing it was silly when he'd seen all of her at one time or another, but feeling shy anyway. His gaze flicked to Caleb, greedily suckling, lingering either on his son or the swell of her now overabundant breast, she wasn't sure which, before settling on her face.

"He's hungry again already?"

"I'm hoping to get him down for the night," she said.

"Greedy little bugger," Will said fondly, then sat in the easy chair facing her. He stretched his legs out, crossed them at the ankles and relaxed, but didn't pick up his book. Apparently he was simply going to watch her.

After a minute of pretending he wasn't, she said, "I should have driven Mom to the airport today."

"She understood why you didn't."

Her mother had come only for a few days instead of the couple weeks she'd offered when Moira thought she'd be on her own with a newborn. Mom and Will had gotten along splendidly, as far as Moira could tell; they'd taken turns cooking and cleaning the kitchen, and had had several long, quiet conversations Moira wished she'd overheard.

As dearly as she loved her mother, though, it was almost a relief to have her gone now. With Will still not working, they hadn't needed the help, which had made Mom really a guest who had to be entertained. Will had made an effort to leave them alone sometimes, but Moira was too confused about how she felt about him and their marriage to have any desire to confide even in her mother.

They'd decided last night that Will would take her to the airport, because it was up to a two-hour drive each way, depending on traffic. Too long for Moira to leave Caleb, since she was nursing, and Will had quietly said, "I'd rather we not take him, with it so cold out there and the roads icy."

Still, Moira felt a little bit guilty now. She frowned, thinking about it. No, that wasn't really what was bothering her. Mom *hadn't* minded. It was more complicated, she thought. Things had changed without her realizing how much it would affect her relationship with her mother. Some of it was little stuff. Already she and Will had developed a kind of verbal shorthand, an ability to read each other's minds, that sometimes had left Mom excluded; a couple of times Moira had caught a fleeting expression on her mother's face that in retrospect Moira realized was sadness. This visit was the first time Moira had ever kissed her mother good-night then gone off to bed with a man, and *that* was different. It just…had felt as if they'd lost some closeness that they'd both always taken for granted.

It was the first time she'd found herself speculating about her mother's choices, too. Moira didn't remember her dating very often, and never seriously. Had Mom not *wanted* to remarry? It had always been her and Moira against the world, although—to her credit—she hadn't tried to cling when the time came for Moira to leave for college.

Moira frowned, forgetting that Will was watching her. Was it an accident that her own life was ending up an echo of her mother's? Or would have, if not for Will's stubborn refusal to take no for an answer?

"What are you thinking?" he asked now.

It took her a second to recall what they'd been talking about. Her not accompanying Mom to the airport. That was it. "Just Mom. About today…I know she understood. It's not that."

When she hesitated, Will said, "You miss her?" His gaze was keen on her face. She wondered what he was thinking.

"I guess I mostly feel bad that we didn't need her more. You know?"

He nodded. "If it had been a busier time of year, I might have picked up some work for Clay while your mom was here to take care of you. To give you two time alone. But he's got crews idled as it is, so I didn't want to ask."

Moira looked at him in surprise. "Are you thinking about going to work for him?"

After a minute Will shrugged. "Maybe later. Not long-term, and not for now. First I want to do the bedroom."

The guest room was to become Caleb's, but they'd agreed to wait to redecorate until Moira's mother came and went. Although they had bought a crib, Caleb was currently sleeping in a bassinet beside their bed. Now that Mom was gone, though, Will was going to paint and put up a wallpaper border. Moira didn't sew very often, but she'd bought fabric to make a valance for the window, too. Will would be taking down the bed and storing it in the basement.

"You know," he said, "we might want to think about putting on an addition."

Moira had been switching Caleb from one breast to the other, something that was easier to do when she wasn't trying simultaneously to whisk the cup of the bra up with lightning speed to cover her breast even as she freed the other one. But that brought her head up. "An addition?"

"To the house?" He looked amused but also…wary, she thought. "Another bedroom or two maybe. Do you really want to be without a guest room?"

"Well, maybe not forever, but…"

"Your office is too tiny to make a decent bedroom. I might want my own office down the line, too. And then if we have more kids…"

They hadn't even decided whether they were going

to stay married, and he was talking about them having another baby? Something that might have been jubilation tangled with apprehension.

"Wow." She cleared her throat. "You're, um, thinking way ahead."

"Why not? I'm free right now, I could do most of the work." He shrugged again. "Think about it."

Moira made herself speak calmly. "I think I'd like to wait until we know better where we stand."

"What the hell does that mean?"

"We agreed we'd talk when Caleb was a little older." Her stomach squeezed into a ball at the thought, and she silently pleaded, *Argue. Tell me we don't have to, that you never plan to leave.*

But…he didn't. His eyes narrowed and she had the sense that he was mad, but he only said tightly, "If that's what you want."

No. No, it wasn't.

Caleb's mouth slipped off her breast. Moira eased him against her shoulder and patted his back until he gave a sleepy burp and nestled into her.

"I'm going to put him down," she murmured.

Will didn't move as she stood and went down the hall. Moira hesitated once she'd settled Caleb into his bassinet. The coward in her wanted to hide out in the bedroom and *not* return to the living room. Will was in a strange mood tonight. She couldn't imagine what had set him off, unless… Had *he* felt excluded while Mom was here?

Heavens. Maybe, Moira thought unhappily, she'd made both of them feel unappreciated.

And maybe that wasn't it at all. Maybe she was seeing Will's naturally pushy personality in action.

But when she entered the living room, he only said,

"Like some ice cream? I was thinking a bowl would be good."

She moaned. "You can't keep tempting me like this."

"Nursing takes a lot of calories."

"Yes, but look at me." Moira laid her hands on her still too-soft stomach. "I have so much to lose."

He pushed himself to his feet. "There's no hurry, you know."

"Easy for you to say," Moira muttered.

"So no ice cream?"

She sighed. "Mocha almond fudge?"

"Yep."

"Oh, God. Just a scoop. Okay?"

Will grinned and disappeared into the kitchen.

He brought two bowls back, hers containing one perfect round scoop, his mounded high. After a resentful glance at his bowl, she concentrated on eating her own ice cream in tiny increments, stretching it out, letting the richness melt on her tongue.

"Why do you worry so much about your weight?" Will asked after a time.

Moira looked up sharply. He sounded too casual.

"What did Mom tell you?"

He lifted those dark eyebrows. "About?"

Okay, maybe not.

After some internal debate, Moira said, "Even before prepregnancy, I wasn't exactly a sylph."

"No, you had a luscious, curvy body that made me want to—" He broke off, color slashing his cheekbones.

Moira's eyes widened.

"You know what I wanted to do," he muttered. "I did it."

"You mean, I begged you to do it."

Abruptly, Will frowned at her. "Begged? I don't re-member any begging."

"You were reluctant."

He snorted. "Yeah, that's why I insisted on walking you to your hotel-room door. Because I wasn't dying to take you inside and peel that dress off you."

"But you were such a gentleman. I thought—"

"Whatever you thought, it was obviously wrong. Any hesitation was only because of me planning to leave the country so soon." He hunched his shoulders. "And I suppose I didn't like the idea of being a stand-in for the creep."

"The creep." She made an awful face. "Do you know, if I'd slept with him, and used that condom..."

Will didn't say anything. His expression was so un-changing, she could tell the thought had already occurred to him. And if it had...he must have wondered how she would have felt about Bruce Girard being the father of her baby instead of Will Becker.

"For your sake, I wish it hadn't happened," she said, meeting his eyes. "But for mine, I'm really glad. Glad you're Caleb's father."

His face relaxed, and she hadn't even been aware how rigid it had been. Voice scratchy, he said, "Don't be sorry. You think after holding Caleb I can regret anything?"

"No." Moira felt inexplicably mushy inside. "That would be awful, not having him, wouldn't it?"

They were both quiet for a moment, and she could see that he was as incredulous as she was at the very idea: no Caleb.

"You've managed to evade my question," Will pointed out.

She pretended not to know what he was talking about, even though she did.

"Do you really not know how sexy you are?" he asked.

With a shrug, she said, "Men tend to see me as best-friend material. I always figured it was the freckles. They positively shout girl next door. You know?"

"I've never lived next door to anyone who looked like you."

With no idea why she was arguing, Moira still shot back, "I'm just saying…"

"I watched you at the gala." Will sounded thoughtful. "For quite a while. I told you that."

She nodded.

"You danced. Men kept coming on to you, and I didn't need to hear you to be able to tell you were saying, 'Thanks but no thanks.'"

"That's ridiculous. I don't remember anyone special."

Will looked at her.

Well, there was Stan Wells, when she'd first arrived at the gala, but then she'd decided she must have imagined the way he had reacted. So maybe…

"I used to be fat," she blurted.

"Were you," Will murmured. It wasn't a question. She had the awful sense that she'd answered all his questions instead.

He might as well know. "When I was a kid," she said. "I don't know why. I was okay until…oh, third grade or so. The fatter I got, the more I wanted to eat. I'd sneak food. Mom would bake cookies and think they'd last for a week, only I'd have eaten the whole batch in two days. That's why I never learned to swim, you know. I didn't want anyone to see me in a bathing suit. I ended up getting dropped by the girls I thought were friends. And boys are such jerks in fourth or fifth grade."

"I don't think they can help themselves."

"They should," she muttered. "I pretended I didn't care, but I did."

"When did you lose the weight?"

"Oh, it was gradual. Being fat in middle school was really horrible. I had crushes on boys, but I knew they'd never in a million years look twice at me." She shrugged. "They probably wouldn't have anyway, but..." Moira heard herself and cringed. "That's what I always think, you know. That no guy could be interested in me."

She hadn't known he could move so fast. One minute Will was lounging in the chair, the next he was on the sofa beside her, his hand grasping her chin.

"You're wrong. Guys can be. I am."

She gulped. "I think maybe my self-esteem issues are left from those days. After a while, you sort of...give up."

His thumb stroked her lower lip. His voice was a low rumble. "You shouldn't."

Wow. Moira gazed into his dark eyes and felt this swell of complicated emotions. "Thank you," she whispered.

He swore and took back his hand. "Damn it, there you go again."

"Again?"

"Why would you thank me for wanting you?"

"I was thanking you for being nice!"

After a moment he sighed. "Okay. I can accept that." He leaned back but kept watching her. "So, go on. How long did it take to *gradually* get slim?"

"I never got slim. It would have helped if I had. But... I'm not built to have skinny hips."

"A woman is supposed to *have* hips."

"Well, I do." She didn't know why he was being so insistent about this, but she was, after all, the one who'd decided to tell him why she maybe lacked confidence. "By the time I was a senior in high school, I'd mostly lost the pudge. Too late to be a social success."

"You mean, the idiots you'd gone to school with didn't notice what was in front of their eyes."

She smiled at him. "You're good for my ego."

His mouth quirked in return. "I'd like to be."

"I finally dated and then had a serious boyfriend in college. End of tale."

"Okay, next question. Why do you hate the freckles so much?"

"Because hardly anyone else has them."

He waited, something he was good at. Moira couldn't help squirming under Will's patient regard. "Maybe because they came from my father." It had taken her a while to figure that out. "He was the redhead."

"Ah."

"What does *that* mean?"

Will took her hand and laced his fingers through hers. "Just that now it makes sense. You don't want to owe anything to him, but ignoring heredity is hard when it's right there every time you look at yourself in the mirror."

Moira made a face at him. "Plus, kids teased me about my freckles, too."

"*I* got teased for being big."

"Really?"

"Oh, yeah." He sounded wry. "I was always the tallest, from kindergarten on up. And talk about middle school. I had all the grace of a Saint Bernard puppy. My feet were huge." He lifted one and they both looked at it. "I wore a size twelve by the time I was in seventh grade. I tripped over my own feet. I was too clumsy to be any good at sports until later. Way later. I was probably eighteen, nineteen, before everything really started working together."

Why was she so dumbfounded? Did she really think she was the only person in the world who'd grown up knowing she was different, that she didn't *fit?*

"I like your size," Moira told him. "You're strong and gentle both. You make me feel…safe. Which I guess is a silly thing to say, since I'm not in any danger, but it's true anyway."

"I like your freckles." He lifted her hand to his mouth and kissed it. "And your hair, and your curves. Skinny, stringy women don't do it for me."

"A match made in heaven." She tried to sound sarcastic.

He grinned. "I keep trying to tell you."

They sat in silence. Will didn't let go of her hand. Moira had butterflies in her stomach that reminded her of Caleb's tumbles in midpregnancy. Her skin tingled. She wanted…

Will released her hand and, before she could feel disappointed, cupped her face and turned it toward him. Then he bent his head and kissed her. His mouth moved softly over hers, not demanding anything, only…asking. Her lips parted, but his kept dancing over them, nibbling, licking, almost kneading them the way his big, strong hands did on her back, seeming to *know* her body better than she did. Moira quit breathing. Eyes closed, she only experienced, wonder filling her.

Finally, Will eased back and waited until she lifted heavy lids and looked at him. "Someday," he whispered, "I want to kiss you all over. Just like that."

She swallowed.

"But not yet. I don't have enough self-control to stop.

For now, we'll pretend we're shy thirteen-year-olds who know Mom or Dad is only a room away."

"Oh."

He stroked one fingertip from her chin down her throat. It was all she could do not to moan. In a low, husky voice, he said, "Okay?"

Moira bit her lip. "Okay."

"I think," he said, "it will be fun to flirt with you, Moira Cullen Becker."

Dizzy with unexpected pleasure, Moira tried for a saucy smile. "I might enjoy flirting with you, too, Mr. Becker."

"Good." He kissed her cheek, his breath warm, the small caress raising goose bumps on her nape. "And now, sweetheart, you'd better go to bed if you're going to get any sleep at all before our tyrant of a son starts screaming."

"Yes." She stood. "I take it you're going to stay up?"

"Yeah." His gaze was heated. "Cuddling you sounds a little too dangerous right now. I'll, uh, be along in a little bit."

Moira nodded, said, "Good night," and fled. Tonight, she loved knowing that he'd risen to his feet and was watching her go.

CHAPTER THIRTEEN

CLAY CALLED AND ASKED if Will was interested in working, if only temporarily, as foreman on a job in Everett.

"Doug Redmond quit on me today," he explained. "No notice. Not really his fault. His parents have been going downhill, and now his dad has had a minor stroke. Doug and his wife decided to move to Texas and take care of them."

Doug was a nice guy who'd worked for Becker Construction as long as Will could remember. He was unimaginative but steady and reliable.

"You'll have to replace him," Will said.

Clay grunted unhappily. "I'm thinking maybe Ward Stevens, but I don't want to pull him from that drugstore we're building in Lake Stevens."

Will opened his mouth to comment, then closed it. The decisions weren't his anymore.

Instead, he said, "I wouldn't mind being busy for a little while. Moira doesn't plan to go back to work for another six weeks or so. It doesn't really make sense for us both to sit around staring at Caleb."

His brother laughed. "Is that what you do?"

"Just wait," Will said good-naturedly. "Man, there's nothing like seeing your own kid be born."

"Does he do anything besides sleep, nurse and piss?"

"He craps his diapers, too. And sucks his thumb. That's riveting."

Clay laughed. "Brother, you need to get out more."

Amused, Will said, "And you're giving me the chance."

Moira seemed fine with the idea when Will told her. Probably more than fine, he thought ruefully; having him hover 24/7 had to be getting on her nerves.

She was the one to catch his mood, though. They were loading the dishwasher and putting away leftovers when she said, "We haven't really talked about money."

"No." He guessed they should have. Knowing she was still paying utilities and a mortgage, if she had one, had been bugging him, but when he'd said something about splitting expenses she'd been evasive. He'd settled so far for buying most of the groceries and gas.

"Well…do you *need* to go to work for your brother?"

Will set down the saucepan he'd dried. "Do you mean, financially?"

"Yes."

He shook his head. "No. I have savings and investments. I put away most of my salary all those years. Living in the house we inherited from Mom and Dad, I didn't need much money."

"Then…why did you say yes?"

"I feel pretty useless sitting around."

"Now that you figure I don't need you anymore?"

That sent a cold chill through him. He hoped like hell she did still need him, if not in the same way. But he nodded.

"The thing is…" Moira hesitated again. "I could be wrong, but I just got an undertone there that you weren't very happy about working for Clay."

He went still, thinking about it. "I didn't realize," he said after a moment. "Hell. Are you reading my mind?"

Her face went blank. "If you don't want to talk about it..."

Damn it, he'd given the impression that he disliked her being so perceptive. He was shocked by a lightning quick thought: Did he? Will didn't let himself stop to examine the idea.

"No, you caught me by surprise. And you're right," he admitted. "It's not that I mind working for Clay. It's that..." He hesitated.

"You're used to him working for you?"

"That's part of it." Will fumbled his way, trying to figure out his own reluctance. Good God, was he oblivious to his own motivations? Did Moira understand him better than he understood himself? Unsettling thought. "Maybe more of it than I want to admit," he said finally, with a shrug. "It's not Clay, it's that I haven't taken orders from anyone in a lot of years. He started talking about promoting this guy and I almost said, 'I think you could do better.' But the truth is, he has to make his own decisions and his own mistakes. It was easier to keep my mouth shut when I wasn't around."

She closed the refrigerator. "I can see that."

"I don't want to work for anyone else." He frowned. "I don't think I want to run a business as big as Becker Construction again, either. I spent too much of my time shuffling papers, overseeing the books, hiring and firing. I guess I really do like building."

Moira smiled at him. "I understand. I didn't like working in a big architectural firm, either."

Will was swept by the odd realization that, in all his adult life, he'd never had anyone he could talk to like this. He'd been the boss at work, the grown-up, the parent, at home. He'd become stuck in his roles. He had never felt able to confide, to talk problems out like this. Even though parts of this conversation had been oddly unsettling, Will thought he could easily learn to depend on having a real partner.

But all he said was, "Thanks," and that came out roughly. "I've committed to this job, but I think I'll say no next time."

"You do take commitments seriously, don't you."

Will tensed. "Shouldn't I?"

She seemed to shake herself. "Yes, of course. Don't listen to me." And she changed the subject, leaving him frustrated by his inability to figure out what she was really thinking half the time.

HE GUESSED HE *HAD* BEEN getting restless, because something settled in him once he started leaving for work every morning and coming home tired but satisfied. A brief stretch of good weather allowed them to get the roof on and walls framed in on a strip mall that would house three businesses. Tenants were already lined up for all three, so they were building to spec instead of planning open spaces. Will made any decisions and Clay didn't attempt to assert authority. During their brief business conversations, they were both tiptoeing around, Will realized, which reinforced his feeling that he shouldn't take on another job for his brother.

Damn, he looked forward every day to getting home to Moira and Caleb. Caleb changed so fast, and that was part of it. Will hated to miss anything. But mostly, he found himself thinking about Moira. He'd want to share something he'd heard, or a joke, or a random thought. He'd remember the plush feel of her lips beneath his, the delicate indentations of her spine when he slipped his hand under her shirt and tugged her close to him. He thought about the nightly pleasure-torture of sleeping with her, of waking up to find her head on his shoulder and her breasts pillowed against his side. He'd remember the luscious white swell of her breast revealed when she was nursing their son, and the occasional glimpse he caught of her nipple, damp and swollen, when Caleb's mouth slipped from it.

He kissed her every day at least twice. The brief good-bye kiss in the morning was becoming a satisfying routine. She'd blush, but lift her face to his so naturally he rejoiced. Come evening, he would touch her whenever he could, and sooner or later he'd bend his head and explore her mouth. Most nights, he read for a while or went online after Moira disappeared to bed. He had to cool off before he could get under the sheets with her so temptingly close. He might have been able to maintain his sanity better if he wasn't sleeping with her, but he loved holding her at night. He was living for her six-week checkup and the all clear from the doctor. Will hoped and prayed she felt the same. Or—hell—that she was at least *willing*.

Weekdays, she'd taken over doing most of the cooking. When he walked in the door, Moira would greet him, hand over Caleb and disappear to the kitchen, giving him some time alone with his son. By three weeks old, Caleb was staying awake more and holding his head up pretty well. He started cooing, a soft sound that always made Will smile. Usually Moira would nurse him again and put him down for a short nap while they ate dinner. Some nights he'd refuse to fall asleep, and they'd take turns bouncing him against a shoulder while they ate.

Painting the bedroom only took a couple of days. Moira commented on how much more quickly he worked than she could have.

"Dad made me learn the business from the ground up," Will explained. "I painted the entire first summer I worked for him. Over the next few summers, I learned to wire and plumb a house along with framing a window, hanging a door, reading blueprints." He shrugged. "I took the same tack with Clay and Jack."

Her brows rose. "But not with Sophie?"

Will laughed at her tone. "Are you accusing me of sexism?"

"Should I be?"

"No. Sophie worked one summer in the office, but letting her even set foot on a construction site was out." He chuckled, thinking about his sister's quirks. "She's really smart. You know that."

Moira nodded.

"She couldn't build a decent tower with wooden blocks when she was a toddler. I doubt that, to this day, she could assemble a Barbie house. She's got a great memory, so she gets herself most places with no trouble, but she can't read a map. We finally figured out it's some kind of spatial thing. She worked in a vet clinic a couple of summers, she's a whiz on a computer, but she'd be a menace with a tool in her hand."

"I've heard about people like that. I'd never have guessed."

"Sophie does plenty of things well. When she has kids, her husband can assemble the toys."

"Are there many that *need* assembling?"

"Are you kidding?" He looked at her. "There was this pink plastic dollhouse that must have taken me four hours to put together one Christmas Eve. I was up half the night, determined to have it under the tree. I did a lot of swearing." He grinned, remembering. "I kept worrying she'd hear me and sneak down the stairs. Maybe she secretly still believed in Santa Claus and found out he had a foul mouth."

He loved Moira's laugh.

Caleb was a month old when she took him for his first doctor visit.

"He's—what a surprise—in the ninety-ninth percentile in height," she reported that evening. "Ninety-seventh in weight. He's going to be big like his daddy."

"You mean, he'll start tripping over his own feet before we know it," Will said, pleased despite himself. He was amused to discover how much he liked the idea of his son taking after him.

"Well…he has to learn to walk first."

Caleb was five weeks old when Moira called Will one day when he was at work. In the middle of talking to the plumber, he was going to ignore the call until he saw Moira's number on the screen.

He felt a jolt. Not Moira's number. *Their* number.

"Excuse me for a minute," he told the plumber, and turned away. God, what if Caleb was sick? he thought with quick panic.

"Moira," he said, walking outside. "Is something wrong?"

"No, I didn't mean to scare you. I had to tell you." Excitement rang in her voice. "Will, Caleb smiled! I was nursing him, and he let my breast go and just beamed. Now, every time I smile at him, he smiles back and flaps his arms. Oh, I can hardly wait for you to get home and see."

"Damn." He closed his eyes, overwhelmed by a flood of emotion. "I wish I'd been there. Oh, hell. You make me want to come home right now."

"He's about to go down for a nap, anyway. I— Well, I probably shouldn't have called, but I had to tell you."

Voice low and husky, Will said, "I'm glad you did. I'll never mind you calling me, Moira."

"Oh." Abruptly shy, she said, "Okay. I'll, um, see you when you get home. I'm making a stir-fry tonight."

Thoughts of stir-fry and smiles got him through the rest of the afternoon. He walked in the front door wondering if Caleb would smile for him, too, or only for his mommy, and not liking the twinge of jealousy.

But Moira, her own smile glowing, was waiting for him with Caleb in her arms, and when Will reached for him and said, "Hey, big guy," his son lit up. He focused hard on his daddy's face and grinned a huge, toothless grin. Eyes that had turned brown sparkled. If Will hadn't already been in love, he'd have gone down for the count.

Moira had trouble pulling herself away to fix dinner, and he didn't blame her. Who needed any other entertainment?

After Caleb fell asleep Moira told Will about her day. She'd grocery shopped with Caleb in the stomach sling he seemed to enjoy. "Mom called," she reported. "I think she'll visit again pretty soon. It's killing her not being able to see Caleb."

"Has she ever considered moving over here?" Will asked.

"I don't know." Moira's forehead crinkled reflectively. "She seems to like her job, and she has friends. On the other hand, she's been grumbling more and more about the cold. She's getting arthritis in her hands, you know, and it's worse during the winter." She was quiet for a minute. "I think I'll ask her."

Will nodded. He thought Moira would like having her mother nearby. He wished the idea didn't feel like a threat to him. Would she turn to her mother instead of him?

Feeling petty and uncomfortable with it, he listened

as Moira continued to chatter. She'd talked to Gray today and to a new client.

"I'm meeting with her and her husband next week. They've bought some property at Port Susan and want me to design a house for them. I thought I could start working here at home."

They'd talked about her doing some of her work from home, and perhaps hiring a part-time nanny instead of putting Caleb in day care.

"You must be going stir-crazy," he realized. "Unless you're getting addicted to soap operas."

Moira scrunched up her nose. "I've taken to watching a couple of talk shows, but no soap operas. And no, I'm not going nuts yet, but...it has been a big change. It's weird, having this completely different rhythm to my days. And no one to talk to. I can't tell you how much I look forward to you walking in the door."

His voice roughened. "No more than I look forward to getting home."

"Oh," she said softly. "I didn't realize."

It was way too soon—too risky—to tell her how much he thought about her, how much she meant to him. She and Caleb gave him a sense of purpose. They *were* his purpose. That made him feel a little uneasy sometimes. He'd wanted to do something meaningful with his life, something bigger than being the devoted husband and father he'd fallen into being. He'd had no choice but to make the decision he had, and he wouldn't change it if he could. He wanted to be here with his wife and son, not in Zimbabwe building medical clinics. He just wished... hell, he didn't know what. That he could have his cake and eat it, too, he guessed.

She was a little shy with him for the rest of the evening,

and Will wondered what she'd seen on his face. When she finally said, "I'm going to bed," he stood with her.

"Let me kiss you good-night."

Her face warmed, but she came to him and wrapped her arms around his neck. Will bent his head and nuzzled her ear, her cheek, her throat, inhaling the scent that was Moira's alone. The rush of desire was almost painful. He'd made love to her once, and that was ten months ago. He'd been sleeping with her now for over two months, and it was killing him.

He brushed her lips with his. "When's your doctor appointment?" he murmured.

"Next week," she whispered. "Wednesday."

He groaned and kissed her with more hunger than he'd meant to unleash. Damn, he wanted her. He ended up with his tongue driving into her mouth and his hands wrapping her hips and lifting her against him, so that she couldn't help feeling how aroused he was. What gave him hope was that she held on tight and danced her tongue around his. They were both breathing hard when he let her go with another groan.

"Go to bed."

Wide-eyed, she took in his expression, then backed away. "Um…good night, Will."

"Good night."

He paced the living room until the quiet sounds of her getting ready for bed had ceased. Then he grabbed his parka and went for a walk. He'd been taking a lot of late-night walks recently. Only heavy rain stopped him. The frigid night air worked as well as a cold shower. He could go back with some hope of actually sleeping.

Will still didn't feel ready for bed after his walk. Instead, he turned on his laptop and browsed the internet. He did that some nights, too, when he wasn't in the mood to read. A foundation employee he'd known in Zimbabwe was regularly blogging and posting pictures. Will always started by checking if Gary had added anything new. Then he browsed for similar projects in Africa, or sometimes went to tourist sites. He wasn't much of a photographer himself, but he liked looking at pictures of Victoria Falls or the fascinating wildlife. He hadn't been in Africa long enough for glimpses of elephants or impala or even a lion lounging not far from the road to become routine.

Tonight Will found photos posted by someone who'd recently gotten home from visiting grandparents still farming near Chinhoyi, and was admiring a spectacular one of cormorants roosting in the branches of a long-dead tree poking from the waters of Lake Kariba right at sunset when he heard a sound and turned his head to see Moira. She wore flannel pajamas with cartoon characters on them. Her hair was loose and tousled, her eyes fixed on the computer monitor.

In an odd voice, she asked, "Where's that?"

"Lake Kariba, along the Zambia-Zimbabwe border. It flows into the Zambezi River then on to Victoria Falls."

"Oh." She was already backing away. "I didn't mean to interrupt you. I just got up to... It doesn't matter."

He had a really bad feeling that it did matter. "Did you want to talk to me?" he asked.

"No, I— It's nothing." She smiled, although it wasn't much of one, said, "Good night again," and disappeared down the hall.

His body tensed with the desire to go after her, but he made himself stay where he was. He'd wake Caleb if he chased her to the bedroom. Something told him she wouldn't want to talk right now, anyway.

Somewhat grimly, he decided that Caleb needed to

start sleeping in his crib, in his own bedroom. Sure as hell before next Wednesday night.

Will had lost interest in browsing scenic pictures of Africa and closed out the internet, then turned off his computer. He rubbed his forehead and felt as guilty as if Moira had caught him viewing pornography. Damn it.

The next moment, anger rose. He'd been doing something completely innocent. He was entitled to his interests. Why should he feel guilty? He'd quit the job for her, he'd married her. He was here, wasn't he, giving her his all? She had no business looking wounded because he was browsing the internet.

A rough sound escaped his throat. He hated his memory of the expression on Moira's face. It made it hard to hold on to the anger.

But maybe he'd been imagining things. Moira probably hadn't read as much into what she'd seen as he feared she had. It was that damn, irrational guilt making him see what wasn't there.

Still, he had no desire to go back online or read. Instead, he followed her down the hall and went to bed. But when he quietly got in on his side, he stayed there, hoping Moira was sleeping and not lying very still, wanting him to keep his distance.

SPYING WAS REALLY LOW and Moira hated herself for it, but the next morning after Will left for work, she turned on his laptop, went online and called up the list of websites he'd recently visited. What she saw made her feel as if she'd been kicked in the chest.

Scrolling down, she realized he was obsessed. She'd let herself believe he wasn't going to bed at the same time as she did because he was having trouble resisting the desire to make love to her. Now she knew. He could probably hardly wait for her to go to bed so he could go online and vicariously live his dream.

The one she'd stolen from him when she told him she was pregnant with his child.

Hastily, half wishing she *hadn't* looked, Moira closed down the computer and went to her office. While Caleb was sleeping, she'd do rough sketches of some ideas for the Russells, the new clients she'd told Will about. Molly Russell had said enough on the phone about what they wanted to get Moira thinking, and she did that best on paper.

But she felt too agitated to accomplish a thing. She wasn't used to not knowing how to handle a problem. It wasn't like her to be so completely clueless.

Of course, there was a reason she was. She had next to no experience in relationships. Worse yet, she'd never been in love before.

But now she was. So desperately in love, and with a man whose life she'd seriously mucked up. A man who probably wished he'd never met her.

She closed her eyes and remembered him gently rubbing her belly and saying, *I wouldn't want to be anywhere but here.* And *You think after holding Caleb I can regret anything?*

Yes! Yes, she thought he did. Oh, she did believe he loved Caleb. The tenderness on his face when he held his son was unmistakable. And she believed that he did want her. A man couldn't fake an erection, which he seemed to have pretty frequently these days.

But then…men liked sex. Getting a hard-on didn't mean much.

What should she *do?* Offering to let him go would be useless; he was fixated on a goal, the same way he'd been after his father died. He might be miserable, but that wouldn't count. Marrying her, being a husband and father, was now his main goal in life, and she was pretty sure it would take dynamite to shake him from it.

And—oh, God—she didn't *want* to let him go. She could have survived without Will, if she'd never let him know she was pregnant. She knew she could have. But now that she'd had him, she couldn't bear the idea of life without him.

If only Gray hadn't bullied her into telling Will.

Moira made a face. She'd have contacted him sooner or later anyway. Later, maybe, without Gray's push, but she knew she'd have done it. Will had deserved to know.

She spent a really unhappy day, but pulled herself together enough to greet him when he got home as though nothing was wrong. She thought his gaze was rather searching as he took Caleb from her, but she had the excuse of needing to stir the spaghetti sauce simmering on the stove. And she got lucky in that Caleb chose tonight not to want to sleep, so he was a distraction during dinner.

Afterward, he would have liked to fall asleep, but she refused to let him.

"He only woke up once last night," she told Will. "And that wasn't until nearly three. Maybe if we keep him awake now he'll sleep through the night. I talked to Charlotte yesterday, and she says Emily did before she was six weeks old."

Caleb let out a frustrated cry.

"Mommy doesn't really mean that," Will told him, holding his son up to look into his eyes. "She'd miss that middle-of-the-night feeding. She told me how much she loves getting up with you. Snuggling you when the house is all quiet and dark. She's grumpy tonight, that's all." He blew a raspberry on Caleb's plump cheek. "Don't listen to her."

"You know," Moira said, "I've been thinking about pumping some breast milk so he could start getting used to taking a bottle. If I did that, *you* could get up and snuggle him in the middle of the night. Just think. It could become your special time."

He laughed and bounced an increasingly disgruntled Caleb against his shoulder. "Now Mommy is getting nasty."

"Goo ga."

"Hey!" Face alight with pleasure, Will looked at her. "Did you hear that? He's talking."

"That was a new sound." Wow. The dumbest things could make her teary-eyed. It wouldn't be that long before Caleb was saying *Mama* or *Dada*.

"What a smart boy," his father crooned, sounding as besotted as she was.

Oh, she had a million doubts, but never that he loved Caleb. Watching Will Becker, big and kind and sexy, walk in circles around the living room with their baby cradled in his arms, all she could think was, *But what about* me? *Can't he love me, too?*

After she put Caleb to bed, Moira returned to the living room. She was in such turmoil, her chest felt crowded inside, as if she was stuffing too many emotions, too many doubts, into it. *Say something,* she ordered herself. *Don't be a coward.*

Will was texting someone on his phone when she came back to the living room. "Jack," he murmured, finishing and setting the phone aside.

"Last night," Moira said. Too abruptly, probably too loudly. "I know you're spending a lot of time online. Do you…do you look at stuff about Africa a lot?"

His jaw tightened. "I'm still interested. I do a little browsing."

A little? she thought incredulously, remembering the list of sites he'd visited.

Feeling incoherent, she began, "It's just..." Swallowed. "Maybe we should talk about it."

"Moira, the fact that I read someone's blog or look at pretty pictures of Africa has nothing to do with you and me." His voice was tighter than usual. Was it temper ruffling his usual calm? "For God's sake, don't read something into nothing."

What could she do but nod? She wasn't sure the lump in her throat would have let her speak anyway. *Nothing?* The very fact that he was defensive told her *nothing* was definitely something.

But she was a coward after all. Enough of one that she wouldn't light that stick of dynamite, that she would keep taking whatever he would give and pretend she didn't guess how deep his regret ran. And she would hope that he meant it when he said he liked her freckles and her hair and her curves; that he did, at least, want her.

CHAPTER FOURTEEN

TUESDAY EVENING, WILL SAID, "Why don't we try Caleb in his crib tonight. Since he's made it through the night a couple of times now."

Call him prudish, but he didn't think he'd be able to enjoy making love with Moira when Caleb was right there, only a few feet away. Will knew it was dumb; it's not as though Caleb would know what his parents were doing, and that was assuming he even woke up. And it took a heck of a lot to wake him up. Will had seen Moira vacuum right around his bassinet while he snoozed on without a twitch. Whatever Caleb did, he *concentrated*.

Not surprising, since Will knew he was known and occasionally reviled for the force of his determination and single-mindedness. And he'd seen Moira lost in her work, oblivious to ringing telephones or conversations around her.

Moira's gaze found and shied from his. "Um…that's probably a good idea. Let's see if we can keep him up another half an hour."

"Good idea." He sat on the far end of the couch from her, stockinged feet on the coffee table. He'd spent a lot of time looking at her tonight. Tormenting himself. "Your doctor appointment still on for tomorrow?"

She murmured agreement and played "This little piggy went to market" with Caleb's toes. He might be getting sleepy, but he smiled with delight nonetheless. She moved on to his other foot. Will might have believed she wasn't thinking about anything else, but her pink cheeks betrayed her self-consciousness.

This last week had been a strain. For both of them, he suspected. It was partly that near-argument about his continuing interest in Africa. The tension between them had never dissipated. His fault, maybe—he'd continued to stay up long after she went to bed, feeling bloody-minded but doing it anyway. Making a point. Marriage didn't mean giving up all privacy, all outside interests. It was unreasonable of her to imply—even if only by one stricken look—that he should. The fact that he'd had no interest since in reading about Africa was irrelevant; if he wanted to, he could.

Guilt still ate at him, and that still pissed him off. But he had also been forced to do some thinking, which was probably a good thing. Truth was, he'd been drifting. Taking this job for Clay just to have something to do. He had a new life now, and he had to make it matter or he was going to end up unhappy.

So he'd actually spent some pretty productive time on the internet, leading to a meeting today that had him excited. He'd been looking forward all afternoon to telling Moira about it.

Truth was, he wouldn't have had the self-discipline to go to bed at the same time as she did, anyway. Sharing a bed as if they were nothing but friends had become an impossibility. If he cuddled with her, she'd notice he had a raging hard-on. It was bad enough climbing into bed beside her once she was asleep. He still stayed on his side, careful not to touch her. Every muscle in his body would be rigid with restraint, when all he wanted to do was reach out for her. He'd relived their one and only lovemaking a thousand times. The feel of her under him, the sounds she made, the tightness of her body when he pushed inside her. Sleep did not come easily. It was worse when she had to get up to nurse Caleb and would slip back into bed beside Will. Knowing she was awake, wondering if she was thinking about him, remembering his touch, too, was enough to make him feel like fire ants were crawling over his skin.

Torture.

They'd never actually talked about whether they'd make love, but the knowledge that soon they *could* had become part of the very air they both breathed. Every time Will looked at her, it was on his mind. The fact that Moira had gotten shyer made him pretty sure she was thinking the same. Wanting the same. Please, God, she wanted the same.

Will had hardly took his eyes off her all evening. Usually, when she nursed Caleb, he made no pretence that he wasn't watching. He was fascinated by the voluptuous swell of her breasts, the moist dark peak of her nipple when Caleb let go of it. In a different way, Will loved the sight of their baby nursing. That small, perfect hand often seemed to pat his mommy's breast, as if in appreciation. The two of them together, mother and child, made his heart swell until it filled his chest.

He changed Caleb's diaper and brought him to her to nurse, as usual. Sat down, watched as she lifted her shirt and reached for the catch that would free one breast, then shot to his feet. He couldn't take it tonight.

Voice hoarse, he said, "I'm going for a walk."

"Oh." Her color heightened. "Okay."

She was tiptoeing down the hall when Will came in, shaking the water from his hair like a wet dog. He took his coat off and said unnecessarily, "It's raining." Then he recognized her unusual caution. "You put him in his crib?"

Moira nodded. "He was already asleep."

"Will he notice when he wakes up?"

"What do you think?" she scoffed.

He grinned. "Of course he will," he said. "Caleb's a smart boy."

"And he's going to be a mad boy."

"Can I go look?"

She narrowed her eyes. "If you wake him up, on your head be it."

Another grin, and he slipped silently down the hall. The ceramic nightlight shaped like a mouse cast a faint, golden glow that allowed him to make out Caleb, a tiny lump under his comforter, his face slack and peaceful. When Will just as quietly stepped back out of the room, Moira was hovering at the other end of the hall.

Will waited until he'd reached her. "He's cute."

"Yes, he is. And I'm going to bed, too."

"I wanted to talk to you about something first," he said.

Moira studied him. She must have heard that he was serious, because she looked apprehensive when she said, "Sure."

She sat on her usual end of the couch, bare feet tucked beneath her, Will in the big easy chair across from her.

"I've been thinking about the future," he said.

Her face stayed unnaturally still, but he saw the way she squeezed her hands together, the fear in her eyes.

"Work," he clarified, before she could do more than stare at him.

Air escaped her with a force that was audible.

Will raised his eyebrows, but when she didn't say anything, he went on, "I'm bored with what I'm doing.

No, more than that—dissatisfied. We build solid, Becker Construction doesn't cut corners, but...this kind of job I'm doing, the best you can say is it's workmanlike." He shrugged. "Nothing wrong with that, but I think I'd like to build something that might endure. Even be admired fifty years from now, a hundred years from now."

"Which means building for clients with money. Lots of money."

He grimaced. "Yeah. The opposite of what I was striving for in Africa. I do realize that."

"So what have you decided?"

"I guess I have two sets of ideals. One pushes me to do something for people who genuinely need help. The other is to build real quality." He leaned forward, letting her see passion he most often kept disguised. It was one of those pieces of himself that he had to share if they were to have any hope. "I think I can do both," he said. "I might start a small construction firm. Build one house at a time. Focus on the details, connect with the real craftsmen in our area who do fine stonework or cabinetry or wrought-iron railings. Do work I can be proud of."

Moira nodded. "That's part of the reason Gray and I struck out on our own."

Will nodded in acknowledgment, unsurprised by her understanding. "The other part of what I'm thinking is that I'll provide my services free or at minimal cost for projects I believe in." He paused. "I've already found the first one."

"Really?" She was leaning forward slightly, too, as though he'd captured her by his intensity.

"I found an organization looking to build an apartment house for women with children who are trying to make a new start. Most of the women served were in abusive relationships. Bright Futures works to provide counseling, help find jobs, whatever the clientele needs. They'd like to be able to offer housing, too, for up to a year while the women get their feet under them. The idea is that the women can turn to each other, that the apartment building will give the residents a community, too."

"Is the funding in place?"

"They've got property in Stanwood, but they thought they were a year or more away from starting. No plans yet, for one thing. If I don't charge for my work as contractor, and I get deals where I can find them for materials, we might be able to break ground this spring."

Moira didn't even hesitate. "I can draw the plans free."

He smiled. "I thought you might say that."

"I've been suckered?"

"Yeah, you have."

He could all but see her brain racing. "There should be a community room. Not only the separate apartments, but a space for the women to get together. Maybe even for some communal child care. How many apartments?"

"Six or eight."

"I'm ashamed that it never occurred to me to volunteer my skill for something like this."

"Don't be." He made his voice low, husky, intimate. "I thought maybe it was something we could do together."

That was one of the things he'd realized this past week, when he'd sat here long after she'd gone to bed. He'd hated the gulf that had opened between them. He wouldn't let himself be disappointed if she didn't want to be involved in whatever project he took on, but...he'd liked the idea of sharing it with her. He'd liked that a lot.

"Yes." Her face was alive with the same excitement he felt. "This is great timing, Will. I could get started any time. As soon as you can set it up for me to meet with whoever will be overseeing us."

"I'll talk to them tomorrow," he promised. He sat back in his chair, looking at her with pleasure. This had gone even better than he'd hoped. "Now you'd better get to bed. Thank you for listening to me."

Moira stood then, in a flurry, came to him and kissed his cheek. He felt his evening beard rasp under her soft lips. "I like your ideas," she said, her voice a little husky. "Both of them."

"Good." He made no move to touch her or pull her down for a deeper kiss although, damn, he wanted to. He had no doubt his expression was rueful. "I think I'd better read for a while. My self-restraint is flagging."

"Oh." Heat bloomed in her cheeks again. "Okay."

All he could do was sit there trying not to hear the muted sounds of her getting ready for bed—water running, the toilet flushing, the glide of the closet door—and try to figure out how he could kill an hour or two, when all he wanted to do was make love to his wife.

WEDNESDAY HAD TO BE THE LONGEST damn day of his entire life. Will considered himself a patient man, but he'd used up all his patience these past few months.

Why hadn't he tried to seduce Moira before she had the baby? She'd probably convinced herself that, as big as she'd gotten, he didn't want her. Truth was, he'd been half-aroused most of the time since their wedding. She'd been carrying his baby and was round and ripe and bursting with fertility. What was sexier than that?

But he'd told himself it was too soon, that she needed to get to know him, decide she could trust him. Will had given serious thought to trying to coax her after he'd made the move into her bed, but her bleeding episode had scared him. He wouldn't do anything that might threaten their child. And…she had gradually relaxed with him, so his original plan had been working.

What he *hadn't* thought about was how torturously long the six weeks until Moira got the all-clear from her doctor would turn out to be. Ten months, one week exactly since he'd made love to her. Hell, since he'd had sex. He didn't know how he'd survived.

He got home at five-thirty to a flustered wife and a cranky baby. Caleb had not enjoyed his first night in his own bedroom. He'd woken up every couple of hours all night long and sobbed. Moira and Will took turns going in and rocking him back to sleep. They were all three heavy-eyed this morning. Under other circumstances, Will might have been thinking about nothing but hitting the sack.

Taking Caleb into his arms and enjoying Moira's pink cheeks and green eyes that wouldn't quite meet his, Will hid his grin. He was thinking about nothing but bed, all right, although sleep didn't have anything to do with it. And it was pretty clear that Moira had her mind on the same thing.

He kissed Caleb's chubby cheek and strolled as far as the kitchen doorway in pursuit of his wife, who'd skittered away the instant she handed off their kid. "Smells good," he said amiably. "What are you cooking?"

"Meatloaf and baked potatoes."

He spotted a pie cooling on the counter. "And you baked."

"Cherry," she said tersely, keeping her back to him as she fussed unnecessarily over whatever vegetable she had steaming in a saucepan on the stove.

"À la mode?" he said hopefully.

Mouth prim, she shot him a look. "For those who can afford the calories."

"You're determined to stick to your diet, aren't you?"

"I will never be fat again," she said in a steely voice.

"Can't you splurge sometimes?"

She rolled her eyes, looking for a moment like a disgusted teenager. "Why do you think I put on almost forty pounds while I was pregnant? Remember the French fries? The milkshakes?"

"I suppose it's natural I eat more than you do," he realized.

"Ya think?"

Amused, he let it go. "Did Caleb sleep all day?"

There was more steel in her voice. "I didn't let him. My sympathy was at a low ebb today, I can tell you."

"Yeah, I almost crawled into my pickup for a nap." Will surprised himself with a jaw-popping yawn. "Damn. Well, let's hope he's resigned himself tonight to his crib."

Moira yawned, too. "Oh, don't get me started."

Very casually, he asked, "How'd the doctor visit go?"

"Fine." She kept her back to him. "Great. She said I'm fine. Everything's…"

Fine.

Under other circumstances, he'd have grinned. As it was, his blood pooled in his groin. "Good," he said after a moment, his voice rusty. "I'm glad you're—" not *fine.* Anything but fine "—recovered," he finished firmly.

She nodded, still without looking at him. Will retreated to the living room.

While he entertained Caleb, Moira dished up dinner. They settled him in a reclining baby seat while they ate. Moira cheered up when Will told her that someone from Bright Futures, the nonprofit organization that wanted to build the apartment house, would be calling her the next day.

"I can't tell you how excited they are. An architect and a contractor. And I talked a buddy of mine who owns an electrical contracting firm into offering his work cut-rate. You remember Dennis Mattson—he was at our wedding."

"Dennis was nice." Sounding thoughtful, she said, "I know a plumber who might be interested, too. Let me give him a call tomorrow."

"Maybe we can build up a network of, er…"

Moira arched her eyebrows. "Persuadable people?"

He chuckled. "Yeah, something like that. Good meat-loaf," he told her.

Seeing Caleb's eyelids sinking, she said, "Oh, no you don't," and tickled his stomach. He started and began to cry.

Will saw her frustration and guessed that she was exhausted. The thought made his heart sink. Was she too tired? Damn it, damn it.

He stood immediately and picked Caleb up, holding him tight to his chest, one large hand engulfing the baby's entire back. He silently begged, *Please cooperate. Please.*

CALEB WAS SO TINY AGAINST the breadth of his daddy's powerful body. The sight of Will with their baby always moved Moira, but tonight she felt especially emotional. Somehow, it was more amazing to see a man as big and strong as Will being so extraordinarily gentle.

His eyes met hers and seemed to darken. "Are you all right?"

She nodded and gave a sniff. "I just…sometimes…" She flapped a hand.

His mouth curved. "Yeah. I know what you mean."

She saw that he did. He so often seemed to. How did he understand her so well? Was figuring her out part of what he'd taken on when he decided she and Caleb were going to be his priority?

"Poor boy," he was murmuring. "I know you're sleepy. But, see, there's a big picture you're missing. Mommy and I are sleepy, too. And if you nap now, we're in trouble."

Caleb didn't care. In the next hour, Moira began to feel that they were tormenting him, keeping him awake. She might have buckled, but Will displayed a more ruthless streak than she'd seen yet. He shook rattles, bicycled Caleb's chubby legs, made obnoxious noises, played bounce the baby. Caleb alternated between grumpy and delighted.

Maybe it was her own tiredness, but a giggle kept bubbling in Moira's throat.

"Mean Daddy," she said.

Amusement and something else in his eyes, Will retorted, "Desperate Daddy."

That didn't strike her as nearly so funny. In fact, she had to clench her thighs together to contain a wickedly physical response to his expression and the low, rough sound of his voice.

They were both watching the clock. At eight on the nose, Will stripped off Caleb's sleeper and quickly and efficiently changed his wet diaper. Then he thrust their baby at her.

She already had her blouse unfastened and her bra unhooked. Caleb latched on with his customary eagerness. She gave him a couple of minutes, then switched him to the other breast. The entire time, Will sat staring. Tingling all over, Moira felt as if her skin was flushed from her toes to the crown of her head.

The suckling slowed. Caleb's small body went slack and his mouth slipped from her breast. Not looking at Will, she eased the baby to her shoulder, patted him until a burp escaped him, then stood. Will rose, too, and by the time she reached the bedroom, the lights in the kitchen and living room had already gone out.

She turned on the nightlight, laid Caleb in the crib and tucked his flannel quilt up to his chin. He never stirred.

Will was already waiting in their bedroom, where the lamp cast the only light. Her pulse skipped.

He watched her walk toward him. "Moira." He spoke barely above a whisper. "Sweetheart."

She swallowed.

"You know I want to make love with you."

She nodded. "I want that, too." In her attempt to keep her voice low, too, she sounded almost sultry. She hadn't known she could. "We shouldn't until…until things are more settled. But I don't care."

After nursing, she hadn't bothered buttoning up her blouse. Will caressed her cheek, then stroked his fingertips down her throat until he reached the front clasp of her bra.

"You have the most beautiful breasts. Watching you nurse has been killing me."

"They're…awfully big these days," she said awkwardly. "I'm always leaking."

"Beautiful," he repeated huskily. He flicked open the clasp and her breasts spilled out. His big hands enveloped them the way she'd remembered. Her nipples peaked against his palms, and he rubbed gently, squeezed, whispered about how much he wanted her. She stood for the longest time doing nothing but soaking in his touch, as if every cell in her body was starved for it. Finally, she had to touch him, too, and she tugged his sweatshirt upward.

As though they'd both lost all patience in that moment, they fought to remove each other's clothes. She was hardly aware of losing her shirt or bra; her hands were already on the metal buttons at the fly of his jeans. So quickly, they were both naked, and only then did she remember to be self-conscious.

She crossed her arms protectively. "Don't look at my stomach."

Will groaned and thrust his fingers into her hair. "How many times do I have to tell you how sexy you are? I like you soft. You just had a baby. You *should* be soft." His voice was ragged, the gaze that swept her so darkly appreciative Moira couldn't help but believe him.

"Where have you been all my life?" she asked, and quit trying to hide herself.

He laughed, scooped her up and laid her across their bed. Coming down beside her, he kissed her, a deep, drugging kiss that tumbled her back in time, to that first night. All the lonely months that had followed, all her fears, slipped away, forgotten if only for this moment.

His mouth finally left hers to nibble and lick and kiss her neck and her shoulders, her breasts and belly, her thighs and calves and the sensitive arches of her feet.

"Such pretty freckles." He was nuzzling his way up her legs. "You make me want to connect the dots. All the dots."

She half sobbed at the pleasure his mouth brought her. She wanted to explore his body, too, but that seemed too leisurely for this first time. "Please." Moira gripped his shoulders, felt the muscles bunch beneath her fingers. "Will. Now."

He surged up the length of her body, found his place

between her legs and thrust into her. Then they were both groaning, their bodies rising and falling in a rhythm that came so naturally, they might have done this a hundred times instead of only once. And yet there was nothing smooth about it. She strained upward, fighting him each time he pulled back, moaning at the depth of his plunges. The end came too quickly. She cried out and faltered; he had to grip her hips and lift her so that he could drive deep inside her again. Once, twice, three times, his body bucking and shuddering above and inside her. And then he sank onto her, and she pressed her lips to his damp skin and couldn't tell whether the vibration and thunder of the heartbeat she felt was his or hers.

THAT WEEK WAS THE SINGLE happiest of Moira's life. When Caleb napped, she eagerly started work on plans for both the Russells' Warm Beach house and the Bright Futures apartment building. She hadn't felt so creative or excited in ages, she realized. Of course, the pregnancy had tired her, but it was more than that—maybe she'd needed the break. She loved talking to Will about her ideas, too. She and Gray used to talk about their work that way, but had done so less and less in recent years. Perhaps they'd both gotten stale, or simply too busy.

She adored being a mother, watching her gorgeous baby boy thrive and change day by day. His eyes had turned a warm, chocolate brown, lighter than his daddy's, but so pretty. She kept wondering whether he'd have freckles. A few would be okay, a dusting across his nose, maybe. A little wryly, she thought, *a sprinkle of cloves, instead of a warehouse club-size canister dumped*. Already she could see him as a tough little boy, missing a front tooth or two and grinning, both mischievous and deceptively innocent. She began to wonder if she really had to go back to work full-time. Maybe she and Gray should start thinking about bringing in an associate. They hadn't so far, but they both had families now.

Then there was nighttime, after Caleb was asleep. From the minute Will walked in the door at the end of the day, Moira could hardly think about anything *but* going to bed. With him. Making love. Falling asleep with her head on his shoulder, her legs tangled with his. Waking to find his hand on her breast, his morning erection pressed against her belly or hip. If they were lucky and Caleb gave them time, they made love then, too.

Life was so perfect, it shimmered like the highway ahead did sometimes in the desert. She had this funny, uncomfortable feeling, as if she were a little girl who'd been trusted to carry a precious family heirloom and was proud and thrilled even as fear curdled in her stomach that she'd trip or do something foolish and drop it. The vision of it shattering was almost more real than the loveliness in her hands.

That was silly, of course, but being scared that this was only an idyll wasn't. Will wasn't in love with her, he hadn't married her because he couldn't imagine living without her. He'd made the best of it, and he did want her, but...for how long? They'd never had that talk, and she wasn't brave enough to suggest that they do. She didn't want to hear any harsh truths, however gently phrased. She didn't want to think about how only days ago Will was waiting for her to go to bed so he could go online and...and visit his former lover. That's what it felt like. As if she knew a big part of his heart was taken, and that it was only because he was a good, kind man that he hid his hurt and disappointment.

For which *she* was responsible.

Moira felt adolescent, the way her worry continued to niggle at her. The fact that Will had loved his project in Africa—had loved Zimbabwe—didn't take away from anything he felt for her and Caleb. She was adult enough to know that. They weren't teenagers, to demand complete and utter devotion of each other. They'd both had lives, had work that was important to them, family and friends, opinions and values and goals that weren't necessarily shared.

This common sense had zilch effect. She kept wondering how the Bright Futures project could possibly compare to what he'd been accomplishing in Africa—an apartment house for a few mothers and their children, a temporary refuge against a dozen medical clinics and community hospitals that would have improved thousands and thousands of lives. Saved many of those lives. Was this another way he was…settling?

She wanted to clap her hands over her ears and shut out the doubts, but how could she? She wanted so much to believe she was lovable, but that didn't mean Will did—or could—love her.

And yet…he seemed happy. And he *was* in love with Caleb. She kept reminding herself of that.

On Wednesday the week after they had begun to make love again, Moira became so engrossed in drawing that she didn't notice when the mail was dropped through the slot in the door. Will picked it up off the floor when he got home, glanced through it and handed most of it to her before taking Caleb with an exuberant grin and a kiss for her.

But he kept one envelope aside.

She wasn't sure what he did with it. She didn't see him open it at all. Maybe it was junk mail. He didn't seem to get much personal mail; Sophie and he emailed and even, occasionally, used Instant Messenger rather than exchanging letters. She knew he talked to her and both his brothers regularly.

Moira didn't really think about that piece of mail until the next day, when she passed the end of the breakfast bar where Will kept his computer, a battered address book and a heap of work-related notes to himself. She loved his handwriting, an emphatic scrawl that was a complete contrast to her own exceedingly tidy, careful script.

A long white envelope, torn open, lay there on top of his notes. The typed letter was beside it. One fold concealed the bottom, but she could see the letterhead—the foundation he'd worked for. It was probably nothing. He hadn't tried to hide the letter. He might have automatically gone on their list of potential donors, for example. But her heart had began to pound hard, and she couldn't stop herself from reaching out and unfolding the piece of paper. Reading. And feeling sick, when words leaped out at her.

We regret losing you… Projects have bogged down… Your skill at dealing with local authority… And finally, their hope that he'd fulfilled the *obligation* that had interrupted his planned commitment to them. Might he be able to return to Zimbabwe?

They wanted him back. And he *had* fulfilled his commitment to her.

An obligation. She felt sick. *I'm nothing but an obligation.*

The last months of her pregnancy had been hard. The first weeks with a newborn, too. But she and Caleb would be fine without Will now.

Except that her knees almost gave away at the thought

of him leaving. The pain that filled her was nearly unbear-
able because she knew she couldn't keep him here. Not if
he truly wanted to go.

But how did she find out?

CHAPTER FIFTEEN

WILL KNEW THE MINUTE he walked in the door that something was wrong. Moira was quiet, closed off. Pre-occupied rather than upset, he wanted to think. Or maybe Caleb had been cranky today and she was tired.

During dinner he asked a few questions about her work, talked about an aggravating delay brought about because he'd rejected the shoddy cabinetry that had been delivered today.

"Damn, I'm going to be glad to be done with this job," he said with feeling.

She appeared to be concentrating on her salad, although he couldn't see that she'd eaten much. "I can imagine."

"Is something wrong?" he finally asked bluntly.

Her eyes, a darker green than usual, briefly met his. "No. I just thought we should talk tonight. Once Caleb's gone to bed."

A sense of foreboding tightened his stomach. What the hell?

The evening seemed interminable. Moira insisted on cleaning the kitchen while he played with Caleb, who then resisted going down for the night. When he finally did and Moira returned to the living room, Will said, "All right. What is it?"

She sat on what he thought of as her end of the couch, well out of his reach. "I saw the letter from the foundation."

Well, shit. He hadn't meant to leave it out.

"It's flattering they thought I did such a good job. But I'm not going back."

Finally, she looked fully at him. Her voice was completely steady. Even cool. "Maybe you should, Will."

"What?"

"I thought about it all day. I've appreciated more than I can say what you've done for me. I hope you know that. But I don't need you the way I did. Not the same way. We'd agreed in the first place this would be temporary. You gave up so much. And now…now it looks like you don't have to."

He let loose with an obscenity. Fear clawed at him. "We're married, Moira. I gave up one commitment for another—to *you*—and I'm sure as hell not going back on it."

"Will, this is your chance." She sounded almost as if she was pleading with him. "We didn't marry for love. Neither of us was thinking about a lifetime when we did it. You've been wonderful, but you can still follow your dream. I'll welcome you to stay whenever you can get back to the States to see Caleb. And…he'll be here when your two years is up. I promise I won't ever try to keep him from you. I swear."

"Moira, what I want has changed."

Her gaze pierced him. "Tell me that you didn't feel longing when you read that letter. Be honest, Will. Please. Please." For the first time her voice faltered. "You read that and thought, I could go back. Didn't you?"

"I won't lie to you," he said hoarsely. "I felt a pang. But that's all."

"You hate the work you're doing right now, and starting your own contracting business isn't what you ever intended to do with your life." She was relentless. "It's second best. All of this is." Her vague gesture encompassed him, her. Them. "I don't want a marriage with a man who came to it reluctantly and stayed out of a sense of obligation. That's…not fair to either of us."

She did deserve better, and he could give it to her. He loved her. But he had the breath-stealing fear that she wasn't asking for his love. Was she telling him that he wasn't what she wanted and needed?

"When we made love, did it feel like obligation?" Now his voice was harsh. Only anger could combat pain. "Is that what you were offering? Did you think I expected payback because I'd taken care of you when you needed me?"

Finally, color rushed over cheeks that had been too pale. "Of course not. We enjoyed sex. We enjoyed sex a year ago, too, Will. That didn't keep you from going to Africa. Why should it now?"

Now the shock, anger and hurt were so damned knotted together, he couldn't separate them. "Are you asking me to leave, Moira? Is that what this is about?"

"No, I…"

He swore. "I'd have sworn last night—this morning—that you were happy. Is it just the letter?"

The flush had left her cheeks. She was marble-white now, her freckles standing out starkly. He wondered if she was even breathing. "You know I'm…not very confident about some things. And you know how much I hated the fact that you gave up something you'd been dreaming about for years. It broke my heart, when I saw your face that night when you were looking at pictures of Zimbabwe online. I suppose I thought you couldn't have it back, once you made the decision. But it turns out you can, Will. It's not like you can't still be a father to Caleb. He'll need you more later, anyway, when he's older."

Granite hard, he said, "I'm not going, Moira."

Eyes huge and beseeching, she said, "Will you think about this? Please? Don't…don't just be stubbornly set on sticking it out because you think you promised. That's not enough. We'll both be miserable later. I need you to be honest. Please," she repeated. "Please don't lie to me."

"Moira…"

She shook her head and stood suddenly. "I can't talk about it anymore. I've said what I had to say. Just…think. Now I'm going to bed. No," she said, when he started to rise. "I'd rather go alone tonight. I'm not in the mood—" Moira stopped as if her throat had clogged, then rushed away.

Frozen halfway between standing and sitting, he heard the quiet snick of the bedroom door shutting. His knees gave out, and he sank into the chair. That damn door hadn't been shut in a long time. Should he be grateful that she trusted him to hear Caleb?

At the thought of their baby, Will felt a huge crack in his almost-numbness, one that let him glimpse such agony he couldn't bear it. How could she know him so little that she'd think for an instant he'd want to spend two years half a world away from his son?

From her?

He sat there for hours, the house quiet and almost unbearably lonely around him. Once Caleb did awaken and cry. Knowing he couldn't be hungry yet, Will rocked him back to sleep. The small weight nestled against his chest felt so sweet, Will only reluctantly laid him back in the crib and retreated from the softly lit room. The door across the hall stayed closed. Either Moira hadn't heard Caleb's cries, or was lying there tensely hoping she wasn't needed.

What if she did kick him out? Will tried to imagine

going home to his brothers' house—and he thought of it that way. It wasn't home anymore. *This* was home now, with Moira and Caleb. And he sure as hell couldn't talk to anybody about what had gone wrong, not even his brothers. Clay was becoming a friend, but still, Will had never in his life talked about his feelings with any of his siblings. With anyone, really, before Moira.

And this… No, he needed to wrap his mind around everything she'd said first. She'd asked him to think, and he would.

He eventually laid down on the couch, not even bothering to convert it into a bed. It was too short, but he wouldn't have slept well, anyway. He waited in the morning until he heard Moira go in to Caleb, then he showered and dressed for work. Thank God for work, he thought, with an edge of desperation. When he came out, Moira had already fried bacon and was scrambling eggs. He ate, they were civil, but he didn't kiss her goodbye. It was the first time they'd parted in a long time when he hadn't kissed her.

The morning was too busy for much brooding. One of the tenants came by to inspect the work and discuss some minor changes. Will's crew was doing finish work, and on impulse at noon he said, "You're on your own this afternoon. Call my cell if you need me," and left.

He drove over to Forest Park and found a bench with a view of the playground. The day was chilly but clear and several well-bundled mothers pushed their kids on swings or watched them scramble on climbers. As he'd be doing someday with Caleb.

Had he been lying to Moira? To himself? If he weren't bullheadedly determined to make their marriage work because he viewed this commitment to the mother of his child as the right thing to do, would he want to take up where he'd left off in Zimbabwe?

He sat for a long time, imagining himself getting back on the airplane, ending up in Harare. Walking into his house there to the smell of cooking, sitting down in solitude to his *sadza,* served by Jendaya. He remembered his last trips in the country, the lengthy negotiations with regional officials, the open-air meetings with villagers, the glimpses of wildlife and ancient rock art. And gradually he relaxed, because what he remembered best was how colored his every day had become by his worries about Moira, his memories of their one night together.

It would be a thousand times worse now. There wouldn't be a minute when he wasn't haunted by thoughts of her and Caleb. He'd enjoyed what he was doing there, he'd found it satisfying, but it didn't compare to being a husband and father.

How could she think...?

He groaned, remembering the night she'd walked in unexpectedly when he was online looking at photos of Zimbabwe. He sat without moving, aching when he pictured the stricken expression on Moira's face as she'd hastily retreated. She'd tried to talk to him, and he'd shut her down. But she'd been right, and he was wrong.

There was a reason he had only gone online after she'd gone to bed, or when she wasn't home. Face it: he'd been trying to deceive her, to convince her that he wasn't thinking anymore about the job and dreams he'd given up. He'd deceived even himself, because what he'd done was leave that door cracked open.

With what she saw, with his refusal to talk about it, he'd confirmed Moira's belief that he'd chosen duty over heart. That wasn't true, but it also hadn't been quite honest of him to pretend he had no regrets.

Had a part of him, hidden inside, still thought maybe he'd help Moira out for a while, then go back to what he'd been doing? He couldn't be sure, but he was ashamed of himself that his commitment hadn't been as absolute as he'd believed it was. He felt sleazy, as if he *had* been looking at big-breasted naked women online.

The door was shut now, but maybe too late. He'd hurt her, and he had refused to see that that's what he was doing. *Please God,* he thought bleakly, *don't let me be too late.*

No matter what, he was done. She and Caleb mattered more than anything else in the world to him. That *was* the truth. He'd finally been finding his way to a life that would satisfy him in other ways, too, he realized. He wouldn't like to disappoint the people at Bright Futures. He'd committed to them, too. Nor would it be hard to keep finding projects like that, ways he could do good here.

But…what if he couldn't convince Moira? The fear devastated him. Just thinking about losing her, he knew how much he loved her. Her, and Caleb. How could he go on without them? He couldn't conceive of being an every-other-weekend father to his son. Seeing Moira only to hand off their child would be hideous.

If she didn't believe in his commitment, would she believe he loved her? Will didn't know.

He kept searching through her words for clues, and not finding them.

I don't want a marriage with a man who came to it reluctantly and stayed out of a sense of obligation. The question was, did she want marriage with *him?*

Leaving that aside, he began to think about why she'd had such a hard time from the beginning believing he would want her enough to give up anything for her. He'd always known that she was strong, but even that first night

Will had seen the vulnerability beneath. He'd peeled back layers since, and could see the scars she tried to hide even from herself. The father who hadn't given a damn. The years she'd seen herself as fat and been rejected socially. The sense she'd always had of being likable, but not... desirable.

Hands shoved in the pockets of his parka, legs stretched out in front of him, Will stared at the playground without seeing a soul. It might as well have been deserted. All he saw was Moira, only Moira. Her face that time he'd told her how much sadness he saw in her. He remembered her telling him once that he was a good man, so good she was afraid he'd lie to her to keep her from thinking she was taking advantage of him.

She had never believed he would want to stay with her. He'd *known* that, without letting himself understand how deep her fears ran. In her memory, she'd had to beg him to make love to her in the first place. The pregnancy was all her fault because all he'd done was be kind to her. His enthusiasm in bed was...hell, who knew? A man getting laid?

That's what I always think, you know. That no guy could be interested in me.

Making love at least once a day this past week, waking up next to her, eating breakfast with her, coming home to her, had been so good, like an idiot he'd believed that her fears about him had been laid to rest. Of course it wasn't that easy. Moira's deep-seated belief that he had made a huge and terrible sacrifice for her and for his baby had only dozed, waiting to be reawakened by that letter he'd so carelessly left out.

Carelessly, because it hadn't meant that much to him. A sound escaped him as he exhaled. Had he really even felt a pang? Reading the letter, he *was* flattered. Sorry the clinics weren't being built as quickly as they had all hoped. He'd had a moment of renewed guilt at having failed to keep a promise. But he hadn't been tempted at all. He'd tossed the damn thing aside without a second thought because he'd found something a hell of a lot more important. Love.

Had Moira really not seen how happy he was? How much he needed her? How many times had he told her he lived to get home to her and Caleb? Will was still baffled that she could really think it was all a lie, him making the best of an obligation he'd reluctantly shouldered...but she did.

What an idiot he'd been, not telling her he loved her. He had known for a long time what he felt. But...that door had still been cracked open behind him, too, and he guessed that's what had kept the words unsaid. Yeah, Moira had plenty of self-doubts. What had she said? *After a while, you sort of give up.* But she'd been married to a man dumb enough not to say, loud and clear, "I love you," and keep saying it. And she wasn't a woman able to hold on to faith in the face of his silence.

He surged to his feet, wanting nothing more than to get in his truck and head home to West Fork to confront her. To tell her he was crazily, permanently in love with her, and she could by God *learn* to believe it.

As the engine roared to life, he felt a hard kick in his chest. Was he kidding himself, thinking she wanted him to love her? Moira had never said anything to indicate she was in love with him. He was judging solely on the way she responded to his kisses, to him in bed, the expression in her eyes sometimes, the trusting way she slept in his arms. The fact that she had agreed to marry him in the first place. He'd presented marriage to her as a sensible solution to their dilemma, but Will knew he wouldn't have gone that far if he hadn't already felt too much for her. And he couldn't imagine that she'd have accepted him if *she* hadn't felt enough to know she could live intimately with him. They'd both gambled on something they hadn't been willing to name, not at that point. And he'd believed—still believed—they had won.

But he had to hear her say those three words, too. *I love you.* Until he did, until he had her in his arms again, he was going to stay scared.

"THERE," MOIRA SAID, lifting Caleb from the small plastic bathtub she'd set on the kitchen counter. "That wasn't so bad, was it?"

The first few weeks of his life, he'd wailed every time he was put in water. He'd progressed to looking worried, and tonight he'd become briefly entranced with a floating soap bubble. He'd grinned once, too, kicking his legs and splashing the counter and her.

Bundled in a towel, he wriggled happily.

"Now I'm wetter than you are," she told him, kissing him on the nose. She carried him to her room and laid him on the bed while she peeled off her shirt and grabbed a dry one from the drawer. But, unable to resist, she picked him up before she put the T on, loving the feel of his plump, naked body against her own bare skin.

She'd read in books about how important touch was to babies. Dry diapers and enough formula weren't enough. Something inside shriveled and died if babies weren't cuddled often enough. They lost the potential to feel emotions and trust for the rest of their lives.

Holding Caleb, Moira wondered if that's what had happened to her. Not when she was a baby, of course; she knew her mother had loved her. But later. After college, she'd had no one to hold her. An occasional hug from a friend or her mom wasn't the same as this, loving and warm, or the thigh to chest, skin-to-skin contact she'd had with Will. His kisses and his arms around her, the way he had of constantly touching her, that big hand making her feel secure in a way she didn't ever remember feeling. Sitting on the edge of the bed, tears welling in her eyes even as her body soaked up the contact with her baby, Moira ached for Will's touch. For Will.

No, she hadn't lost the potential to feel these emotions, but hope had certainly shriveled in her. The belief in forever.

Cheek pressed to her baby's head, she gasped with the pain, and tried to believe she'd done the right thing in giving Will an out. The only thing possible, for the man she loved.

Caleb began rooting for her breast and, no matter her inner turmoil, she opened the cup of her bra. He happily latched on.

Even as she bent and kissed the silky, damp hair on top of his head, she let herself consider an idea that would once have been unthinkable.

What if Will had meant what he said? What if he really *had* felt only a pang? What if he truly *wanted* to stay with her and Caleb?

What if she hadn't been acting out of love for him at all, but out of her own fears? Her own belief that he couldn't possibly choose her over his dreams?

He'd been angry, she knew he was. If he didn't think she wanted him to stay, might he be mad and hurt enough to call the foundation today and say, sure, what the hell, I'll go?

An awful sound escaped her. Caleb let loose of her breast and lifted his head to stare at her with perplexed brown eyes.

Moira made reassuring sounds despite the anguish that tore through her. She kept looking at her baby—at *their* baby—and thought as she often did how well he blended parts of her with parts of Will. The eyes were Will's, if a lighter shade than his. The square, determined chin was his, too. The red in Caleb's hair was from her, the nose, she thought, hers. He probably *would* have freckles, but also his daddy's size and, someday, powerful shoulders and big feet.

She wished desperately that she'd been brave enough to tell Will she loved him. He'd have been kind no matter what. Why had she been so afraid of baring herself?

Now, all she could think was that, while Will had been angry, mostly what she remembered was the pain in his eyes, the hoarse disbelief in his voice. And she hadn't listened to what he tried to tell her, had refused to hear.

Caleb had fallen asleep. Moira slipped away, fastening her bra and pulling on her T-shirt. He only scrunched his eyes tighter closed when she put on his diaper and carried him to his crib.

She stood for a moment, looking down at him, her chest hurting. Will would be home after work. They could talk then. It wasn't as if he'd left her because of the things she'd said. All she had done was ask him to think, to be honest with himself. That wasn't so bad, was it? She *wanted* him to be honest.

And maybe it was better that she'd never told him she loved him, even if that was cowardly. Because he might tell her tonight that what he really wanted was to go back to Africa. If so, it was better that he never knew. She wouldn't bind him further with more guilt, barbed to draw blood.

WILL STOOD ON THE PORCH and actually thought about ringing the doorbell. The way he and Moira had left it last night and this morning, he didn't know how welcome he was.

But, damn it, he lived here, and after a minute he shoved the key in the lock and opened the door. The foyer was empty. There was a moment of silence and he had the sudden, irrational fear that the house was empty.

But the next instant, she stepped from the living room with Caleb in her arms, as if he was coming home from work any other day.

"Will," she whispered, her face pinched and eyes huge.

Caleb beamed at the sight of his daddy. Without saying a word, Will held out his arms, and she put his son in them. Damn. His eyes burned.

Moira backed up, as if to give him space. For a moment he laid his cheek against Caleb's head and inhaled the clean, milky scent of baby.

"How could you think even for a minute that I'd walk away from you?" he whispered. He had to blink away the blur in his eyes to focus on her face. "I miss you every day, just going to work."

"Oh, Will." She flung herself at him. He barely got his free arm out in time to catch her. He lurched back and pushed the door closed.

Their baby was squished between them. Moira wrapped both arms around Will's torso as if she were drowning and he was the life preserver. She burrowed her face against his chest. She was trying to talk, but the words were muffled in his shirt.

Caleb struggled in protest. Heart pounding, Will said, "Let me put Caleb down. Sweetheart, let me set him down."

It seemed to take her a minute to hear. Then she slowly let her arms fall and backed away. Her face was wet. Will looked around and saw a crib-size comforter on the arm of the sofa. He grabbed it and spread it on the floor with one flick, then laid their son down on his tummy. Caleb pushed up right away, stronger than he'd been a few days ago.

Will turned and hauled Moira into his arms. Once again, she pressed herself to him as if she wanted to crawl inside him. He wanted that, too. Holding her as close as was humanly possible meant more to him right now than anything else on earth.

He heard himself saying things, but he didn't know if they were any more coherent than whatever she'd mumbled into his chest. He was crooning to her more than making any sense.

It had to be a couple of minutes before she began to relax. Just a little, then a little more, until her body didn't feel as frantic to him and he could loosen his own grip some. Finally she stepped back, her wet, puffy face wrenching his heart, and cried, "Oh, I've got to blow my nose." She fled for the bathroom.

While she was gone, Will swiped his eyes with his forearm. He crouched beside Caleb and patted his diaper-padded butt. "Look at you," he murmured. "Man, you're going to be crawling before we know it."

When he heard the bathroom door, he stood and watched Moira come down the hall then, more hesitantly, across the living room to him. Her face was still puffy and the red splotches didn't go well with the golden dust of freckles, but she wasn't crying anymore and, damn, she looked beautiful to his eyes.

After a hesitant moment, she said, "I kept being afraid you wouldn't come home. That you were mad, and I'd hurt your feelings, and you wouldn't want to see me."

"You did hurt my feelings," he said gruffly, but he was reaching for her to draw her close.

"I just…needed to know…"

"I understand," he heard himself say gently. He rubbed his cheek against the top of her hair. "I gave you every reason to wonder."

"I…" Moira went very still in his grip. "Did you get in touch with the foundation?"

"Yeah. The day the letter came. I sent them an email saying thanks, but I'm not available."

She pulled back enough to look up at him, searching his face with grave eyes. "You truly didn't want to go?"

"And leave you and Caleb?" His voice sounded rusty now, the hurt thickening it. "No. I didn't want to go."

Moira retreated farther. The hands that had been pressed to his chest writhed as she wound her fingers together. "I thought I was doing the right thing for you. But today I realized I was listening to my fears more than anything." She swallowed. "Did you think, Will? The way I asked?"

"Yeah. I thought. And I realized that I'm not very good at communicating with people. Not about what I feel. I've never had to try before. I also realized that I wasn't completely honest with you. I was trying to hide the regrets I did feel. And that was stupid. I can talk to you. I just thought—" He stopped, lost for words.

"That I'd assume exactly what I did last night."

He frowned. "But maybe you wouldn't have, if I'd been open all along. If I'd said, 'I loved it in Africa, but I love it here, too. With you, Moira.'"

"Is that what you'd have said?" she whispered.

He nodded.

"Will." The strain on her face was heartbreaking, but

no more so than the hope. "Do you really want to stay married to me?"

His throat closed, his chest spasmed. In a harsh whisper, he said, "More than I've ever wanted anything in my life."

"Oh, Will." She rushed into his arms again, and they were ready for her. She pressed her face to his shoulder, and he buried his in her cloud of copper curls. They rocked in place, a subtle, reassuring motion that came instinctively, comfort at its most primal. He knew he was probably holding her too tightly, but she didn't seem to mind, and he couldn't make himself unlock his arms from around her.

"I love you," he said to the top of her head. "Maybe you can't feel the same way about me, but don't ever doubt me. I love you so damn much, it about ripped me apart when I was afraid you didn't want me."

Without loosening her arms at all, Moira tilted her head back to look at him. "You love me?" she asked, her voice cracking at the end, the vulnerability and uncertainty in it as excruciating as a blade between the ribs. "You really love me?"

He tried to smile. "I think I must have fallen in love with you that first night. I knew I shouldn't do something as dumb as go in that hotel room with you, but…I couldn't not. From the minute I saw you in the ballroom, I couldn't look away. I never got your face out of my mind. You'd have heard from me as soon as I got back from Africa. I think I'd have spent two years praying you didn't meet someone and get married while my back was turned."

Her eyes filled again with a rush. "I fell in love with you, too. And, oh, so much more when you came to see me. And listened to Caleb's heartbeat, and laid your hand on my stomach to feel him move. The expression on your face—" She choked to a stop.

"I should have told you," Will said. "I thought you weren't ready to hear those words. But I should have said them anyway. Maybe you'd have known that I wouldn't leave you. *Couldn't* leave you."

She was the one smiling now, although her lips trembled. "I don't know if I'd have believed you."

His fingers tightened. "Do you now?"

There was something dazed in her eyes. After a moment she gave the smallest of nods. "Yes. I do. Part of me thinks I'm dreaming, but...I do believe you. Oh, Will. I love you so much!"

He kissed her then, using mouth and teeth and tongue to show her how hungry he was for her. The kiss wasn't just about wanting her body. Although he did. God, he did. She kissed him back so fervently, he knew she felt the same. She still wanted to get inside him, and she wanted him inside her just as much.

Caleb let out a cry. When his parents ignored it, he got serious with a frustrated wail.

Will and Moira separated, only a few inches. He felt a grin stretching his mouth and loved the answering smile on hers.

"Oh, dear," she said. "He thinks this is his time of day with Daddy. He's not used to us ignoring him."

Will stooped and picked up Caleb, murmuring, "You felt left out, didn't you? I'm so sorry, buddy. So sorry."

Moira kissed Caleb's cheek, then briefly rested her cheek against Will's arm. "This is my second favorite time of day. When you come home."

"What's your favorite?" he asked in a low rumble.

She gave a little laugh. "You know."

Cradling Caleb in both arms, Will bent his head and

nuzzled his wife's ear. "Mine, too," he said huskily. "And I'm already thinking about it."

A little shyly, she said, "Good."

Gently bouncing Caleb, Will said, "So, what's for dinner?"

Moira laughed. "A pot roast."

"Even though you were afraid I wasn't coming home?"

Her smile, glorious and uncomplicated by any doubt whatsoever, stole his breath. "But you see," she said, "I was being optimistic."

He lifted his eyebrows. "I've cured you of pessimism?"

As if startled, she was quiet for a minute, her lips parted. When she answered, she sounded bemused. "I think maybe you have. Or at least, that I'm learning. What a funny feeling."

On a surge of emotion that filled him to aching, Will said, "You'll get used to it. I'll help. I promise."

"You're a good and kind man, Will Becker," she told him.

"And an honest one."

"Yes, I believe you are." Her mouth curved once again. "There I go again. Optimistic." The smile turned into a laugh. "I'll get dinner on. That will bring bedtime closer."

"Our favorite time of day." Will took a deep breath. "Damn, it's good to be home," he said, and headed for the bathroom. Their son needed a clean diaper.

Bedtime would come soon enough.

* * * * *

COMING NEXT MONTH

Available January 11, 2011

#1680 A LITTLE TEXAS
Hometown U.S.A.
Liz Talley

#1681 HER GREAT EXPECTATIONS
Summerside Stories
Joan Kilby

#1682 HERE COMES THE GROOM
Going Back
Karina Bliss

#1683 HOME TO HARMONY
Dawn Atkins

#1684 BECAUSE OF JANE
Lenora Worth

#1685 NANNY NEXT DOOR
Single Father
Michelle Celmer

REQUEST YOUR FREE BOOKS!

2 FREE NOVELS PLUS 2 FREE GIFTS!

HARLEQUIN®

Super Romance®

Exciting, emotional, unexpected!

YES! Please send me 2 FREE Harlequin® Superromance® novels and my 2 FREE gifts (gifts are worth about $10). After receiving them, if I don't wish to receive any more books, I can return the shipping statement marked "cancel." If I don't cancel, I will receive 6 brand-new novels every month and be billed just $4.69 per book in the U.S. or $5.24 per book in Canada. That's a saving of at least 15% off the cover price! It's quite a bargain! Shipping and handling is just 50¢ per book.* I understand that accepting the 2 free books and gifts places me under no obligation to buy anything. I can always return a shipment and cancel at any time. Even if I never buy another book from Harlequin, the two free books and gifts are mine to keep forever.

135/336 HDN E5P4

Name _____ (PLEASE PRINT)

Address _____ Apt. #

City _____ State/Prov. _____ Zip/Postal Code

Signature (if under 18, a parent or guardian must sign)

Mail to the **Harlequin Reader Service:**
IN U.S.A.: P.O. Box 1867, Buffalo, NY 14240-1867
IN CANADA: P.O. Box 609, Fort Erie, Ontario L2A 5X3

Not valid for current subscribers to Harlequin Superromance books.

**Are you a current subscriber to Harlequin Superromance books
and want to receive the larger-print edition?
Call 1-800-873-8635 today!**

* Terms and prices subject to change without notice. Prices do not include applicable taxes. N.Y. residents add applicable sales tax. Canadian residents will be charged applicable provincial taxes and GST. Offer not valid in Quebec. This offer is limited to one order per household. All orders subject to approval. Credit or debit balances in a customer's account(s) may be offset by any other outstanding balance owed by or to the customer. Please allow 4 to 6 weeks for delivery. Offer available while quantities last.

Your Privacy: Harlequin Books is committed to protecting your privacy. Our Privacy Policy is available online at www.eHarlequin.com or upon request from the Reader Service. From time to time we make our lists of customers available to reputable third parties who may have a product or service of interest to you. If you would prefer we not share your name and address, please check here. ☐

Help us get it right—We strive for accurate, respectful and relevant communications. To clarify or modify your communication preferences, visit us at www.ReaderService.com/consumerschoice.

HSR10R

HARLEQUIN®

A Romance

FOR EVERY MOOD™

Spotlight on

Classic

Quintessential, modern love stories
that are romance at its finest.

See the next page
to enjoy a sneak peek from
the Harlequin Presents® series.

*Harlequin Presents® is thrilled
to introduce the first installment of
an epic tale of passion and drama by*
USA TODAY *Bestselling Author*
Penny Jordan!

*When buttoned-up Giselle first meets
the devastatingly handsome Saul Parenti,
the heat between them is explosive....*

"LET ME GET THIS STRAIGHT. Are you actually suggesting that I would stoop to that kind of game playing?"

Saul came out from behind his desk and walked toward her. Giselle could smell his hot male scent and it was making her dizzy, igniting a low, dull, pulsing ache that was taking over her whole body.

Giselle defended her suspicions. "You don't want me here."

"No," Saul agreed, "I don't."

And then he did what he had sworn he would not do, cursing himself beneath his breath as he reached for her, pulling her fiercely into his arms and kissing her with all the pent-up fury she had aroused in him from the moment he had first seen her.

Giselle certainly *wanted* to resist him. But the hand she raised to push him away developed a will of its own and was sliding along his bare arm beneath the sleeve of his shirt, and the body that should have been arching away from him was instead melting into him.

Beneath the pressure of his kiss he could feel and taste her gasp of undeniable response to him. He wanted to devour her, take her and drive them both until they were equally satiated—even whilst the anger within him that she should make him feel that way roared and burned its resentment of his need.

She was helpless, Giselle recognized, totally unable to withstand the storm lashing at her, able only to cling to the man who was the cause of it and pray that she would survive.

Somewhere else in the building a door banged. The sound exploded into the sensual tension that had enclosed them, driving them apart. Saul's chest was rising and falling as he fought for control; Giselle's whole body was trembling.

Without a word she turned and ran.

Find out what happens when Saul and Giselle succumb to their irresistible desire in

THE RELUCTANT SURRENDER

Available January 2011 from Harlequin Presents®

MARGARET WAY

Wealthy Australian,
Secret Son

Rohan was Charlotte's shining white knight
until he disappeared—before she had
the chance to tell him she was pregnant.

But when Rohan returns years later as
a self-made millionaire, could the blond,
blue-eyed little boy and Charlotte's heart
keep him from leaving again?

Available January 2011

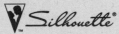
Silhouette®

ROMANTIC
SUSPENSE
Sparked by Danger, Fueled by Passion.

Cowboy Deputy
by
CARLA CASSIDY

Following a run of bad luck, including an attack on her grandfather, Edie Tolliver is sure things can't possibly get any worse....

But with the handsome Deputy Grayson on the case will Edie's luck and love life turn a corner?

LAWMEN
of BLACK ROCK

Available January 2011
wherever books are sold.

SRS27709